Limboland

Leigh Goodison

This is a work of fiction. Names, characters, places, and incidents are products of the author's imagination or are used fictitiously and are not to be construed as real. Any resemblance to actual events, locales, organizations, or persons, living or dead, is entirely coincidental.

SHEFFIELD PUBLICATIONS

The text for this book was set in Garamond.

Printed and bound in the United States of America.

10 9 8 7 6 5 4 3 2

Leigh Goodison

Limboland / Leigh Goodison / 1st edition

Summary:
Psychiatrist Rand Morrissey, still haunted by his sister's death, must overcome his childhood demons to save the lives of two half-sisters, inextricably tethered between life and death.
[1. Medical thriller-Fic. 2. Psychological thriller-Fic. 3. Suspense-Fic.]

I. Title

St. Augustus Chronicles [Fic]

ISBN-13: 978-1945136047 (Sheffield Publications)

Cover design and Copyright: SelfPubBookCovers.com/L.Blair

DEDICATION

This book is dedicated to my baby brother, Wayne,
who died at the age of four and never
got to live the life he deserved.
You inspired this story.
I think of you often.

And to my sister, Vicky, and brother, Bob.
There was never a sister more blessed than I,
to have you as siblings.

Limboland

Leigh Goodison

Chapter One

"What shall it profit a man, if he shall gain the whole world,
and lose his own soul?" (Mark 8:36)

The morning's commute might well be a metaphor for her career and marriage, Melanie Moran thought. Going nowhere.
Though her tenet to be punctual and precise controlled her life
and everything around her, displacing the congested freeway
traffic that more closely resembled the parking lot of the half-
yearly sale at Nordstrom's Rack than a main thoroughfare
would take more than willpower. Her foot hadn't touched the
accelerator for miles.

She had nearly worn out the touch pads on the car's radio
by repeatedly switching stations when an unexpected cleft in
the traffic allowed her to move through. She veered into the
fast lane and as she flew past the other vehicles, their left signals blinking, her cell phone rang. At this early hour the call
could only have originated from one of three people, no doubt
selfishly demanding her time or presence. In a perfect world a
woman should be able to seamlessly dovetail work and family,
she reflected. Her face hardened as she took her hands off the
wheel to tap the screen of the phone.

A black Mercedes whipped around to avoid her car. The
driver rolled down his passenger window and shouted, "Hang
up and drive!"

Melanie ignored him, noting wryly the bumper sticker on
his car that read, 'Wife for sale: take over payments.' Still holding the cell phone, she flipped him off. The motorist accelerat-

ed, leaving her enveloped in dirty rainwater spray and the smell of hot rubber from his squealing tires. She slammed the BMW's vents shut with her free hand.

"What?!"

It was an inadvertent response to the most likely caller, her husband Tim, no doubt checking to make sure she'd driven their daughter Chelsa to school because of the rainstorm. But Melanie had told Chelsa she'd have to walk or she wouldn't have enough time to get to work if she had to take Chelsa to school. After all, as a child *she'd* walked to school. It wouldn't hurt Chelsa to do it for once, either. And a damned good thing she hadn't or she'd have been trapped inside the car with a yappy kid all this time. Too late she realized that she should have checked the caller ID. It wasn't Tim.

"Is that how you answer the phone when it's your husband? Or your next lover?" Melanie swallowed hard.

"John." She willed her reply to a husky softness. On hearing his voice she'd expected a reprimand for being late to work. Now a rush of conflicting emotions surged from the bottom of her pelvis to her rib cage. Her new boss at Excel Electronics couldn't be subtle if he tried, but it brought an element of danger into her otherwise dull life.

"Meet me at the Sleep-Inn Motel, Melanie," he urged. "You know where it is, right? You take the last exit north of the office. I'm in Room 211."

She hesitated, her lips tightening until they nearly disappeared. Although she'd never been there, she knew she could find the location of the motel without any trouble, but it irritated her that he'd already booked a room. It *was* sexual harassment, though she couldn't 'cry wolf' when she'd been flirting outrageously for weeks. Then there'd been their 'sexting' via cell phone. She could refuse or she could file a complaint. But she wouldn't. In spite of wanting to say 'no' out of principle, this would be a shortcut to the promotion she'd been waiting for.

"Well?" said John. The terse impatience in his voice inflamed her already black mood. She hesitated a little longer, purposely keeping him waiting for an answer. She was at the top of her game and they both knew it. But she would play along with the game for a prize as substantial as the one she envisioned.

* * * * *

Eight-year-old Chelsa Moran had slept in by a half-hour, and to make things worse, her mother had refused to drive her to school on Portland's northeast side. Her father had already left for work, or he would certainly have given her a ride. She was on her own. Though she tried to rush, each movement she made seemed calibrated to prolong time rather than hasten it.

As she set out on the five-block trek to school, her clothes were soon dampened. The rain spritzed her cheeks and turned her curly blonde hair into tight tendrils. But her childish euphoria at encountering mud puddles remained. She skipped through their centers, oblivious to the scolding she'd receive when she got to school. She reached up to loosen the ponytail that ached at the roots from her mother's perfunctory straightening, and smiled with satisfaction at the muddy splashes on her socks.

Turning her face skyward, she stuck out her tongue to taste the rain. As if in response, a carload of teenaged boys driving by stuck out their tongues at her. Chelsa's already flushed cheeks turned brighter yet. She shifted her soggy book bag further onto her right shoulder, swinging it like a pendulum to take pressure off the cast on her broken left arm.

More comfortable now, she kicked free the clumps of cherry petals clinging to her wet sneakers and danced down the rutted concrete sidewalk that led to her best friend Lisa's house. Then one foot caught the other and she stumbled. Giggling, she regained her footing as Lisa emerged from her house.

"You're late!" Lisa admonished.

"Maybe *you're* early," Chelsa countered.

Lisa rolled her eyes and waved goodbye to her mother

while Chelsa waited on the front step. Though she knew they'd both get 'tardies' from their teacher, it would be her mother's fault. Chelsa had told her so, which had only resulted in a disinterested shrug from her mother. Her father, she knew, didn't like her to walk that dangerous piece of road and wouldn't have let her. He'd be angry when he found out she'd had no choice.

By the time Chelsa and Lisa reached the crosswalk that led to their brick and mortar elementary school their clothes were drenched by the now steady downpour. School buses pulled away when the buzzer sounded, leaving their young passengers to scamper into the school. Lisa and Chelsa exchanged glances and quickened their pace. But as they were about to cross the street, they were momentarily distracted. A half-grown Golden Retriever puppy galloped toward them, his leash dragging along behind with no owner at the end. Chelsa reached out to grab the leash as it shot by, but the puppy panicked and raced onto the street. Without checking for cars as they'd always been warned to do, Chelsa and Lisa dashed after him.

Then a silver Eldorado seemed to come from nowhere. The elderly driver squinted blindly through the condensation on her windshield as the girls ran after the dog. Panicked, the woman brought up both hands to cover her eyes. But instead of braking, the car accelerated and swerved, jumping onto the curb and throwing the girls in opposite directions. And the last things Chelsa saw was her own startled reflection in the car's chrome bumper and one of Lisa's fresh white Keds spinning crazily into the air.

* * * * *

Far across town, Tim Moran, Chelsa's father, planed another slice of cedar in the sawmill where he had worked since dropping out of 11th grade at the age of seventeen when Melanie had become pregnant with Chelsa. He'd never regretted marrying Melanie, the only way he could dissuade her from having an abortion. Whether she regretted it or not, he couldn't say. But even the bone-grinding monotony and bodily stress of a mill job never detracted from his joy each evening watching Chelsa at play or doing her homework.

He stopped for a moment and rolled his shoulders to relieve the stiffness from feeding one lengthy plank after another into the machine. A couple of years ago he'd tried to talk Melanie into having another child. He laughed out loud at the memory, causing a couple of his coworkers to cast curious glances at him.

"I'm a career woman," she had said, "not a brood mare." And her vehemence effectively ended *that* subject. She'd made it very clear that having another child would be nonnegotiable and birth control was his responsibility. It didn't matter, he thought. At their current salaries, they could only afford to raise one child. Even so, he made a mental reminder to pick up yet another surprise for Chelsa from Toys 'R Us on his way home. Melanie's exasperation would be gift enough for him.

* * * * *

As Melanie listened to a morning show blaring in the background from the motel television, and the softer sound of John's breathing, coming through the cell phone, she pondered over his interest in her. How far would her power extend after this assignation with her boss? she wondered. The rendezvous would be a temporary solution. Nothing more. When she'd gotten what she wanted she would tell him what he could do to himself. And if he made an issue out of it, she'd have a chat with Human Resources. She sighed in resignation, willing her mood to transform from irritation to a sense of adventure.

"The traffic is horrendous," she growled. "I'll be there when I get there."

She dropped the cell phone into her purse and made a U-turn at the next intersection. But her excitement dissipated when she pulled into the rutted parking lot next to John's Mercedes, and gazed in disgust at the seediness of his choice for a tryst. She took a couple of seconds to turn down the visor mirror and smooth her long honey-blonde hair, fuzzy from the humidity, before heading up the sagging walkway to his room.

John answered the door, wrapped in a dingy white motel towel.

"What was wrong with Motel 6?" she asked, her voice heavy with sarcasm.

As she brushed past him she surveyed the tacky monochromatic brown-and-browner room. The lumpy mattress, predictable southwestern art and stained carpet would be there long after the damp stench of cigarette smoke from years gone by had faded. A gold plastic starburst clock that could have been vintage chic, though too cheap to transcend any fashion period, had ceased permanently at 12:15.

She stepped into the bathroom and grabbed a handful of tissues, blotting the perspiration from her forehead and upper lip. As she stared back at her reflection, an overwhelming sense of uneasiness crept over her. She took a deep breath and forcibly shook it away. Then she headed back into the room, tossing her purse onto the night table. She turned toward John and closed her eyes, leaning against his hard, naked body as he began kissing her neck. And this time when her cell phone chirped she didn't even open her eyes.

* * * * *

After switching off the planer to take a smoke break, Tim rubbed away a stream of sweat that threatened to trickle into his eyes. He pulled a pinch of loose tobacco from his shirt pocket and deftly rolled a cigarette with one hand. Then he flicked open the five-year-anniversary lighter he'd been given for company service, lit the cigarette and inhaled deeply. For a few seconds it obliterated the sickly-sour smell of pulp mill that clung to his clothes and stuck to his skin.

He stared across the plant at his coworkers and the whining machines that caused most of the crew early hearing loss. A country and western song popped into his head and almost involuntarily he began to sing, "Don't break my heart, my achy, breaky heart..." He groaned aloud, knowing the song would stay with him all day. Then he dropped the cigarette butt to the floor and ground it out with his heel.

Picking up another slice of cedar he began feeding it carefully into the planer. The whirring whine started again as tiny flecks of cedar sprayed around the plank. He didn't raise his head as the Plant Manager of Clarkson Timber hurried through the building in search of him. Looking up could cost you a finger, and Tim only had eight left to spare now.

* * * * *

Melanie slid her gym-toned backside under the sheets as she surveyed the latest conquest in her struggle to scale the ladder of success. She began patting herself dry with the towel John had tossed her while he got dressed, ignoring her the way men always did once they'd got what they wanted.

This time she would get what she wanted. Instead of considering the newly hired Cantrell an obstacle, she'd drafted plans for her future. Standing there physically and professionally vulnerable, pulling his boxers up to a belly that gave away his drinking habits, she knew that stepping up and over him would be no more difficult than removing her panties. She sighed. *Just no slip-ups this time*, Melanie, she said to herself.

* * * * *

When the steel-toed boots belonging to the Plant Manager didn't move away from the opposite side of his work area, Tim finally shut down the planer and peeled off his leather gloves and safety goggles. He glanced up at his boss for an explanation to the interruption. It struck Tim as odd that the man's mouth moved but no words emerged. Then a trickle of coldness he couldn't attribute to any draft seemed to slither between his clothes and down his back until goosebumps tickled his arms. For what seemed like an eternity they stared at each other. Finally the Plant Manager spoke.

"There's been an accident," he said, his voice scarcely rising above a whisper.

Tim heard something drop and crash to the floor but the sound seemed to be coming from far away in the distance. Almost as if he stood in a smoke filled room he saw the outlined form of the Plant Manager bend and pick up the plank he'd been working on and slide it atop of the others. A burning pain began to form the back of his eyes until he could no longer see the man in front of him.

"I can drive you to the hospital." He placed his arm around Tim's shoulders and held him tightly as Tim let out a cry of anguish that caused all heads in the warehouse to turn his way.

Tim didn't wait to hear anything more, nor did he notice the curious stares from his coworkers as he ran out of the building toward his car, the pressure on his chest as intense as though someone had reached under his ribs and ripped out his heart.

Chapter Two

Tim searched out the hospital wall clock for what seemed like the hundredth time then checked his own watch to confirm that it hadn't stopped. Despite the comings and goings of hospital workers wheeling carts, carrying trays and balancing charts, there had been no word yet from the ICU on Chelsa's condition.

He reached over, picked up an ancient, dog-eared copy of *People* magazine and set it back down again. A tiny bleat started up in his pocket. But when he checked he saw that the sound came from his cell phone battery getting low. His heart sank when he realized there were no messages.

He caught the eye of another grim-faced man who sat quietly across the room from him, also pretending to read a magazine, and glanced discreetly away. *Where the hell was Melanie?*

After the Plant Manager had told him of Chelsa's accident, he'd forced himself to be calm until he could safely drive. Once he arrived at the hospital he'd called Melanie's work number from outside the hospital, but the secretary informed him that Melanie hadn't come in yet.

He'd tried her cell phone but each time he did he got her voice mail. The only thing he could do would be to leave another message. He'd spent the last hour watching other families come and go; heads together as they shared their crises. He had no one and he ached for emotional support.

He turned, taking in the nursing station with its constant stream of pastel uniforms. Two nurses chattered amicably while they pillaged a box of chocolates. A large bouquet of blood-red roses, their heavy damask scent cutting through the smell of disinfectant and all the way to where he sat, blocked his view to the phone. Every time it rang he expected it to bring news of Chelsa.

The muted scuff of rubber-soled nursing shoes approached. He glanced up in anticipation, but it wasn't for him. The nurse smiled sympathetically as she walked past. This was just another work day for them, he supposed. After she'd gone he exhaled loudly, feeling as if he'd been holding his breath since he'd left work. He yearned for a cigarette and unconsciously fingered his tobacco-filled pocket, glaring resentfully at the No Smoking sign on the opposite wall. An enormous throbbing began in his temples. If only they'd give him some news. But maybe no news was good news after all.

Then he heard another set of footsteps approaching. Familiar ones. He turned toward the corridor to see Melanie click-clicking toward him in a body-fitted, grey pinstripe suit and strappy black stilettos that always made her look as if she were about to topple over. As usual, all the heads in the room turned to watch her. Melanie didn't see him at first and walked calm and deliberately, not rushing frantically as he had done, toward the call desk.

"Melanie." He spoke her name in a loud whisper. Her head jerked around. She saw him then and whirled away from the desk, dropping onto the seat beside him.

"What's happened?" She scanned his face for information. Apparently reading everything she needed there, she dropped her face into her hands and let out a whimpering cry. Tim encircled her in his arms, rocking her as if she were a child.

"We don't really know anything yet. I've been here about an hour and all they were able to tell me is that she had been struck by a car and has head injuries."

Melanie pulled back, the dreaded question showing in those brandy-colored eyes that had always reminded him of a cat's. He shook his head.

"It's my fault," she moaned. "I thought, just this once she could walk..." Her voice trailed off. She raised her eyes to

Tim's for reassurance but he glanced away.

"You let her walk to school. On *that* busy road." His voice dripped with recrimination. Almost as if to himself, he repeated the words. "You let her *walk* to school."

"Tim, I'm so sorry." Her contrition failed to move him though he distractedly stroked her hand. "Please tell me she's going to be all right."

"They haven't given me an outcome."

"Isn't there anyone who can tell us what's going on?" Her cry shrilled to such a pitch that several people cast glances their way.

Tim put his finger to his lips. "I don't think they know yet. We will just have to wait." His eyes narrowed. He'd left half a dozen messages at her office; at least that many on her cell phone.

"Where the hell *were* you all morning? Didn't you check your voice mail?"

Deftly avoiding his stare, Melanie unsnapped her purse and withdrew her iPhone. As she began punching the keys Tim wrenched his gaze away. He couldn't even figure out how to turn the damned thing on.

"I had to run a few errands and forgot I'd turned my cell phone off. When I got to the office Linda told me the hospital had called and there had been an accident." Her eyes dropped to Tim's hands. "I just figured you were down another finger."

Her lips twisted with the kind of nervous tension that comes at inappropriate times from stressful situations, like getting the giggles at a funeral. Tim's face crumpled.

"So I guess it doesn't matter if..." Before he could finish he noticed a short, heavy-set man in a white lab coat approaching them. He had the dark shadows under his eyes that come from working the graveyard shift, dealing with life and death, dishing out good news and bad with the finesse of a TV anchorman. Tim and Melanie stood simultaneously and took a few hurried steps toward him.

"I'm Dr. Elias." He glanced at each in turn then rested his gaze on a point past Tim's shoulder. "Are you Chelsa's parents?"

Tim nodded. Melanie clutched his arm and though her nails dug into his flesh, the pain helped him focus on the reality around them. He didn't like the distress on the doctor's face. He didn't like the way the man's eyes wouldn't meet theirs. In an overwhelming surge of panic Tim knew what the doctor was about to tell them even before he said it.

"I'm so sorry," he began, then hesitated for what seemed an eternity. "There's not much more we can do for her other than make her as comfortable as possible."

The blood drained from Tim's face. The trepidation of the unknown had flipped his stomach upside down. For a moment he thought he would vomit. He felt his body weakening until his knees threatened to crumble beneath him.

"Let's sit down," said Dr. Elias, his voice softening. He took Melanie's arm and tried to lead her to a chair but she stayed standing, frozen like a mannequin. Helplessness seemed to overcome the doctor. His hands began to shake and that alarmed Tim even more. The doctor saw Tim looking at his hands and quickly thrust them deep into the pockets of his coat.

"I examined Chelsa when she arrived at the Emergency Department. She has a skull fracture. We reset her broken arm because the impact destroyed her cast. She also sustained internal injuries from the force of the car hitting her. She's been in a coma since the accident."

He hesitated. "The good news is the internal bleeding has stopped and her other injuries are not life threatening."

Tim swallowed hard and forced himself to take a slow breath. He felt so dizzy he knew he could pass out at any moment. He stole a glance toward Melanie, her face a frozen white mask as she waited for the doctor to continue.

Obviously uncomfortable with what he had to tell them the doctor's words emerged in a rush. "The bad news is we're not seeing any brain activity on the CAT Scan."

No matter how hard he tried, Tim found himself unable to speak. He yearned to drop to his knees and begin praying, but this wasn't the place. He gripped Melanie's hand, trembling and clammy with cold sweat. Though she made no sound, tears ran down her cheeks, leaving little black rivulets of mascara dripping off the end of her chin. The questions he should be asking the doctor would not come. When Melanie spoke for both of them he felt weak with gratitude.

"Isn't being in a coma after a head injury a good thing?" she said, her voice quivering. Though she managed to disguise it by clearing her throat, she still sounded as if any moment she would burst into tears. "A way for the brain to take time out to heal itself?" She snaked her arm around Tim's waist for support. He tightened his hand on hers in response.

Dr. Elias shuffled uncomfortably. The room became so silent that the random hospital noises and voices seemed to recede into the background. The stillness made Tim believe he could hear everyone in the room breathing, could almost hear individual heartbeats.

"That's true with occasional brain trauma cases," Dr. Elias said, "but in Chelsa's case there's been too much brain damage. It's unlikely she'll ever regain consciousness. Or that she'll ever make a full recovery." He inhaled deeply. "I know this is probably more bad news than you're able to handle at the moment, but I would recommend discontinuing life support."

Tim's legs finally gave way. He stumbled to a chair and sat, staring straight ahead at nothing. Only a few hours ago he'd left for work, saying goodbye to Chelsa as she ate a bowl of cereal. He squeezed his eyes shut, muttering a prayer. Any minute now he'd hear *His* voice. *He* would guide him.

When Tim stopped praying he'd made his decision. Melanie stared down at him with a kind of terror in her eyes. He stood.

"We're not taking her off life support. It would be no different than murder." He felt Melanie grip his hand.

"Tim," she began.

"No!" His voice escalated with anger. "She's a tough little girl and she's gotten through other injuries in the past. I want to give her a chance to heal."

"They weren't like this one, Mr. Moran," said Dr. Elias. "There's really no hope." He turned to Melanie, eyebrows raised with the unspoken question. She shook her head.

"I agree with Tim," she said. "We need to give her more time. It's too soon."

"I understand," the doctor replied, clearing his throat. "There's no rush. We can keep her here until she's physically out of danger. She'll be monitored continually and you'll be notified if there's any change in her condition."

"I want to see her." Tim's voice broke. He jerked his arm from Melanie's grasp. "I want to see her now."

Dr. Elias nodded. He walked over to the nursing station and whispered to a tall, dark-haired nurse. She shot a glance at Melanie and Tim, then turned back to Dr. Elias and patted his arm as if to reassure him before she pulled away.

When the nurse reached them she said, "I'll take you to see your daughter." She led the way down the corridor to the Intensive Care Unit, Tim and Melanie following a few steps behind.

"Tim, we need to talk," Melanie lowered her voice so the nurse couldn't overhear them. "Alone."

"There's nothing to talk about," Tim answered. "We're not disconnecting her from life support."

"I agree with you. I know it's too early to make that kind of decision. But think about what the doctor said. There's no hope of recovery and even with my health insurance, the hospital bills are going to be enormous."

They walked for a few moments in silence. He glanced at Melanie and saw her eyes narrow as she chewed on the inside of her lower lip, her way of processing information.

"Do they know who drove the car that hit her?"

Tim heaved a sigh. "It was an elderly woman. I spoke to the police when they were filling in their accident report in Emergency. They think she may have had a heart attack or stroke, or maybe the rain prevented her from seeing the girls."

"Girls?"

As they walked along, Tim stared at the back of the nurse

who led them on without looking back at either of them. He couldn't tell if she purposely made an effort not to hear what they were saying or if she'd tuned them out.

"Her friend Lisa was hit, too. They're keeping her for observation. She'll probably get out tomorrow."

"But what about the driver?" Melanie persisted. "Is she going to be charged with reckless driving? They've got to take away her license. We should contact a lawyer so we can sue to help with the medical bills."

"We can't do that."

"Why not? If it was negligence..."

"She died at the scene."

Melanie exhaled loudly. "Then we'll go after her estate, surely she's got some money."

"Jesus Christ, Melanie," he hissed. "I don't want to think about that right now."

The nurse had stopped at the door to the Intensive Care Unit. She kept her face impassive, though she gave them a grim but sympathetic smile as she handed them dull green cotton gowns and face masks from a cart outside the room.

"I'll leave you with her," she said. "Ring the buzzer if you need anything." Tim nodded his thanks and they stepped inside.

Together they walked over to Chelsa who lay in a white enameled hospital crib, strapped to IVs and machines that monitored everything left alive in her body. Her eyes were swollen to tiny slits in an almost unrecognizable face; the skin on her forehead and cheeks raw and abraded. Her head had been shaved and so heavily swathed in gauze she looked like a mummy. Vague yellow and red stains seeped through the bandaging. Melanie's hand snuck into Tim's and she gripped it hard. At that moment they were closer than they'd ever been.

"Can't we dim the lights?" Tim said, irritated at nothing other than the frustration of being completely powerless to help his daughter in her precarious condition. Melanie's mouth dropped open.

"She doesn't even know we're here," Melanie whispered.

"She's not going to be bothered by the lights."

I know you're here. The lights hurt my head.

"Besides, the doctors and nurses need to be able to check her vital signs for any changes." Her voice quavered. She held her lip between her teeth until she'd gained control. "What am I saying? There's not going to be a change."

Why am I here, Mommy?

But Tim only nodded, numb with grief. He relinquished Melanie's hand, dropped to his knees beside Chelsa's bedside and began to pray. Deep in prayer, he didn't notice as Melanie bent over Chelsa and kissed her on the forehead. Nor did he see her leave the room, or the anguish on her face as she swung the door closed behind her.

Chapter Three

Balancing a cardboard box that contained candles, a crucifix and a small leather-bound Bible, Tim eased open the door of the tertiary care unit where the medical staff had moved Chelsa after she'd healed from her physical injuries. As the doctors predicted, she hadn't regained consciousness since having been struck by a car six weeks earlier. But each night after leaving Chelsa's side in the hospital room, he'd head to St. Augustus' chapel, light candles for her recovery and pray for a miracle.

He wondered whether Melanie would be visiting Chelsa that evening. He'd given up trying to change her mind about turning off Chelsa's life support. She'd given her daughter two weeks to emerge from the coma, but refused to budge on her decision once it became apparent that Chelsa would remain in a persistent vegetative state, as the doctors had called it.

Melanie had become less confrontational, seeming to accept and adapt to their virtually childless situation better than he. Their family life had lapsed into a routine of either one or the other being home alone, or with Chelsa. They were seldom together now, not even at night. Melanie had moved to the spare bedroom.

In fact, Melanie's mood had become increasingly mellow over the past few weeks. More like the girl he had fallen in love with. It both puzzled and concerned him because she actually seemed happy and he had no idea why this could be. Though she and Chelsa had the typical mother-daughter conflicts, she would never have consciously desired Chelsa out of their lives. She was a good mother. *Is* a good mother, he corrected himself.

He began setting candles around the room, on every

available counter and windowsill, hung the cross on a coat hook on the wall near the door, and placed the Bible on the table beside her bed. He tiptoed around the room again, lighting all the candles until the room glowed. After kissing Chelsa's cheek, he knelt by her bedside to pray. Without warning, the door opened, smacking the wall behind him. The cross fell to the floor with a crash and shattered. Tim leapt to his feet, shaking.

"What the hell do you think you're doing?" Melanie marched into the room, picked up the candles and blew them out. She flung them into the box, a couple of them snapping under the impact.

"Lower your voice," Tim hissed, raising his hand as if to quiet her. He detected an unfamiliar scent on her clothes as she brushed past him, and it wasn't a new perfume. She looked as if she'd gained weight, for her clothes were fitting a bit tighter these days. Even her face had become puffy. This was unusual for Melanie who fastidiously guarded her weight, traveling every day to a local gym where she worked out for at least an hour.

"Or what? She'll hear me?" Melanie sneered. "Face up to it, Tim. All your religious hocus-pocus and praying is not going to bring her around. She's dead. The sooner we let her go, the sooner we can get on with our lives."

I'm in here. Don't let me go.

Tim grabbed Melanie's jacket by the collar and forcibly pushed her outside the room. Tearing herself free she whirled and whacked him hard across the face. He reeled back, hand flying to his mouth. His eyes darted around the hallway. None of the nursing staff had witnessed the altercation. He let out a sigh of relief.

"She just might be able to." His voice wavered with emotion. "You may have set her back forever when you said she's dead. Coma patients are aware of what is going on around them."

Melanie stood speechless, her fists balled up angrily on her hips as if she were having difficulty in preventing herself from hitting him again.

"I've been praying," he said and almost involuntarily his hands clasped together.

Melanie saw the movement and rolled her eyes. "So what's new?" A humph of obvious disapproval escaped her lips.

"And yet," she continued, pausing dramatically as she tilted her head and glared at him from under narrowed brows, "nothing has come of your prayers, has it, Tim? Or am I missing something?"

Tim stared at her as if she were a stranger. "God spoke to me."

Melanie trembled visibly and stepped back. Tim felt a tiny thrill of satisfaction. He knew his unquestioning faith bothered her, but it had only grown stronger since Chelsa's accident. Before the accident Chelsa had shared his beliefs, attended church services with him, even gone to Sunday school; customs that had further alienated Melanie from them.

"He said that we'd be faced with challenges like this, but that I should never doubt my faith in Him. If I continued to pray and have faith, He'd show me a miracle."

Melanie's face tightened. Little white spots dotted her reddening cheeks. She stared at him in disbelief.

"We can't go on like this anymore. When are you going to wake up?" Her voice shook as if tears were close to surfacing. "You have to let her go."

Tim set his chin and refused to meet her eyes. Melanie moved to stand directly in front of him, placing her hands on his shoulders until she forced him to make eye contact with her.

"Tim, we're over our heads in debt. We're going to lose the house. And Chelsa is never, ever going to get any better. Can't you see that? The insurance settlement gave us enough for a funeral, not a lifetime of hospital care."

Tim recoiled and pushed her hands away, his face congealing with hostility.

"We can move back into my mother's house," he argued

stubbornly.

Melanie's eyes became angry slits. "The only way I'd move back in with your mother would be if I was in the same condition as Chelsa. Dead. Besides, living with her wouldn't save us anything. Remember how she kept raising the rent on us?"

"It's always about money with you, isn't it? You would let your child die because of money."

"It's not the money," Melanie persisted, "it's that there's no hope. We got second opinions, third opinions, and all the doctors were in agreement. If there had been any brain activity at all, or any chance of her recovering, they'd have told us. But there isn't."

Tim shook his head. "I can't believe that. I refuse to believe it. We'll just have to work longer hours to pay for her care."

"Not we," Melanie corrected. "I'm through. I can't do it anymore. It's draining me; it's draining us. Financially and emotionally." She took a deep breath. "And physically."

She turned away from him, her voice scarcely audible as she said, "I'm pregnant."

Tim stayed silent for a very long time. Finally he slid to the floor and sat against the wall, cradling his head in his hands.

"How far along?"

"About six weeks. I only found out today."

He looked up and felt a scorching behind his eyes as he regarded her. That explained her weight gain. The recent change in her mood. And her move to the spare bedroom. Everything had become crystal clear to him now.

"Six weeks? That would put conception about the time of Chelsa's accident." Melanie stared at her hands.

"Are you trying to tell me I'm the father? Because we haven't had sex for a couple of months. At least not since well before the accident."

"Of course you're the father," Melanie retorted, but with a touch of wariness in her voice. "How dare you say that to me?" She gnawed on the inside of her lower lip and glanced away. "Maybe the test was wrong and I'm farther along than the doctor thinks."

Tim scrambled to his feet. He stared at her, his eyes narrowing until their reddened slits seemed as if they were burning.

"Think back, Melanie. You told me that taking birth control pills made you gain weight. You talked me into having a vasectomy." His eyes were devoid of expression, his face hard as a mask. His whole body felt rigid. It took every bit of self-control he possessed not to hit her. He'd never resorted to violence before, but a woman like Melanie could provoke men to do things they'd never dreamt of.

"Remember that, Melanie? After Chelsa ended up in hospital with a broken arm? I did exactly what you demanded, as usual, because you didn't want any more kids. Now I wish I hadn't." Then the resentment that had been simmering for years finally boiled over.

"You're no different than your mother," he spat. The moment the words were out he regretted them, though his regret came too late to take them back. It was the worst thing he could have said to her.

Melanie looked as if she were about to reach out and choke him. Her face had drained of all color. She stumbled to the doorway, clutching the door handle to Chelsa's room as if it were the hatch that stood between safety and a chasm into the unknown. Scarcely breathing, her mouth worked but no sound emerged.

"I want you out of the house by the time I get home," Tim said.

He moved towards Melanie who shrank away as if afraid that Tim would slap her. Instead, Tim threw open the door and gave Melanie a shove toward the hallway. Before he stepped back into Chelsa's room he said in a cold, dead voice, "You're on your own now."

After that, Tim had very little contact with Melanie. She rarely came to see Chelsa and if Tim happened to be there, they usually fought over keeping her on the life support. The fear that the negative effects the fighting would have on their comatose child gnawed at him. When it came time to sign the divorce papers, he nearly refused; for the first time in their relationship he reveled at having all the power. Finally he acquiesced, if only because of Melanie's innocent unborn child. Having Melanie out of his life was the best thing he could do for Chelsa.

Melanie took nothing of the marital property with her as there was nothing left to take. They'd sold all their furniture and anything of value. All his income had gone to pay Chelsa's medical bills. He'd mortgaged and remortgaged the house until finally, unable to keep up payments, it had been foreclosed upon by the bank. Chelsa had been relocated to a state-run facility with sparse care, and so too with cleaning and personal attention to his child. It nearly broke his heart to see her there.

After Chelsa had been transferred to long-term care, Tim made arrangements for her to be baptized, something Melanie had always refused to let him do. He'd waited years for this. His mother had passed away a couple of months after Chelsa's accident and it had been her last request before she died. Though it came too late for his mother to see it, it gave him comfort to finally fulfill her dying wish.

He did his best to dress up for the occasion, having found a pair of barely worn Dockers and a nearly new dress shirt at the local Goodwill. Because no one at work cared, his grooming rarely consisted of more than a morning shower. When he shaved for the first time in a week it shocked him to see the reflection of a haggard man with sunken brown eyes and scraggly, shoulder-length, prematurely greying hair. He reached for the scissors and with the help of a hand-held mirror, snipped away until he had a passable haircut.

He'd requested that Reverend Maloney from his church, a grandfatherly man with a round florid face and bright blue eyes, perform the ceremony. Only Tim would be present. He had no friends and he'd long since lost contact with Melanie, who had moved several times since the birth of her new baby. Now there was no one else in his life but Chelsa.

The Reverend Maloney came prepared with all the vestments of his station. He placed a Bible and a bottle of holy water on the night table beside the bed then peered down at Chelsa.

Get away from me.

A look of aversion passed across Reverend Maloney's face. He retrieved the Bible and bottle of holy water in haste, backing away from the bed.

"I'm sorry, Tim," he said. "There can be no baptism." His gaze of apprehension remained fixated on the girl in the bed, as if he was uncertain whether he should remain or leave at once. Tim grabbed his arm. Reverend Maloney stared at the hand holding him until Tim dropped it.

"What do you mean?" Tim demanded. "Why can't you baptize her?"

The Reverend shook his head, a strange mixture of sadness and trepidation on his face. "You didn't tell me the severity of her condition. She may not be technically dead, but in the eyes of the Lord, she is." As he was leaving the room he turned back to Tim. His last words were chilling. "The best I can do is to bless her and give her last rites in preparation for her final journey..."

Though Tim began to protest, Reverend Maloney hurried away without another word. But as he disappeared into the elevator, Tim heard him mutter, "Keeping her that way is an abomination."

Tim's shoulders slumped in defeat. Even when the doctors had told him there would be no chance of Chelsa recovering, his faith had kept him going. Reverend Maloney's hapless remark had more impact on him than anything that had been said or done by the so-called experts. Was it selfish of him to keep her hanging on like this? Had Melanie and the doctors been right? Would it be best for Chelsa to take her off life-support, in effect, ending her life? He sighed heavily. Not even God would give him an answer.

That evening he left Chelsa's bedside at around 11 p.m. Shortly after midnight the nursing station was empty because every medical professional on the ward of the short-staffed nursing home was working on a Code Blue at the end of the hall. So no one saw the door to Chelsa's room slide quietly open and a person wearing a long dark coat with the collar up-turned to obscure the face, slip inside unnoticed.

Who's there?

Once in the room, the person walked over to the life support system and monitors that metered out Chelsa's life.

What are you doing?

The person bent down and pulled the plug from the wall socket, then left just as quietly. And though the breathing machines were now silent and the light from the LED readout extinguished, there came the soft sound of an eight-year-old girl letting out her last machine-fed breath.

Chapter Four
Six Years Later

It seemed to psychiatrist Rand Morrissey that his morning was crazier than usual. He'd arrived at his office to find his receptionist, Angela, fending calls from distraught patients, and before he'd even removed his jacket a terse call came in from a patient's attorney. The patient had taken an overdose of sleeping pills after child pornography had been discovered on his office computer. Fortunately, the wife had found him in time to have his stomach pumped. Now the patient rested in a hospital ward under suicide watch, investigation by the police, and waiting in the wings, his wife's divorce lawyer.

Later that morning, a 26-year-old female patient whose flirtatiousness made him uncomfortable enough to always have Angela present, sent Angela out of the room for a glass of water and proceeded to remove her clothes in front of Rand, all the while professing her love for him. And that was even before the exhausted Angela popped in to inform him it was noon and she was heading out for something to eat.

By the time the call came from Kate Petroski, a pediatric neurologist at St. Augustus Hospital, Rand was prepared for anything. Although he rarely received calls to go into St. Augustus to see patients, he'd heard of Dr. Petroski through the nurses' gossip channels. A workaholic dedicated to her young patients, she had been on staff at the hospital for a couple of years. Though in that time, it seemed, very few had come to know much about her.

"What can I do for you?" he said, vaguely wondering why a pediatrician would be calling. For personal reasons, he limited his practice to adults. He cradled the phone carefully between his jaw and shoulder and picked up a pen so he could scribble notes about the previous patient's visit before he forgot them.

"I've got a five-year-old female who was brought into Emergency several times this last week because she'd lost consciousness. We've admitted her to hospital for further investigation."

"Why are you calling me?" Rand only half listened; he'd heard enough already.

"I'd like you to do a consultation on her," Kate said.

"I only see adult patients," Rand stated in a tone that anyone could tell was non-negotiable.

As if she hadn't heard him or deliberately ignored what he'd said, Kate continued, "Since the intermittent blackouts began we've done a complete neurological work-up, CAT Scans, the whole bit. I consulted with a pediatric cardiologist who ran EKGs, but none of us can find anything etiological to account for the blackouts."

She paused and several moments of silence followed.

"There's no evidence of epilepsy," she said finally. "We've ruled out nearly every medical possibility. We know that it is syncope, but we've questioned the parents and there are no indications as to why they're happening."

"Refresh me on syncope."

"It's the medical term for childhood fainting spells. Like when a kid is having a tantrum and holds their breath until they pass out. I had a few episodes as a child. Sienna's not in any real physical danger except if one occurred at the wrong moment, like riding a bike or while in a playground. But if they go on uncorrected, or if we don't figure out what's causing them, she may not grow out of it. Then it will become a problem as she gets older."

"Maybe you didn't hear me before," Rand interrupted, wincing because he didn't mean to sound rude, but he couldn't help it. She wasn't getting the message. "I don't see children. My practice is limited to adult psychiatry."

"I'm aware of that." Kate's exasperation was evident in

her voice as well. "But because we're not finding a medical cause to explain her symptoms, we're getting ready to release her. I thought maybe a psychiatric exam as a last ditch effort might reveal what we've missed. I wanted to get a consult from a child psychologist, but a mutual friend insisted I contact you."

"So I'm your 'last ditch effort'?" Rand gave a short laugh.

An awkward silence filled the line for a moment until Kate said, "Well, I didn't mean..." But at least the earlier tension had been broken.

"That's okay," Rand reassured her. He passed a hand over his face and rubbed at the corner of his right eye.

He hated doing psychiatric consults on kids. Hated it with such a passion that during his psychiatric residency he'd avoided seeing children except only when it became absolutely necessary to fulfill requirements for his medical license. For personal reasons he'd decided to limit his practice to adults. God, he didn't even know how to talk to children. His own childhood had ended so abruptly he'd forgotten what kids were like. They really should get another doctor. He fumbled for the right excuse.

"You mentioned you were referred to me by a mutual friend," Rand said. "Who was that?"

"Dr. Irving Silverstein. Do you remember him?"

Hearing the name brought back such a kaleidoscope of memories it made Rand lightheaded. He focused on the ceiling fan that seemed to sway as if it was about to crash downward. He closed his eyes and an image of the diminutive doctor with his year-round chestnut tan and shock of maestro-style white hair came back to him. He swallowed hard to steady his nerves. He hadn't thought about Dr. Silverstein in many, many years. Hadn't even realized he was still alive, for that matter.

"Of course I remember him," he said, his voice almost a whisper. And he knew then that he'd have to see this little girl because he owed it to Dr. Silverstein. He had a definite, intangible debt that needed repayment. But why the doctor would want him to see this child was incomprehensible. And more importantly, what had Dr. Silverstein told Kate about him?

"You win," he said. "I'll talk to her." He mentally crossed his fingers. "How mature is she?"

"She's very mature," Kate replied in a rush. "You might think of her as an old soul—very wise and very deep. Almost weird, in a way. But she's an only child growing up among adults, so maybe it's to be expected."

"All right." Rand suppressed a sigh. "I'll drop by to visit her after I've seen my last patient this afternoon."

"I'll hold off on the discharge papers," Kate said. "I'm on call this week, so I'll be around. Page or text me when you get to the hospital. My number is 555-7654."

Rand made a note of the number then hung up the phone. He half-turned when he heard a noise in the doorway. Angela entered the room carrying a full pot of coffee in one hand and a submarine sandwich in the other.

"Tough day, huh, Dr. Morrissey?" She set the sandwich on his desk and refilled his coffee cup.

"It's about to get worse," he groaned.

She smiled and blushed, turning quickly to hide her reddening cheeks. Either the fifty-something Angela had a crush on him, a fact he largely ignored because he'd done nothing to encourage it, or she was becoming overly protective. But it was hard not to notice the overt signs: she'd gone from grey to blonde overnight, she'd joined a gym and lost at least three dress sizes, and home baking showed up in the office several times a week. It puzzled him. He'd never thought of himself as being particularly attractive to women. Or maybe it was because he'd never given it much effort.

Too lazy to fuss with his spikey black hair each morning, he kept it cropped short and tamed with a little gel. His coloring was so dark he was often mistaken for Italian instead of the Irish that he was. Black Irish, they called them, those descendants whose ancestral blood was Spanish and Italian mixed with Irish. Only his ice-floe blue eyes gave away his heritage. His sister Carrie had been blessed with dark blonde hair and freckles, the more typical Gaelic coloring of his parents that he'd envied, wishing he weren't so swarthy that his high school classmates had called him a derogatory term for people of Italian heritage.

"Where'd you get this one?" friends and relatives would ask as they ruffled his hair, referring to his appearance being opposite from the rest of his family.

"Oh, he looks just like the milkman," his mother would joke and everyone except he and his father seemed to find that hilarious.

At the end of the work day after Angela had gone home, Rand walked around his office, adjusting the times of his clocks. The office could have been mistaken for an antique clock store were it not for his named engraved in a bronze plaque on the door. As a child, his grandmother had given him a cuckoo clock she'd bought from Germany: a man and a woman in lederhosen and peasant dress respectively, who pursued each other through the open doors of a miniature wooden house.

Once he'd put it on display, well-meaning relatives took it to be the beginning of a collection and almost, it seemed, before he'd had a chance to deny being a collector, he had ten of them of varying themes and sizes. His favorite was a baseball pitcher sending a fake pitch, with the batter swinging at nothing. It had been a gift from Dr. Silverstein, who'd no doubt been prompted by his mother.

Then he'd become intrigued by them and as his psychiatric practice flourished, had expanded to include everything from a Seth Thomas Westminster chime clock to a Roger Wood's Buck Rogers. The first time a patient had called him an horologist he'd almost punched him until he learned what it meant. But the effect of thirty clicking and chiming clocks would drive a sane person to lunacy, so he'd stayed the workings of the most inaccurate of them and kept the others set. Even so, many of them continued to run either fast or slow. An annoyance to several patients who'd reset their watches only to later discover they'd been misled.

Shortly after five o'clock, Rand slid his silver Volvo into the physicians' parking lot at St. Augustus Hospital and headed toward the pediatric ward. He stopped briefly at the front desk to have Dr. Petroski paged, eschewed the elevator, and by the time he'd sprung up three flights of stairs, Kate was already busily filling in patient charts at the nursing station.

He'd managed to do a bit of homework on Dr. Petroski before he'd left the office. He'd heard that she was single, but considered somewhat cold, or too interested in a career and paying off student loans, to have a social life. Or so it was reported by Rand's womanizing informant, who perhaps was not a reliable source. By her peers she was considered to be a brilliant diagnostician. So if she was unable to come up with a diagnosis for this child, the problem had to be unusually elusive.

Dr. Petroski appeared to be on the sunny side of thirty, although she was so petite, in her blue hospital scrubs she looked much younger, and was probably mistaken for a child herself on occasion. Her rich mahogany hair was pulled tightly back in a ponytail and as he approached he could see that behind her round rimless spectacles, her grey-green eyes were fringed with thick black lashes. She smiled at him and it lit up her whole face.

Stunning, he thought, surprising himself by blushing. Then his smile became rigid. An angry red port-wine birthmark, only partially covered with concealing make-up, extended from her left ear and disappeared under her chin. Almost involuntarily Kate's left hand flew to the side of her neck in a pre-rehearsed gesture to cover it up. With her right hand she gave him the patient's medical chart.

"You'll see most of what I told you in there." She inclined her head toward the chart. "There are a couple of other things you should be aware of. Maybe I should say 'beware' of, and that would be the mother. She's always there so it's difficult to speak directly to the child. I'd tread carefully with her."

Rand studied Kate's face to see if she was joking. She wasn't.

"That's not a problem," he said. "I'll ask her to leave the

room while I'm evaluating the child." He reflected for a moment on his female patient earlier that morning. It never hurt to be prepared for any situation. "I'll make certain there's a nurse or other assistant in the room."

Kate shook her head. "Not that simple. She'll never leave you alone with the kid. But if you can interview Sienna by herself you might be able to get more answers than we could."

"Is there a father in the picture?"

Kate's face crinkled into a wry smile.

"Yeah, there's a father. He's hard-nosed and all business. Difficult to read. He doesn't come down often because these episodes of Sienna's only last for a couple of hours. She's usually released first thing in the morning after we've run the so-far inconclusive tests."

Rand opened the chart and began reading the notes made by Kate and the other professionals who'd been consulted on the case. He paged through the lab work and scan results, but it was as Kate had said. Nothing to indicate a medical explanation for her fainting spells. Not much history to a five-year-old. *Or was there?*

He tore his attention away from the file and back to Kate. "Is she awake?"

"She wasn't the last time I checked. But the syncope comes and goes. We should get you in to see her right away because they serve dinner to the peds first."

With Rand at her side she set off down the child-friendly, balloon and teddy bear painted corridor, stopping in front of a small private room. Kate slowly turned the handle and eased the door open.

Rand hesitated, a wave of foreboding sweeping over him. It was just an ordinary hospital room door with a small cross-wired rectangular window inset. A couple of dirty fingerprint smudges overlooked by the custodial staff framed the door handle. Missing paint chips revealed that at separate times the door had been alternately moss green and dusty rose instead of the current eggshell. But the door demarcated a line that he feared to cross: a hospital room with a little girl inside. He took a deep breath and pushed the door open.

The Venetian blinds had been drawn, but one indirect lamp spotlighted a tiny, dark-haired figure curled up in a fetal position in the hospital crib. Rand could see the child, her face distorted with green lattice reflections from the raised sides of the hospital crib and mossy walls. A woman sat on the opposite side of the bed with her head bent over a magazine, one finger distractedly twisting her long blonde hair. As she heard their footsteps, she stood, dropping the magazine onto the chair. She peered from one to the other with an anxiousness in her eyes that should have been maternal, but somehow wasn't. It puzzled him. Kate walked over to the mother. The mother raised a finger to her lips and pointed to the child, who appeared to be asleep.

"Mrs. Cantrell, this is Dr. Morrissey. He's the psychiatrist I told you about," Kate said in a low voice. She seemed annoyed at having been shushed by the mother.

The woman scrutinized Rand and the pale, freckled face that had at first appeared aloof, illuminated with a smile that transformed her so she looked angelic. Almost. Her eyes were an unusual cinnamon brown and the way she had used eyeliner and mascara gave her a feline look. She held out her hand.

"Melanie," she corrected, casting him a friendly glance from under those long-lashed eyes.

He shook her offered hand and studied her for a few moments. She was the kind of woman who, despite all his training as a psychiatrist, unnerved him. Self-assured and prepossessed, she spoke and moved as if she had nothing to fear of anyone or anything. The world was hers and there was no one with the power to take it away.

He considered himself a good judge of character, and not only because he was a psychiatrist. Disreputable people disconcerted him. His ability to spot them was like built-in radar. In his practice this trait occasionally turned out to be detrimental. But Melanie did not seem like the sort of person Kate had described. He shrugged off the notion. Maybe a woman would be a better judge of another woman's motives.

"There's a visitors' room at the end of the corridor," Kate said, her words emerging a little clipped as she glanced from one to the other.

She steered Melanie outside, motioning Rand to follow them. Silently they walked three abreast, stopping at the dull waiting room with its stock hospital furniture upholstered in mauve and grey. The clanging of food trolleys signaled the dinner hour. And though the lukewarm scent of broccoli and creamed something-or-other was unappealing, Rand's stomach growled in anticipation. He faced Melanie who looked like a teenager being held for detention after class.

"Dr. Petroski told me that Sienna's had several fainting spells and brief periods of unconsciousness," he said. "Do you recall anything unusual happening before the first episode?"

Melanie Cantrell frowned. She turned to Kate and crossed her arms. "It's all in her charts. Do we really have to go through her whole history again?" Kate's eyes sought Rand's and her eyebrows raised a little as if to say, 'I told you so.'

"No, no," he reassured Melanie. "I haven't had a chance to go over her charts and test results as much as I'd like. I wanted to see if we could establish a pattern of behavior prior to them taking place."

Melanie leaned back against the wall and folded her arms tightly around herself again as if she were cold. Or it could have been a defensive gesture. He watched her collect her thoughts, and out of the corner of his eye noticed Kate's impassive face as she too scrutinized the mother.

"It started about two weeks ago. One minute she was playing alone—then when I didn't hear any sounds coming from her room I went in. At first I thought she was asleep so I shook her. When she didn't respond I called 911. But the paramedics weren't able to bring her out of it either so they brought her to the hospital. When the doctors couldn't find anything physically wrong they discharged her. Since then she's had two more blackouts."

Rand glanced from Melanie to Kate and back again.

"I'd like to talk to her once she's awake and had dinner."

Kate nodded in agreement. "There's no point trying to interview a hypoglycemic child."

He headed back to Sienna's room with Kate and Melanie following close behind. An empty food trolley waited outside her room and as he reached the door a nurse emerged. She smiled and held the door open for the three of them to enter. Rand walked over to the side of the child's bed and carefully lowered the side of the crib so as not to startle her. A tray of food sat unnoticed on the bedside table. Sienna still appeared to be sleeping.

He reached up and turned on the bright overhead light. It didn't seem to affect her. He lifted her wrist. It hung limply in his hand. He turned her hand over and noticed a small birthmark that looked almost like a bird in flight on the inside of her wrist. He laid her hand back down on the covers. Then he pulled back each eyelid and examined her eyes. At that moment the child rolled away from his touch and moaned.

"Don't," she said aloud, eyes still tightly closed.

"Sienna?" he whispered. Sienna's little face frowned in her sleep as if she were having a bad dream.

"Sienna, what don't you want me to do?" Her eyes opened then and she sat up, gazing blindly at the opposite wall. He followed the direction of her stare but could see nothing unusual. He looked back to see Kate and Melanie's gaze riveted on Sienna, their expressions frozen in horror. Alarmed, he turned back to the child.

Sienna was now sitting upright, rigid as a mannequin. As they watched she began emitting high, ear-splitting shrieks that filled the room and reverberated off the walls. Kate leapt to Sienna's bedside, folding the child tightly against her. Sienna fought her, thrashing against the confinement.

"Can I get some help here?" she shouted to Rand. Melanie cowered near the door. Rand moved forward to help restrain Sienna just as a nurse rushed into the room.

"Wrap the bedding around her and hold her tight until she starts to calm down," Kate ordered.

Together the three of them swaddled the perspiring child,

holding her until her thrashing slowed to a slight tremble. Within seconds she'd relaxed in their arms. As Rand and the nurse stepped back, Kate lowered Sienna gently back onto the bed.

She let out a ragged breath of suppressed tension and gave a short laugh. "That was exciting."

Rand passed his hand in front of Sienna's still open eyes, but she made no move to indicate she was aware of it. Without another sound she closed her eyes, seeming as if in a peaceful sleep. Rand pulled back her eyelids once more to examine her pupils, but the child made no further movement.

He turned to Melanie. "Has this ever happened before?"

Melanie shook her head violently as if still dazed from the episode. She whirled around and rushed out of the room.

Rand and Kate exchanged a long contemplative look.

"What do you make of that?"

"Are you talking about Sienna or the mother?" Kate asked drily.

Rand grimaced, rubbing at the underside of his chin as he considered what had just taken place. "It's very strange."

"You don't think she could be faking it, do you?" Kate asked. "To get attention."

"It's unlikely. She'd have to be a darned good actress. Most kids that age couldn't hold out for very long without giggling."

Kate didn't reply. She began straightening the hospital bedding that had been churned into disarray during the scene with Sienna. Rand took one last look at the child in the bed then turned to leave. As he exited the room, Kate quickly grabbed the child's medical chart and followed. Once outside they searched for Melanie, but she was nowhere to be seen. Then Rand noticed her pacing the hall near the end of the corridor, her back to them.

He glanced back at Kate when her beeper buzzed in her hospital lab coat pocket. She checked it and made a frustrated clicking sound between her teeth.

"I'm needed in the ER," she said. "I'll let you deal with

Mrs. Cantrell and I'll catch up with you later." She hesitated.

"I'm going to keep Sienna here another twenty-four hours for observation. Unless something else happens in that time I'll have no choice but to release her."

She reached into her breast pocket and pulled out a business card.

"Call me if anything happens." She turned to leave and stopped. "Call me even if nothing happens."

A little perplexed, he watched her leave, considering her cryptic comment, trying to interpret her meaning. He frowned, wishing he hadn't been left all alone with the mother and child. He wasn't used to working with children, nor had he much experience with parents. Melanie, leaning against the wall with her back to him, looked as out of place as an exotic dancer at a church picnic. He took a deep breath to consider what he should say to her and headed in her direction. When he reached her, he touched her arm to get her attention. She jumped.

"Sorry," Rand said, studying the sudden pallor of her cheeks. "Are you going to be all right?"

She nodded, looking vulnerable and scared.

"I'll be back to see her again. There's nothing I can do until she's conscious," he said, feeling helpless at his inability to comfort her. "Have the hospital call me when she wakes up. As long as she's under medical observation, she'll be fine." But the look of apprehension in the mother's eyes told him otherwise.

Chapter Five

Nearly six years after Chelsa's accident, while watching late night television Tim Moran experienced a revelation of sorts. A psychic hotline advertisement purported the possibility of seeing into his future. Or more importantly, Tim believed, Chelsa's future. And when he called the toll free number, he was absolutely dumbfounded at how much the company spokesperson knew about him and Chelsa. It occurred to Tim then that perhaps all that time spent in prayer hadn't been wasted. This could be the new route to Chelsa's recovery.

When Chelsa's life support had been unplugged after her accident she'd begun to breathe without help from the ventilator. The doctors had told him that happened occasionally. Families taking the final step prepare themselves for the death of their loved one; but when the life support is removed the patient may continue to live, though they cannot eat or function normally. The feeding tube must remain to sustain life or the alternative is starving to death. Tim refused to allow that and so the feeding tube, and the medical bills, remained. But none of the nursing staff were ever able to explain how Chelsa had become disconnected from her life support.

Sometimes Tim felt as if he'd aged thirty years, though time had stood still with Chelsa. She'd spent nearly half her life in this bed. She only moved when the nurses bathed her or they performed her physical therapy exercises. And even then it was the nursing staff making her move. He asked them to keep her curly blonde hair cropped short, not only because it made it easier to care for, but with long hair her resemblance to Melanie had begun to emerge, giving him a disquiet he couldn't explain.

To his knowledge Melanie hadn't seen Chelsa since that last night when she'd told him of her pregnancy. As they had had no further communication except through divorce attorneys, he didn't know if she was even aware Chelsa was alive or what nursing facility she languished in. Frankly he didn't care. With a new child and another man in her life, he and Melanie had been through for many years.

He'd tried not to blame her for Chelsa's accident, but he couldn't help it. If only she had driven her to school that day as he'd asked, this wouldn't have happened. So the loss of Melanie had never upset him the way losing his daughter had. Not having a woman in his life gave him more time to devote to Chelsa's care. Things had once looked hopeless. Traditional medicine had failed them. And though they'd been all but abandoned by his church, despite what Melanie thought, his prayers had worked. A miracle had happened. Chelsa could breathe on her own. And now God had shown him a new direction.

On Chelsa's fourteenth birthday, Tim called in a psychic to perform a séance to see if she could break through to Chelsa. The psychic's name was Madame Noella. Tim had hired her sight unseen through the telephone number on the psychic hotline. She offered to give references, but Tim couldn't see the point. Besides, he felt secretly ashamed of having called her, scarcely able to admit to himself what he was preparing to do to his child.

Madame Noella arrived like a battleship setting off to fight a war on foreign shores. Her long, oily black hair had been braided and rolled up in a bun then pinned to the right side of her head, making it look like a giant black wart. Her smallish eyes were outlined in black kohl, and her garish red lipstick had smeared onto her chin. Tim judged her to be over 300 pounds, but she disguised it well behind a curtain of flowing black polyester caftan covered in gold-embroidered astrological signs. A heavy black hobo bag with twisted tassels was slung over her shoulder. As she breezed past Tim, she inadvertently whacked him with the bag and an acrid tang of body

odor, strong, musky perfume and something else that reminded him of the smoke left by exploded fireworks assailed him.

"You done this before?" She had a bit of an accent that
sounded like the Southern U.S. mixed in with an attempt at
Jamaican. It was probably invented for the part. When she
smiled he saw that more of the red lipstick was stuck on her
yellowed teeth. She glanced at the comatose girl on the bed and
contemplated Tim with curiosity.

Tim shook his head, his mouth twisting up in a kind of
grimace that must have given away his true feelings.

"You don't believe in it?" she observed, "what you doin'
it for then?"

Tim stole a glance at Chelsa, oblivious to everything
around her. He really didn't believe in it, he believed in prayer,
but maybe this was God's way of having his prayers answered.

"I've got to keep trying," he said. "I know I can get
through to her if I keep trying."

Madame Noella shrugged. "We'll see," she said. She stood
and began arranging tiny incense cones around the room, lighting them as she went, filling the room with a sickly sweet
smoke that caught in Tim's throat. Then she sprinkled what
appeared to be ashes in a circle around Chelsa's bed.

"Ashes represent the cleansing fire," she explained. She
set a brass metronome beside the bed where it ticked rhythmi-
cally. Then she took a little purple velvet sack with a gold cord
drawstring from her bag and began tying it around Chelsa's
neck. To Tim it looked like a miniature version of the satchels
that envelop bottles of Crown Royal whiskey.

"Wait," he protested.

"It's just a medicine bag." She sounded defensive. "It
contains elements to protect her from evil spirits while her
body is in this vulnerable state."

Tim sighed helplessly and stared down at his scuffed
sneakers while he considered her words. Of course he needed
Chelsa to be protected from evil. He'd devoted his life to her
welfare. Finally he glanced up at the woman and nodded once,
unable to meet her eyes. This hocus pocus was what he was

paying her for, wasn't it?

Finished for the moment with the pre-seance rituals, Madame Noella stood on one side of Chelsa's bed and motioned for Tim to move to the other side, opposite her. Then she peeled back the threadbare hospital bedclothes that covered Chelsa and picked up her hand. Reaching across the girl's stomach, she held out her hand to Tim and indicated for him to pick up Chelsa's as well. As soon as he was holding both Madame Noella's and Chelsa's hands in his, Madame Noella's eyes closed and she began muttering under her breath.

Within minutes the heat of the room and the thickness of the burning incense began to affect Tim. He closed his eyes. His thoughts started to drift as Madame Noella chanted, her voice choreographed with the metronome. While he couldn't make out the rough, guttural words that sounded almost like English spoken backwards, they had a hypnotic effect. For a moment he was unable to open his eyes or move his limbs at will. And though that would normally have given rise to panic, with Madame still chanting, and the tick-ticking coming from the side of the bed, he felt only peace and calm. Then there was silence.

Tim forced himself to raise his eyelids. He stared across at Madame Noella. Her head was thrown back and the rolls of flesh on her neck hovered gelatinously above her caftan. His hand still in her grip, she began to rock slowly back and forth, back and forth. Then she spoke in English.

"Chelsa," she commanded. "Chelsa, we need you to come back to us." She continued rocking and chanting in the backward gibberish for several minutes. Now fully out of his reverie, Tim was beginning to lose both patience and interest. He was about to tell Madame that he'd made a mistake when he was interrupted.

"Mommy," said a child-like voice that came from Madame's mouth, yet scarcely seemed possible. "Mommy, where am I...?"

It wasn't Chelsa's voice. It wasn't any voice Tim had heard before other than perhaps Madame Noella's trying to sound like a child. He wondered if he should speak or respond, but Madame gave no indication that she was even aware of his presence.

Then just for an instant, Tim thought he felt Chelsa's bony hand squeeze his.

"Mommy, make it stop!" the voice from Madame Noella screamed. Madame's head fell back with a jerk, then forward again as if she were awakening from a nap in front of the television. She dropped his hand.

"What happened?" Tim asked. Madame Noella stared past him, unfocused for a few moments until she appeared to snap out of her trance. Her heavy bosom heaved with some internal exertion. Then she placed Chelsa's hand back upon the bed cover.

"Whose voice was that?" Tim demanded. "I don't think it was Chelsa and it wasn't you. Who was it?"

"I don't hear the voices when I'm with the spirits," Madame said. "I simply serve as the channel for them to speak. If you don't know who it was, then I can't tell you." She backed away from the bed and began dispersing the ash ring around Chelsa's bed with the toe of her shoe.

She squinted at Tim through her piggish eyes. "What I do know is that this child is as dead as anything I've ever seen. She may be breathing and her heart may pump blood, but there's nothing in there. Nothing at all."

She paused for a few moments, appearing to soften at the devastating impact her words had upon Tim.

"I'm sorry, Mr. Moran. It's my belief that her soul has traveled to the other side."

I'm not dead.

Tim stared at Madame Noella, feeling cold all over.

"Can't anything be done to bring her back?" he asked. "She's in a coma but she's breathing. There must be a way."

Madame Noella began picking up the incense cones and stubbing them out. She blew on them to hasten the process then dropped the still smoking cones into her bag.

"The only way this child will live again is if she regains the soul she's lost." She seemed to ponder this information. "It might be too late."

"What do you mean, too late?" Tim narrowed his eyes, a stab of fear twisting between his shoulder blades. For the first time since beginning this bizarre ritual an unwelcome thought nagged at him. After hearing the strange child's voice he was no longer convinced of Chelsa's recovery.

Madame shook her head and began hurriedly throwing her belongings together.

She stared back at Tim for a few minutes, her eyes raking up and down him, stopping at the holes in the knees of his jeans that hadn't been washed for a week. He wasn't embarrassed. What did it matter? There was no one who cared how he looked. In fact, apart from Chelsa, there was no one who even needed him or would notice if he lived or died. His life and hers were intertwined. They lived for each other. Because of each other.

"Forget what I said."

Tim grabbed her arm. "Tell me!" he insisted.

She tore free from him, her eyes blazing. "I can't tell you what I don't know." She huffed loudly as if she'd walked up a steep flight of stairs. As she grabbed the last of her props she turned to him. "I take cash. No checks or credit."

Tim pulled out his wallet and hastily counted out the money, having to resort to singles to make up the balance. She snatched the cash from his hand and stuffed it into her bag.

"You have to let go," she said, her voice taking on a kinder tone. "It's not natural to hang on so long. She wouldn't want you to throw away your life, too." With those words of advice she turned and left the room.

Tim watched her leave with an overpowering ache in his heart because he knew she was right. He stared down at the immobile girl on the bed, shriveled and emaciated from being bedridden for so long. Over the years her adolescent body that should have been budding into that of a young woman, had instead regressed to a tight fetal position. The delicate little hands that had once floated so gracefully when she danced had become bird-like claws. That he'd exposed his beautiful child to such a charlatan brought a flush of shame.

"Forgive me, Chelsa," he whispered. "I had to try."

He began massaging the stiffened limbs the way the physiotherapists had taught him. If she ever regained consciousness her atrophied muscles would need hours upon endless hours of therapy. Then he noticed that Madame Noella had forgotten to remove the velvet medicine bag from around Chelsa's neck. No doubt it was included in her fee otherwise why would she leave it behind? Curiosity overcame him. He had to see what was inside.

With gentle hands he untied the string around her neck and removed the bag. Then he dumped the contents onto the tray beside Chelsa's bed to reveal a hard, reddish-black lump that resembled a desiccated chicken heart, a foul-smelling bundle of dried herbs tied with a gold thread, and a folded piece of paper. He opened the paper, peering closely to read it in the dim hospital light.

<pre>
ABRACADABRA
ABRACADABR
ABRACADAB
ABRACADA
ABRACAD
ABRACA
ABRAC
ABRA
ABR
AB
A
</pre>

Tim stared at it for a few moments, trying to discern the pattern and meaning of the words. As he pondered their implication the letters began to slowly fade, one by one, from the bottom line to the top, until only the top line remained. ABRACADABRA. Then that too was gone, just as if it had never been. Tim rubbed his eyes and squinted at the paper, perplexed. Then it came to him. Of course. Disappearing ink.

He started to laugh at the absurdity of it. Suddenly he found he couldn't stop. He had to sit on the chair beside the bed to steady himself. When he'd finally regained control he wiped his eyes, annoyed that he'd thrown away his precious money on such a ridiculous notion as a psychic. He placed the folded paper and the other items from the medicine bag back inside and pulled it shut. Then he slipped it around Chelsa's neck and retied it. It probably wouldn't help anything, but it couldn't hurt either. At least not as far as he knew.

Chapter Six

It was late when Rand finally arrived home, and his floating home was aglow with the afternoon sun setting over the horizon of the Willamette River. He grabbed a Heineken from the refrigerator then climbed the spiral stairs to the top deck. Dropping into a lounge chair, he picked up his binoculars and gazed along the riverbank toward Oaks Park. A couple of runners passed by, one pushing a stroller as she kept up her workout pace. That's dedication, he thought. After he'd finished his beer he headed back downstairs, kicked his shoes off in the living room and flung his jacket across the room toward the cobalt blue leather recliner. It missed its mark and fell onto the polished oak floorboards.

Though he kept his office overflowing with a collection of clocks, he only kept one alarm clock at home to get him to the office on time. His furniture had been chosen for comfort and serviceability alone. The framed Oregon seascapes were from a poster shop and each room contained prearranged suite packages from a local mid-range furniture store. The color scheme was neutral blues and greys, matched to perfection. Only the bookcases that filled every wall with volumes ranging from Nietzsche to the Chronicles of Narnia indicated the occupant had any imaginative side at all.

He heard a soft growling and felt his Cocker Spaniel, Goldie, tugging frantically at his pant leg. He glanced down at the dog and the tawny coating of hair on his black slacks. He sighed heavily and gave him a gentle caress behind his ears.

Dodging the amorous Goldie as the dog crisscrossed between his legs, Rand walked across the living room and opened the screen door to let him out onto the tiny front deck.

Leaving Goldie leaping frantically after several resident gulls he'd never be able to reach, he padded toward the white enamel and stainless steel kitchen, pulled out a bottle of scotch and poured a juice glass half-full. Knowing he'd later regret drinking it on an empty stomach he nevertheless took a couple of long swallows, reveling in the satisfying burn it produced in his esophagus and the resulting warmth that flowed down through his body. He squeezed his eyes shut, the events of the day clicking past like movie stills.

Taking on the case of Sienna Cantrell was probably the most ridiculous decision he'd made in a long time. It had all happened so fast it hardly seemed like it *was* his decision. Still, he wasn't sorry he'd agreed to see her. In his ten years in private psychiatric practice he'd never encountered anything like it before. Kate Petroski had been very convincing, and when she'd mentioned Dr. Silverstein, well...

Then there was the mother. Melanie. He didn't quite know what to make of her. Though her concern for her daughter's welfare seemed genuine, and what mother wouldn't be concerned in a situation like that, he couldn't help feeling she had to know more about the lead-up to Sienna's episodes than she'd let on. Though why she would want to hold anything back was yet another mystery.

He removed a beef burrito from the freezer, stuck it in the microwave, and took another long swallow of scotch. Beginning to feel a comforting buzz, he settled down on his recliner with his makeshift dinner and drink and flicked on the T.V. Several hours later when the phone awoke him he couldn't even recall having sat down. The caller was Melanie Cantrell. She sounded distraught.

"Sienna's awake now," Melanie gasped. "I don't know how long it's going to last. If you get down here right away you can talk to her."

He could hear the desperation in her voice. He'd heard it before whenever he ventured into St. Augustus to consult on an adult patient. Parents at a complete loss as to how to help their child. It gave him the jitters. One more reason not to work with children. And not for the first time he was thankful that he had no kids of his own. He checked his watch. It was nearly 11 p.m.

"All right," said Rand, thankful that he hadn't retired yet for the night. "I'll be there as soon as I can."

As he rapidly brushed his teeth to get rid of the smell of the scotch, a thought kept nagging at him. How had she managed to get his unlisted number? It wasn't as if he were an Emergency Room physician, or even on call, for that matter. Though he gave an emergency number to his answering service for at-risk patients or new ones he hadn't built a relationship with yet, it was rare for him to get calls at home from patients. But she no doubt had gotten patched through by the St. Augustus switchboard. He had to hand it to her: Melanie Cantrell was a resourceful woman.

She was waiting for him outside Sienna's hospital ward, pacing the hallway like a captive animal. Though the hospital was deathly quiet at this time of night, she didn't appear to hear him approach. She wore tight fitting designer jeans and a low cut pink sweater with sleeves that reached her elbows. She'd clipped her long blonde hair to the top of her head with an ornate barrette, and scrubbed her face free of makeup. As she checked her watch she finally saw him, and at that moment her expression morphed from annoyance to a disquieting eagerness.

"Thank God, you're here," she said. "She's sitting up and eating Jell-O right now. Just as if nothing had happened." She took his arm and the heat of her touch on his bare skin coursed through his body. He managed to slip away from her grasp without being obvious about it.

"Were you with her when she woke up?" Rand asked. He half-turned toward her out of courtesy while he reached for the door handle to Sienna's room. He was anxious to get inside and talk to the child, but Melanie seemed determined to engage his attention.

She shook her head. "I just got here. I went home to have dinner. When I came back to her ward and walked through the door the first thing I saw was Sienna watching TV. She said, 'Hi Mom' when I came in. Just like that. Like nothing had happened."

Her lips trembled and she choked back a muffled sob. She bent her head as if to prevent him from seeing her defenses weaken. Rand reached out instinctively to put his arm around her then thought better of it, instead awkwardly patting her shoulder. He pushed open the door and she followed him into Sienna's room.

At first it was hard to see the child, sitting in the dim light with the strobe-like flashing of the television screen alternately illuminating and darkening the room. Then as his eyes adjusted he could see her, a miniature, dark-haired version of her mother. She turned to them as they walked in.

"Hi, Sienna," he said softly as he approached the bed. "I'm Dr. Morrissey."

She scrutinized him carefully, giving him the same appraisal that her mother had earlier in the day. She was one of those kids you felt could see right through you. Precocious little demons who'd grown up with adults and no friends their own age. They spoke to you using your first name without being given permission and made you uneasy because you could never be certain what they were thinking. Adult thoughts or childish ones? Was it a bluff or were they really forty-year-olds trapped in a preschooler's body?

He studied her right back.

"Hi," she said. But she had already lost interest in him and turned back to the TV. No doubt by now the constant stream of lab technicians, nurses and doctors over the course of her several hospital visits had become routine to her.

"Do you mind if I sit down?" he asked. She turned to look at him and those cinnamon brown cat's eyes she'd inherited from her mother widened as if she were surprised. Perhaps no one had ever asked her permission for anything before. Still, she offered a shy smile of acceptance. He sat on the chair beside her bed. Inwardly he breathed a sigh of relief. It was easier to treat a willing patient than a hostile one.

"How are you?"

"Okay," she said nonchalantly with her eyes glued back to the TV.

"Good." He patted the blanket covering her knees. "It's pretty late. Do you want to go back to sleep?"

Sienna shook her head.

"All right then. I'd like to ask you a few questions, but we'll have to turn off the TV."

"Okay." She flopped back against the pillows. Without prompting she pushed a button on the right side of her bed and the light on the TV extinguished. Rand heard the scraping of a chair behind him as Melanie sat down. He turned in his seat.

"I'd like to talk with Sienna alone for a while," he said firmly. Melanie started to protest until Rand gave her a hard deliberate stare that convinced her she had no choice in the matter. As Melanie hovered by the door he caught a glimpse of Sienna's face. She looked pensive and strained, as if torn between loyalty to her mother and obeying Rand's request. Melanie shot Rand a silent plea that he only partly understood.

"I'll call you back in when we're done." He waved his hand in a 'shooing' motion and glowered at Melanie until she began to move. Her lips tightened but she said nothing as she reluctantly exited the room. Rand reached over and pressed the buzzer for a nurse, then turned to Sienna.

"It's all right that your mom isn't here. A nurse is coming to sit with us."

At that moment a solidly-built, grey-haired nurse with the gait of a silverback gorilla lumbered into the room. She grabbed a metal chair from the corner and scraped it across the floor. Though she lowered herself gingerly, as if in protest the chair gave a loud squeak. Sienna snickered, but the nurse didn't seem to notice. She appeared bored and a little vexed, no doubt thinking she was unnecessary here and needed elsewhere.

Ignoring her, Rand turned his attention to the child. "Do you know where you are, Sienna?"

"I'm in hospital."

"Have you been in hospitals before?"

Sienna nodded.

"Lots?"

Sienna shrugged and glanced at the nurse whose face crinkled into a lukewarm smile.

"I guess."

"Why do you think you have to come to the hospital so often?"

"Because I fall asleep when I'm not supposed to." She picked at the nap on the hospital blanket, tearing off tufts and making a small pile of it.

"What happens just before you fall asleep?"

"I don't know." She sounded petulant now.

"Do you have any memories from before you fall asleep?"

"No."

"Is anyone with you then?"

"No."

"No one at all?" he persisted.

Sienna's face clouded. She wasn't a very good liar. He didn't need his doctorate in psychiatry to realize she was being deliberately evasive. He got the feeling she was about to stop answering his questions but he had to build up her trust in him and keep the session going as long as possible.

He repeated the question.

"Sometimes my friend is there." She frowned, reflecting. "She never stays if Mommy comes in the room."

"Is this a friend from school?" said Rand.

"No."

"From where, then?"

Sienna pursed her lips.

Then Rand had a chilling thought. A thought about people who befriend children and coerce them into not revealing anything about them.

"Is this a secret friend?" She gave no reply.

"But your parents don't know about her."

"No."

"Your friend's a girl, though, am I right?" When Sienna didn't respond he resumed his line of questioning, feeling certain her friend was most likely female or her responses would have most likely been quite different.

"What's her name?"

Sienna shook her head. "I don't know."

"You don't know your friend's name?"

She shook her head again.

"Have you told anyone else about this friend?"

"No," she whispered.

"Is she imaginary?"

She shook her head violently. "No, she's NOT imaginary. She's real." She began kicking at the sheets on the bed.

"Does she tell you things?"

"Sometimes."

"Like what?"

Abruptly Sienna glanced away. He reached over and took her chin in his hands, forcing her to look at him. Her face puckered with fear.

"Don't tell my mom. She'd be mad if she found out. My friend said she'd be mad."

"It'll be our secret," Rand promised. He was anxious to discover more details about this friend of Sienna's. How long she'd known her or what else this friend might have asked her not to tell Melanie. But then the door opened and Melanie walked in.

"We're not quite done yet," Rand said. He ran his fingers through his hair, annoyed and exasperated with her. "Can you give us a few more minutes?"

"I don't understand why I can't be here when you're talking to her," Melanie insisted. "I *am* her mother."

But when Rand reverted his attention back to Sienna he saw that any further questioning would have to be done at a later date. She'd already switched the TV back on and lay back, arms folded defiantly, propped against the pillows. Essentially closing herself off to further communication. It was apparent she'd decided not to say anything else in front of her mother.

He patted the blanket beside her. "I'll come back another time and we can talk again. Okay?" He smiled conspiratorially and gave Sienna a wink that Melanie couldn't see. She returned the smile and waved her hand briefly. The nurse stood and left the room. He gave a curt nod to Melanie who had parked herself in the chair vacated by the nurse, and followed the nurse out the door.

After leaving St. Augustus, Rand headed to his car, so exhausted and lost in thought he almost missed it in the parking lot. He'd been making substantial progress with Sienna until Melanie came back in. And although he hadn't gotten to the nucleus of what was wrong with Sienna, it was abundantly clear that nothing could really be solved without first getting rid of the mother.

Chapter Seven

It hadn't surprised Tim that Chelsa showed no improvement after the visit from the psychic. From her contrived accent to the bag of rubbish she'd tied around Chelsa's neck, everything about the woman had reeked of fraud. The only thing he hadn't been able to explain away was the voice of the unknown child. Maybe you had to be a true believer in the arcane to witness results, he thought, just as you had to believe in God to expect miracles. Even the psychic had been able to tell he was skeptical.

Whenever he sat at Chelsa's bedside he imagined she could hear and understand what he was saying. He insisted on speaking to her as if she were conscious and could comprehend the books he read aloud, the songs he sang to her. Occasionally he even turned on the television so she could hear the latest news, know what was going on as the world progressed, though it was obvious to everyone else she did not.

A few weeks earlier when he'd come in he'd experienced a bit of a shock. Though she hadn't developed the way a normal teenager does, she'd begun to resemble Melanie. The first time he noticed, it was as if someone had wrenched his heart out. After all, he was quite certain Melanie thought Chelsa was dead. Why else wouldn't she have come to see her? But then, he'd never sent any news of Chelsa or spoken to Melanie for many years.

He tried not to let the resemblance between Melanie and Chelsa get to him. He'd loved Melanie for a long time. He'd even loved her when she wanted to disconnect Chelsa's life support. But the love had died when she'd told him she was pregnant. And there had been no question in his mind, and no rebuttal from Melanie, that he'd been wrong about it being another man's child.

But then, several months after the incident with the psychic, he read a news article about a medical breakthrough with coma patients. An experimental treatment using an electronic device called a Median Nerve Stimulator had been successful in 'awakening' a teenaged girl who had suffered head injuries in a car accident. When he called the doctor who had been conducting the research he was filled with a renewed surge of hope. Chelsa would be evaluated within a week. He truly believed it was a gift, a sign from God.

The day of the procedure, Chelsa had been transported by ambulance to the clinic. Tim drove by himself and arrived shortly afterward. The clinic where the Median Nerve Stimulation was to be conducted was a bright open building with floor to ceiling windows supported by stainless steel and glass brick partitions. Areca palms, dracaenas and crimson hibiscus flowering in a huge oval atrium loomed like a mirage in a desert of marble flooring. Completing the effect was a recirculating fountain in the center of the atrium. Everything looked and smelled clean and new and fresh. So different from the haphazard state-operated nursing home where Chelsa had been living.

They were met by a friendly receptionist with purple spiked hair, a spider tattoo on her neck, and spike piercings through her lip and eyebrow. Though she wore a white lab coat he could see her long black dress and laced Doc Martens under the desk. He shuddered at the overtly Satanic overtones, knowing he'd have never let Chelsa fall victim to that fad. He'd raised her to be a God-fearing child.

Earlier Chelsa had been given a complete medical work up and neurological exam to rule out any complications with performing Median Nerve Stimulation. But it was mostly routine lab work. Although still comatose and in a persistent vegetative state, she'd been medically stable for five years. Dr. Choudry, a darkly handsome immigrant from Bombay who would be performing the treatment, had told Tim she was a good candidate for the procedure.

"We'll start her out at thirty minutes per session, three times each day. Her vital signs will be monitored constantly for any changes," Dr. Choudry said in such a clipped, cultured accent that even Tim could tell he'd been born or educated in Great Britain. "The idea is to get the brain to wake up during the daytime then rest at night."

"How soon will we be able to tell if it's helping?"

Tim had more than one reason for the question. He hadn't checked with his insurance company to see if they would cover the procedure. He was quite sure they would not. Dr. Choudry had warned him of this. Each treatment cost thousands of dollars. But he couldn't put a price on Chelsa's life.

Dr. Choudry shook his head. "We could see results in as early as the first treatment, or it could take months. The key is to note any improvement and keep building on it."

Tim considered this for a moment. "Is it possible she'll ever be normal again?"

"Only time will tell," said the doctor. "It's all up to Chelsa now."

Tim was allowed to be present during the first treatment although he had to remain in the viewing section behind glass. Even so, he could see and hear all that went on. The doctor again cautioned him not to expect much, if anything, at first. Chances were that she might not respond at all. Or if she did, it would be after several sessions.

Tim watched as a technician stuck two small electrode pads, which were attached to a small cigarette-pack sized box, to the inner side of Chelsa's right wrist, just beside her birth-mark. That must be the stimulator, he thought. It was hard to believe that a device as tiny as that little box could resurrect a person from the land of the living dead.

Although they didn't appear to notice him, he could see the nurse and technician clearly. He strained to hear their words, hoping for an insight as to what was going on.

"What do you think her chances are?" the technician, a

burly, red-haired man who looked to be in his 40's, said to the doctor.

Even from this distance, Tim could see the doctor's face crinkle into a frown.

"Let's just say I'd be more optimistic if we'd seen her five years ago."

"We wasting our time?" asked the nurse, a short dark-haired woman with an olive complexion. She spoke with an east coast accent.

The doctor's mouth twisted grimly. "There's no waste of time here. Even if it's only for the benefit of the father."

The doctor checked the electrode pads once again, then switched on the stimulator. Tim half-expected Chelsa to sit bolt upright, stiffly coming to life like Frankenstein's monster, a corpse raised up from the dead. With great difficulty he forced the image from his mind. There was nothing to suggest that the MNS made patients react in that way.

"Once when I was a kid I saw my father butcher a chicken," the nurse said. "Even when the head was only dangling by a sinew, that damned chicken leapt around the yard like it was in the troupe of Riverdance. That didn't mean it was still alive."

The technician guffawed. He heard the doctor make a grunting derisive sound to the nurse and his eyes lifted to the viewing window to look at Tim then back to the nurse. He could barely make out the doctor's words, 'don't ever let me hear you say anything like that again,' and the nurse's face above the mask turned a bright scarlet. She dipped her head in embarrassment and the procedure continued.

He knew he shouldn't get his expectations raised too high. The doctor had warned him about that. The procedure had only worked in a couple of cases. And the degree of results were inconclusive too, depending on variables such as age, amount of brain damage and length of time the patient had been in a coma. There was virtually no way to predict an outcome, good or bad.

So now he watched and waited and prayed. Prayer and this new therapy would bring her through, he believed it so fervently he could almost see her sitting up. But of course at this point, that was still his imagination working.

After watching the repetitiousness of the nurse noting Chelsa's vital signs on the chart, he began to get sleepy and lose concentration. It really was no different than waiting for any other special occasion—this could be his Christmas, birthday and Thanksgiving all rolled into one. He wasn't even aware he'd drifted off until someone gently shook his shoulder. He looked up to see the sympathetic dark eyes of the nurse.

"She's done for the day, Mr. Moran," she said. "There's nothing more we can do until tomorrow morning when we'll start again."

Tim swayed toward the wall, a little groggy and unfocused, blinking in an odd, owl-like way of one eye closing then the other. "Was there any change?"

The nurse shook her head. "Not yet. There's a lot of work to be done and a lot of time to do it in. We can't expect a miracle right away, you know."

Though she sounded like a schoolteacher scolding a student, he weighed her words. A miracle, he thought, yes, we can expect one. I need to pray harder and it will happen. The nurse watched him, waiting for him to leave so she could close up the treatment room.

"Chelsa has been taken back to her room," she said. "My shift is ending but I'll show you the way there."

He stood and stretched to uncramp his aching muscles. Then he followed her down the long, brightly lit corridor lined with abstract paintings he couldn't comprehend. They stopped when they reached the door of Chelsa's room. The door opened and another nurse slipped out.

She looked up. "I'm the evening nurse. I'll be back to check on her later, Mr. Moran, but you can go in now."

He opened the door and stepped inside. Though he recognized the size and shape of Chelsa's shriveled body, he could scarcely see her. He didn't approach the bed, just stood watching until he was satisfied that she seemed to be breathing normally. He gave a little shiver. It was cold in the room and

Chelsa's arms and legs were exposed.

He moved forward to cover her with the hospital blanket and began tucking it snugly around her shoulders and hips. Then he thought he saw her leg move, just a little. For a second his heart jumped in excitement. But the reality of it set in and his shoulders sagged in defeat. He could have accidentally moved her leg while he was tucking in the blanket.

He turned away from the bed. It was time to go home and get some much needed rest. But as he did a tiny sound reached his ear. He spun back around and his eyes once again caught a movement from the bed. Chelsa's fingers, for years frozen in a grasping position, had hardened into fists. She'd brought them up to her face in a protective gesture, as if trying to defend herself. He rushed to the side of the bed.

"Chelsa," he murmured. "Chelsa, can you hear me?" She remained rigid and unresponsive, not giving any indication she had heard him.

Daddy, I can hear you, please don't leave me.

He put his hand over hers and began unfolding her clenched fingers. They were as firm as those of a corpse in rigor mortis, so tightly bound together that the knuckles gleamed white from the pressure. He began massaging them, trying to insert his fingers underneath hers. Then with a motion so quick he could hardly believe it happened, she jerked away from him. Her hands snaked out and clutched at the air as if she were attempting to grasp something she couldn't see. Then like a coiled spring that has been stretched and rebounded, she resumed the posture she'd held for six years.

He took her hands again in an attempt to move them back and then, without warning, he heard her speak.

"Don't," she said. Heart pounding, Tim leaned closer.

"Chelsa?" he said, "Chelsa, what is it you don't want me to do?" But there was no response. Had he really heard her? She looked no different than when he'd entered the room five minutes ago. Was his mind playing tricks on him?

Shaking, he backed hurriedly away from the bed, stumbling over a chair and nearly falling. He groped his way to the door like a blind man. Jerking open the door, he leaned out into the hallway, frantically scanning the expanse. Where was everyone?

"Nurse!" he screamed, at the top of his lungs.

Chapter Eight

Events took a turn for the unexpected several days later when Rand received a call during office hours from the Portland Children's Services Division about a case of alleged child abuse. CSD was frustratingly short on details. They didn't know the identity or location of the child in question. And they didn't know the type or extent of abuse. But they could tell him who had reported it. It was Sienna Cantrell.

Rand mulled over why Children's Services had specifically called him. Summoned was more like it as his presence was requested at their office. He could only deduce that as part of their investigation the social workers had found his name in Sienna's medical records. But if she wasn't the victim, why would they look at her records?

He had Angela reschedule his last patient of the day and after checking his appointments for the next morning was ready to go. As he left, Angela tossed him a cable knit pullover, the same color as his eyes. He caught it deftly with his left hand, a ritual that always made her smile. He preferred sweaters and corduroy trousers to suits and sport coats and rarely had to shop, for his mother kept him in a constant supply of hand knit variations. Although this particular sweater had been a gift from Angela.

The CSD office was located in a concrete box of a building with several other state government offices. The main reception area was lined with orange plastic stacking chairs and chipped Formica tables, suggesting either a temporary location or severe funding cutbacks. Maybe both. He gave the receptionist his business card, which she took, scarcely glancing at him as she set down the dog-eared paperback she'd been reading.

As if limiting her movements were a requirement of the job, she reached out her right hand, punched in a number and muttered a few words, then hung up the phone. She pointed to a door down the corridor, only having moved one hand in the entire process.

"Just walk into 112," she said, her eyes dropping back down to her book.

At Room 112 he lightly tapped the door. It was opened by a tall, stern-faced woman wearing a voluminous white dress patterned with plate-sized red roses that contrasted sharply with the dark tones of her skin.

"I'm Georgia Rollins," she announced, "please have a seat." She lowered herself into a threadbare plaid chair and smoothed the folds of the dress over her knees.

"What's this about?" Rand asked.

Mrs. Rollins picked up a thin file folder, opened it and glared at him. Or maybe it was just his imagination.

"You've treated Sienna Cantrell for an unidentified psychological condition recently, is that right?"

Rand started at hearing her name. "She's all right, isn't she?"

"Sienna's fine." She hesitated.

"Then why did you ask me to come in?" Rand responded in a rather terse voice.

Mrs. Rollin's eyebrows raised questioningly at his tone before continuing. "The children were having free play time today. Sienna was playacting with two dolls, speaking for them and performing actions, as it were. Her kindergarten teacher became disturbed by something she overheard Sienna say. But when she tried to question her, Sienna wouldn't talk about it."

Mrs. Rollins settled a pair of gold rimmed bifocals on her nose and glanced down at the file, then peered over the lenses at him.

"Was it physical abuse the teacher suspected, or something sexual? Because when I saw Sienna several days ago, she didn't give any indication..."

Mrs. Rollins closed the file. "It was definitely physical abuse. Sienna re-enacted the beating and mistreatment of one person by another with the dolls. The teacher also heard her using foul language." She frowned.

"Dr. Morrissey, she *twisted* the arm of the doll until it broke. Then she took a pencil and stuck it in the bottom of the doll's foot, all the while telling the doll that this was being done to her because she was a terrible person. The teacher was very upset."

Rand's pulse rate jumped a few beats. He could not fathom the behavior she'd described emerging from the disinterested child he'd interviewed in the hospital bed. Finally his eyes met those of Mrs. Rollins.

"Although I don't see children in my practice, when I was a medical resident I dealt with abuse victims. Sienna doesn't have any signs of physical abuse. I haven't even seen signs of mental abuse. She doesn't fit the pattern."

Mrs. Rollins stood and walked around to the front of the desk, perching on the outside corner. She stared down at him until he felt as if he were back in school himself.

"That may be. But children don't just make this up. They have to have heard it somewhere."

"Have you questioned Sienna about her behavior?"

"She said the things she was doing with the dolls happened to her friend. When we asked her who the friend is, she clammed up. She refuses to talk to us now. The teacher being the responsible adult that she is immediately called us, thinking that the 'friend' was probably Sienna herself."

Until this moment Rand hadn't realized the seriousness in being called by the CSD. He scanned the cramped office where Mrs. Rollins's diplomas and certificates lined the walls, sharing space alongside the photos of children of varied ages, sex and race. He noticed there were no photos of children on her desk, although she wore a gold wedding ring on her left hand. He shifted uncomfortably in his seat.

"Is Mrs. Cantrell here?" he asked finally.

Mrs. Rollins expression didn't waver. "Yes, she's here."

"With your permission, I'd like to try talking to Sienna, although I'm not sure I'll have much more success. Can you get me in to see her without my coming into contact with her mother?"

Mrs. Rollins nodded. "Follow me." She led him out the front door of her office and then into a side room next to hers that had an additional door at the back. This led to a hallway with a series of closed doors. She pulled one open and stepped back for him to pass. "Wait here. I'll bring Sienna in and take care of Mrs. Cantrell while you're with her."

As he entered the room, he became aware of its undisguised attempt to appear child-friendly. Boxes filled with stuffed animals and anatomically correct dolls, designed to entice a child to 'open up' to adults, lined the perimeter of the daffodil-colored walls. Using the dolls with Sienna had briefly crossed his mind. But as there had been no reason to suspect sexual abuse, he'd decided against it. He preferred to enlist the child's trust rather than manipulate her with props.

He picked up a textured picture book and was beginning to examine it just as Mrs. Rollins reentered the room. Close behind her was Sienna, who appeared to be pouting. Even so, her unsolicited shy smile at seeing him gave him a sense of accomplishment. Inadvertently they had formed a bond.

She entered the room aloof and puppet-like, as if someone else were working the strings. Her toed-out walk suggested that of a dancer, someone who had taken ballet lessons as soon as she could walk. And in spite of heavy soled Maryjanes, she tiptoed in on the balls of her feet. Yet it was without talent or grace, almost is if the walk was meant to be on someone else.

Rand felt a little rush of affection for her. She had the precocious vivacity of a teenager in a five-year-old body. He immediately recognized Melanie in her though it was still with the innocence of a child. In fact, it was virtually impossible for him to imagine Melanie as a child.

"Hi, Sienna," Rand said. He glanced up at Mrs. Rollins. "We'll be fine." She smiled and backed out the door, pulling it closed.

Rand led Sienna to a red plastic child's chair then dragged a floral upholstered armchair so they could sit face to face. He folded his hands in his lap and scrutinized her. Her expression was impassive. It was difficult to tell what she was thinking or feeling. Given her docile appearance, it was hard to believe that anything out of the ordinary could have recently taken place.

"Mrs. Rollins says you have a friend who's been hurt. Is that the same friend we talked about in my office?"

Suddenly everything changed. Sienna turned pale, apprehension spreading across her face like a veil. Her eyes were troubled, frightened even.

"Don't be afraid. It'll be our secret. Don't you want to help your friend?"

Sienna cast her eyes downward and didn't answer.

"Has she told you her name yet?"

"No," she murmured.

"Does she go to your school?"

Sienna shook her head.

"Does she live in your neighborhood?"

"No."

Rand hesitated, knowing he would have to choose his words carefully. The last thing he wanted was Sienna to become uncomfortable with his questions and withdraw her cooperation again.

"How did you meet her?" He did not dare to take his eyes off her for a second. Any flinch, gesture or flicker of expression could speak volumes. And possibly save them both hours of time in therapy.

Sienna looked up then and tears start to fill her eyes. "I see her when I'm sleeping," she said.

Rand stifled a huge sigh of relief. Her 'imaginary friend' and outbursts at school had to be the result of recurring nightmares. There was no victim of abuse here. At least not that he could see. There was only a little girl having bad dreams. Her nightmares could have been initiated by food, play or television triggers, or possibly a scare she'd experienced. That was an investigation he'd have to pursue with the parents.

And that would explain the syncope as well. Emotional triggers could stimulate the fainting spells. A huge weight seemed to rise off his chest. Although he knew the dangers of latching on to an easy, or the most likely, diagnosis, a medical Occam's Razor if you will, he figured he'd probably solved the mystery behind Sienna's malady.

After he'd dried her tears, Sienna regained her composure. He rang the extension number for Mrs. Rollins. "We're done for today," he stated into the receiver. After hanging up he turned back to Sienna.

"Your mom and I are going to discuss how to get rid of these bad dreams so you won't have them anymore."

Her face crumpled. "Will I still see my friend?"

Rand shifted in his chair. "Is she important to you?"

Sienna swung her legs, seemingly fascinated by her sneakered feet as they disappeared and reappeared from under the chair.

"Does your friend tell you secrets?"

Sienna's eyes shot to his face. He'd struck a chord of truth.

"Like what?" he asked. She pursed her lips.

"Her mom is mean."

"How mean?" Sienna lifted her eyebrows as if to say, how mean should a mom be? But before he could continue, Melanie swept into the room. Mrs. Rollins rushed up behind her, an "oops" type of apology on her face. Melanie's expression flattened when she saw Rand. She whirled around to face Mrs. Rollins.

"What's this? What's *he* here for?"

Mrs. Rollins raised her hands in a defensive move, almost as if to protect herself.

"We obtained Sienna's medical records and saw Dr. Morrissey had been evaluating her. We felt he might be able to get some answers."

Melanie's eyes flickered from Rand to Sienna, and back to Rand again. "And?"

"It seems as if she's been having bad dreams." The look

he flashed her was one of reassurance. "Nightmares. That's all. It could explain hypertension that would also cause her fainting spells. We can evaluate what she's eating or drinking or seeing on TV before bed time. If we eliminate the cause, the nightmares should stop. And maybe, just maybe," he stressed, "they'll stop her fainting spells as well."

He could actually see the tension sliding off Melanie's face like a veil being removed. He had convinced *her*, but he hadn't convinced himself. Were they really only nightmares? Or if it was something else, there was a lot more behind them than too many sweets or scary movies. And what sort of horror show could this child have been exposed to? he wondered.

Chapter Nine

An interview with John Cantrell, Sienna's father, was now long overdue, Rand decided. He had no idea how much of an influence or role model Cantrell was to Sienna. Nor had either his daughter or his wife made any mention of him. Either the man was practically a nonexistent entity in the family, or he had purposely chosen to stay out of the fracas of his daughter's problems. Rand had a difficult time believing this to be the case. It was easier to assume that Melanie had deliberately kept him out of the loop.

Getting Cantrell to come into his office was a feat of no small undertaking. In addition to whatever Melanie had told him of Sienna's problems, Cantrell apparently placed a stigma on speaking with psychiatrists. He couldn't see what all the fuss was about and told Rand so in fairly blunt terms.

"So, you're telling me that my daughter needs a shrink? Well, I think you're full of shit. She's just a normal kid with a cold who may have blacked out from taking adult cough syrup. Or as you told Melanie, she's been having nightmares. That doesn't make her a candidate for the nut house."

Rand winced at the man's volume, and his use of 'shrink,' a term he despised for a number of reasons. Nor did he like the words 'nut house.' He forced himself to collect his thoughts before speaking. Cantrell seemed like the kind of person who would pounce on a person's words and then twist them to his advantage.

"You see the problem," Rand explained, with as much patience and diplomacy as he could, "is that now the Children's Services Department is involved. Once CSD thinks there's the possibility of a child being abused we have to get to the bottom of it or you risk having Sienna taken from your home. I don't think either you or your wife would want that." Put that way, Cantrell had to agree, finally acquiescing to see Rand later in the week.

Cantrell showed up at his office late Thursday afternoon. He was a large man, but his custom tailored grey suit proportioned his size and weight so he did not appear to be what was probably well over six-four. He had the squarish, tenacious head of a pit bull, with thinning, sandy hair styled in a minor comb-over. Hooded grey eyes like those of a wolf regarding prey from behind a thicket glared at Rand from under heavy brows. His peevish expression seemed to be a permanent fixture. He looked to be in his late forties, which placed him much older than Melanie. In fact, Rand had difficulty placing him with Melanie at all.

The two men shook hands and Cantrell sat down on the navy blue leather sofa opposite Rand's matching chair. They studied one another silently for a moment like two male dogs facing off.

"Thank you for coming in to talk with me," Rand said. "Since CSD consulted me on the case I have little choice but to give them what they want. There are now two things going on with Sienna that we're aware of, maybe more. The sooner we get to the nucleus of it, the sooner we can figure out how to help her."

Cantrell came right to the point. "I think it's bullshit, clear and simple. There's nothing medically wrong with the kid. The doctors all said so. Until recently she's always been our perfect little angel. But her so-called 'episodes' these past couple of weeks have almost destroyed our family."

Though Rand could discern no emotion underneath Cantrell's hard, cold demeanor, he had the impression the man had little respect for his profession, and probably thought of him as nothing more than a snake oil salesman. He was fascinated at how quickly Cantrell's temper flared, and relieved to see it extinguished almost as fast.

"What do you mean, destroy? When did you first notice a

change in Sienna's behavior?"

Cantrell snorted. "The change wasn't so much with Sienna as it was with Melanie."

"Tell me about that."

"Are you trying to insinuate now that there's something wrong with her mother?" Cantrell's voice had escalated. The annoyed expression had morphed to hostility.

You're quite a jerk, aren't you? Rand thought. I wonder how your wife and child can stand to be around you. He'd been right about the man's personality. It was okay for Cantrell to divulge that Melanie was having problems, but if Rand acknowledged it, he turned on him. Rand took several deep calming breaths and gave a sympathetic smile to disarm him.

"I'm just following your lead. You said the change was with Melanie. Please continue."

His composure seemed to relax Cantrell. "It started last month. Sienna had come down with a bad cold so Melanie stayed home from work to look after her, which was unusual."

He paused, a frown wrinkling his upper brow. "She's the Public Relations Director in my company and never takes personal time off from work. I remember being upset because I was getting ready to leave town on a business trip. Melanie called to say that Sienna had fainted and wasn't coming around. She was taking her to Emergency."

"How long was she unconscious?"

Cantrell contemplated. "Maybe a half-hour or so. By the time I got there she was conscious and well enough to be released. The doctors couldn't find anything more than just congestion from her cold. They thought it was possible she'd had an allergic reaction to the over-the-counter cold medication or maybe was given a little too much. Anyhow, they sent her home with a prescription for antibiotics and everything was fine for a while."

"Then what?"

"She had another episode about four days later. She'd fallen from the swing in the backyard and lost consciousness. The funny thing was that the doctors couldn't tell if she'd lost consciousness before the fall or after. They decided to run some tests then, to rule out epilepsy, a brain tumor, narcolepsy or any kind of brain damage."

"Did they find anything?"

John Cantrell shook his head.

"Was your wife present during either of these incidents?"

Cantrell glared. "What are you implying?"

Rand raised his hand to placate the man. It seemed as if John Cantrell would not malign Melanie in any way. To pursue a line of questioning in that area would not only be divisive, it would probably result in the man stomping angrily out of the office.

While others might have disliked Cantrell, especially Kate who had earlier made no apologies about her aversion to him, his straightforwardness and blunt honesty was refreshing. Especially in his psychiatric practice where nearly everyone lied or manipulated facts. Cantrell was one of those rare individuals who stated their mind and told the truth, no matter how unpalatable it might be.

"I'm not implying your wife had anything to do with it. I wondered if she might have seen what happened prior to the attacks."

"She claims she didn't see or hear anything," Cantrell said angrily, "and I believe her. She loves that little girl."

"I'm sure she does. How many more episodes has Sienna had since then?"

Cantrell pondered for a few moments. "It's been over two weeks now. I'd have to say maybe two or three. But she's never been 'out' more than about a half-hour or so."

"Sienna told me about a friend who talks to her when she's sleeping. And that the friend leaves whenever Melanie comes into the room. Has she ever mentioned this 'friend' to you or your wife?"

Cantrell looked uncomfortable and shifted his bulk on the sofa. Finally he said, "I overhead her once talking to her dolls and the interaction sounded much like what her kindergarten teacher described. But I didn't think anything of it. I thought she was acting out what she'd seen in the playground. I gave her a smack on the bottom, told her not to use bad language, and left it at that. I never even told Melanie about it."

"Do you smack her often?" Rand ventured. Cantrell half-rose from his chair, looming over Rand.

"Now wait a minute. What are you insinuating...?"

"Please sit down," Rand interrupted. "I'm not accusing you of hurting her. Let's establish this right now: she doesn't appear to me to be an abused child. That's not what I meant. I am trying to find out what else is happening with her and only you, your wife and Sienna can help me."

At that, Cantrell's entire demeanor softened and for the first time since he'd walked through the door his body relaxed. "It's not Sienna I'm so worried about," he said. "At least now that all the tests have come out clear. It's probably just a childhood thing she'll grow out of. It's Melanie who concerns me. If she lost another child, I don't know what she'd do..."

Chapter Ten

The mystery of Sienna's illness had scarcely left Rand's conscious thoughts since interviewing her father several days earlier. He had sensed that Melanie, for reasons known only to her, was becoming reluctant to let him delve deeper into Sienna's problems. It appeared that though the father trusted him with his daughter, regaining the mother's confidence might require extra effort. The time between excluding her from the hospital room and encountering her at the Children's Services Division had spooked her.

So it was much to Rand's amazement to find that his first patient on Monday morning was Sienna. Even more surprising, Melanie had booked the appointment herself. He thought he'd be the last person Melanie would have come to. Was she finally recognizing that he was making progress with Sienna? Or had her husband managed to change her mind?

Melanie breezed into his office wearing a pale yellow sun dress, belted at the waist. Skinny spaghetti straps exposed her bare shoulders, showing off a light tan that brought out her freckles. She'd rolled her hair back at the nape of her neck and tied it with a gold ribbon that brought out an amber glow in her eyes. With just a hint of mascara on her lashes, she didn't look old enough to buy beer. Sienna was dressed in a sweatshirt, Hello Kitty T-shirt and rolled-up jeans. Melanie pulled off the pink hooded sweatshirt as Rand walked over.

"Hi, Sienna," Rand said softly, squatting down to her level. Her eyes met his then she quickly glanced up at her mother as if waiting for a cue. Melanie didn't appear to notice the plea. She had Sienna's hand in hers and passed it to Rand the way one would hand over a suitcase.

"You go with the doctor now, and be good. He needs to talk to you a little more."

Rand glanced questioningly at her, wondering why she had brought Sienna back. As if reading his thoughts, Melanie shrugged.

"It would be wonderful if she would open up to someone about what happened at school the other day, and she seems to have a connection with you." Almost whispering under her breath, she said, "Whatever she's keeping bottled up inside is not good for her. She's not eating properly or sleeping at night. John thinks more therapy would help."

Rand frowned. He hadn't expected Cantrell to be in his corner. Maybe the man had more compassion than he'd shown during the interview in his office.

"What do you think?"

She glanced away. "I want whatever is best for Sienna."

Rand forced himself to smile empathetically. He observed her for a moment, trying to read whatever it was that motivated her, without much success. Then he remembered the sullen child at his side. He turned his full attention upon her.

"Why don't we go into my office and get to know each other better." He gave Melanie a dismissive nod and led Sienna into his office. Melanie looked as if she was about to follow them until Angela blocked her way. She opened her mouth to protest, but when she caught Rand's eye he shook his head slightly. Pouting like a two-year-old, she flounced back to the waiting room and threw herself into a chair.

The room wasn't the most child-oriented office, with adult-sized navy leather sofas and French impressionist prints on the walls. But then he'd made an exception by accepting Sienna as a patient. A smaller, wingback chair upholstered in pink floral brocade and too tiny for most of his patients was suitable for a little girl, though. And there were mostly cuckoo clocks in this room, which were enough to fascinate any child.

Fortunately, a few days earlier Kate had stopped by to bring over Sienna's medical records. Not seeing anything that would interest a patient under twenty-five, she had asked skeptically, "This is *it*? How on earth do you expect to elicit information from a child in this petri dish of an office?"

He tried not to show that she'd hurt his feelings. "I don't see kids in my practice, remember? Anyhow, what's wrong with it?"

Kate gave a kind of a huffing sound that could have been a laugh or a derisive putdown.

"Never mind," she said. She walked back out to the reception area and returned with Angela. They eyed him piteously.

"I have some things that my grandkids have outgrown," said Angela, winking at Kate. The next day his office had a makeshift playroom complete with child-sized furniture, art supplies and a box of stuffed toys.

He steered Sienna toward the brocade chair and pulled his own up beside her. For a moment he was at a loss at how to begin. All his training was geared toward adult patients. He took in her ladylike posture, sitting with her ankles crossed and her hands folded in her lap. What was he so afraid of? She was only an adult-in-training. Her behavior was more mature than a lot of his patients. He decided then to make his approach to her no different than with any other patient. She watched him, waiting for him to make the first move.

He gave her a lukewarm smile. "Let's draw some pictures." As he retrieved a couple of sketch pads and a handful of colored pencils, Sienna looked dubious, but stayed silent. He placed one sketch pad in front of her and kept the other for himself, then spilled the pencils onto the table.

He picked up a blue pencil and began to draw randomly, carefully viewing her out of the corner of his eye. She watched him sketch for a few seconds, stretching a little to see what he was drawing, then picked up a pencil and began a series of deft strokes that an accomplished artist would have envied. Rand stopped drawing, gazing at her while she worked on her picture.

It was really rather an elaborate sketch for the abilities of a typical five-year-old. It consisted of what appeared to be a family unit of four people. He recognized the long blonde hair of Melanie, the smaller blonde figure he wasn't sure about, although the man with dark hair must be her father. But what surprised him was a larger figure of a woman with curly grey hair that was double the size of all the others. She had a hooked beak of a nose and a straight, cruel mouth. In her right hand she held a large stick, which was larger than any of the human figures.

Rand frowned, waiting until Sienna had set her pencil down and looked at him.

"Is that your family?" he asked.

Sienna's mouth twisted. She held the picture up, staring at it as if she hadn't seen it before. Suddenly she ripped it into pieces and threw them across the room. For a moment Rand was rendered speechless.

As he began picking up the pieces of the torn picture, placing them on his desk to analyze later, he said very calmly, "Sienna, why don't you check out the playroom? I just had it redecorated." At that she jumped from the chair and headed over to the newest addition to his office, an area that had already raised the eyebrows of several of his patients.

He followed her to the white enameled toy chest Angela had brought in, pulling out a tattered pink chenille rabbit and a velour teddy bear with only one button for an eye, and set them on the floor in front of her.

"Now we have an audience," he said.

Sienna laughed out loud.

"That's better," Rand said, relieved that the tension had been broken. "What would you like to talk about today?" Sienna began swinging her legs idly and pursed her lips.

"I think you have something on your mind or your mother wouldn't have brought you here." He had to find a way to relax her, to get her to open up, but his expertise with children was limited. With most of his patients it was difficult enough to get them to shut up when their visit was over.

He searched his memory for any fragments of things little girls liked to do. Then it hit him. He'd try some make-believe.

He picked up the tattered rabbit and began bouncing it around.

"I'm Mrs. Floppy Ears," he said in his best, made-up girl voice. It sounded ridiculous even to his own ears. But it worked. Sienna giggled and snatched the rabbit from him.

"No, I want to be the rabbit. You be the bear."

Rand picked up the bear. "I'm Mr. One-eyed Bear. What's new with you, Mrs. Rabbit?"

"Miss Rabbit," Sienna corrected. "She's not married."

"Oh, Miss Rabbit is it? Well, Miss Rabbit, tell me all about your day."

Sienna squirmed in her seat, looking uncomfortable. Finally she said, "Sienna's friend came to visit last night while she was sleeping."

Rand held his breath for a moment. "And what did she have to say, Miss Rabbit?"

Sienna hesitated. "She's tired of the hospital and wants to go home. Her arm hurts, too."

While Sienna was playing with the rabbit, Rand very quietly reached back and flipped on the switch of his hand-held tape recorder. It would be impossible to take notes while trying to hold her attention.

"Why is she in hospital? Is she sick?"

Sienna contemplated this for a while, almost as if she were waiting for someone to feed her the answers.

"She doesn't want to tell me."

"Is it because of her arm?"

"No. She wants to sleep now. She says I shouldn't talk to you anymore."

Whoever this friend is, thought Rand, she's a manipulative little brat. Or perhaps it was only Sienna herself.

He watched her shaking the soft toy and then to his amazement a subtle change came over her. Her gaze began to drift and her eyelids drooped. But just as Rand was about to re-engage her attention, her eyes snapped open.

"Daddy's taking me to see the ballet Swan Lake tomorrow," she said.

Rand sat up, surprised. "That's nice. Do you like ballet?"

Sienna nodded happily. "I want to be a ballerina when I grow up."

Rand laughed. "You'll have to take years of dance classes, you know. It's hard work dancing on your tippy-toes."

"I know," she replied in a stern voice. "I've been taking classes with Miss Patty for three years."

Rand frowned, thinking about what she'd just said. Three years? They must have started her not long after she'd learned to walk. He wondered why parents rushed their children through life like that. There was time enough to get them started later while still allowing them time to have a normal childhood.

He watched as her eyelids began to fall shut again. He repressed a sigh. It was impossible to keep the attention of a sleepy child. He was exhausted himself.

"That's enough for today," he said. Sienna stirred as if she were awakening from a nap.

"Stay there and I'll get your mom." He stood and walked to the door. But Sienna jumped up and ran out the door in front of him. When she saw her mother she threw her arms around her waist and began swinging on her.

"Careful of my dress, Sienna," Melanie warned, bending over and peeling Sienna off her. She placed her hands on Sienna's shoulders and turned her toward the coat rack.

"Go get your sweatshirt. Quietly." She looked up at Rand. "Same time next week?"

Rand nodded. He watched as Sienna came bouncing back with her pale pink sweatshirt.

"Sienna's very excited about going to the ballet with her father tomorrow," he said. "She told me about her dance teacher, Miss Patty. She wants to be a ballerina..." He stopped. Melanie had gone dead white.

"What's the matter?"

"Sienna doesn't take ballet classes. She's never even asked about them." Her eyes raked his face as if searching for answers, then she turned abruptly, grabbed Sienna by the arm and almost ran from the office.

If the lack of results from the medical tests hadn't already proven it, after this last appointment Rand was convinced that Sienna's problem was mental, not medical. Kate had been right. She was old beyond her years. Conversation with her was no more difficult than with an adult for she immediately grasped whatever he said. He wondered when it was that her childhood had ended. And without even asking, instinctively he knew that she no longer believed in Santa Claus, the Easter Bunny or the Tooth Fairy.

Judging from the dysfunctional picture she'd drawn and the playacting scene, she was also displaying classic signs of Dissociative Identity Disorder. Once called Multiple Personality Disorder, DID patients exhibit two or more distinct identities, which ultimately take control over them. And in Sienna's case, he realized, the other notable symptom was an extensive loss of memory.

What he needed to do was to get permission from the Cantrells to hypnotize her and find out who else was lurking within the walls of her five-year-old skull. But when he called Melanie to ask her, she wouldn't hear of it.

"She's too young," she said. "Who knows what residual effects might show up later?"

"Do you really think that would be worse than what she's already gone through? The blackouts, the hospital stays, the tests, the psychiatric sessions? All that can have a lasting effect. With hypnosis she won't remember a thing afterward." But he couldn't convince Melanie.

"No," she stated in a flat voice. "If you don't think the sessions are helping you can stop them, but no hypnosis."

Rand hesitated, wondering how he could convince her. "I know it's hard to see results, but I think we're making progress. Please reconsider."

"It's unnecessary and dangerous," Melanie insisted. "I forbid it."

Rand sighed in disappointment. He had no choice. What was she so afraid he'd be able to retrieve from Sienna's subconscious? But after he'd finished speaking with Melanie, he called John Cantrell at his office, hoping it would be too soon for Melanie to have brought up the subject with John first. Maybe it wasn't playing fair, but when he proposed his plan, John seemed at ease with the idea. With Rand's encouragement, he finally agreed for Sienna to be hypnotized, but only if they didn't immediately disclose it to Melanie.

"I can't do it without both parent's permission," Rand advised. "I need you to get her to change her mind."

"Melanie's out of town next week," Cantrell said. "I'll bring Sienna to your office. How about then? You'll only need my signature."

Reluctantly, Rand agreed. It bothered him to deliberately deceive a family member, but the last couple of sessions with Sienna had been alarming. For such a young child she appeared to have several deep rooted psychoses. If he was to discover the source of her problem and override an unscrupulous mother, he was left with little choice but to use subterfuge.

Cantrell brought Sienna to Rand's office the following Friday afternoon. He seemed frazzled, as if he'd been trying to accomplish too many things at once. Or perhaps it was that he was unaccustomed to having a child in tow. Sienna looked bored at being there, hanging onto her father's hand as if hers were only there because he would not relinquish it.

Rand raised his eyebrows in a question.

"We just took Melanie to the airport. She's on her way to Tucson for a conference." He let out a ragged sigh, as if releasing stress.

Rand smiled, pleased at the way things were working out. He was grateful to Cantrell for using common sense and not wasting time with his daughter's well-being. He bent down to greet Sienna.

Although she was dressed in clean, pale green pants and matching tank top, her jacket was buttoned lopsided. Today her thick, dark hair that Melanie kept so tidy, had been hastily tied up in a loose ponytail with strands of hair poking out the sides. Rand suppressed a smile. It appeared that some fathers just didn't have the same touch with little girls as their mothers.

Leaving Sienna busily scribbling in a coloring book in the waiting room, Rand took John into his office. The normally self-assured man still seemed jumpy. Perhaps his conscience was bothering him.

Rand hesitated for a moment. "Before I bring Sienna in here I want to show you something." He reached into his desk and pulled out the picture Sienna had drawn and ripped to pieces. He'd reconstructed it as best he could with Scotch tape. He smoothed it flat on the desk in front of Cantrell.

"What's that?" asked Cantrell, glancing up at him.

"That's what I hoped you could tell me."

Cantrell leaned closer. "Did Sienna draw this?" Rand nodded.

He leaned back into his chair and frowned. "Apart from the blonde woman, I'm not sure who they'd represent."

Rand put the paper back in the desk drawer. "No matter," he said. "It may not have any significance. We can bring Sienna in now, if you like."

"First I need to know how this is done," Cantrell demanded. "We have to make sure Sienna won't suspect what's going on and report back on it to Melanie."

Rand patted him on the shoulder.

"Relax. There'll be hardly any difference between this and her regular sessions. We're going to put her into a sleeping mode so we can dig a little deeper; get into her subconscious."

Cantrell let out a relieved sigh. "I trust you. I'm assuming you've done this before?"

"A few times, but this is my first with a child," Rand admitted. "I don't think that will make much difference." He motioned toward his office. "I'm going to get started now, will you be all right here?"

"Can't I be in the room?"

Rand shook his head. "I'd rather you weren't. It could get disturbing and potentially dangerous if she heard you react in any way."

Cantrell walked over to Sienna, took her hand, and together they followed Rand into his office. Cantrell seemed reluctant to leave, biting at a nail as he stood awkwardly in the doorway. Rand patted his shoulder to reassure him. But his hand kept pressure on the man's back to guide him out the door as he closed it behind him. He didn't have time to worry about Cantrell.

Once in the room, Sienna bounded over to the stuffed animals and chose her apparent favorite, Miss Rabbit, which she clutched tightly to her chest. She scrambled onto the leather sofa beside Rand's chair and lay down on her back. Rand walked over to his desk and pulled out a hand-held tape recorder from the drawer. He moved back to the chair beside the leather sofa and flipped on the record switch. Then he placed the recorder on the coffee table between them.

"Sienna," Rand said. "We're going to do things a little differently today."

Sienna hugged the stuffed rabbit as if it was a life preserver.

"Have you ever been to the beach?"

Her face lit up with delight. "Mommy and Daddy took me and I played in the sand. The water was too cold to swim. Mommy wouldn't let me get close to the waves."

Rand smiled. "I want you to imagine that you're watching the waves rolling in on the sand." He lowered his voice. "Watch them as they go rolling slowly out, then come rolling back again. Slowly, back and forth, back and forth. Can you do that?"

Sienna nodded.

"All right." His voice dropped to a soft persuasiveness. "Now I want you to close your eyes, see those waves. Concentrate really hard. The waves are creeping slowly up, they almost touch you, now they roll back again. Back and forth. Back and forth. It's making you sleepy watching those waves, going back and forth."

Sienna squeezed her eyes shut the way a small child does when they're told to close them.

"If you can see those waves, Sienna," he said, "I want you to nod your head."

She nodded, eyes still closed.

"Are you asleep now?" he asked. "If you are, nod your head again slowly."

Instead of responding, Sienna jumped up and ran to the toy box that Angela and Kate had placed there and began rooting to the bottom of the box, tossing aside rejects until she came to a baby doll with most of its hair missing

Rand groaned inwardly, wondering how on earth he could distract her. These last few days had removed all doubt that Sienna would be the last patient under the age of eighteen he ever counseled.

"Sienna, why don't you bring your doll over here and introduce her to me." She didn't look up from inspecting the doll. Rand repeated the request. Pouting, she jumped up with the doll cradled in her arms, went back to the couch and sat on the edge.

"Can you lie down like you did before?"

With a petulant flounce, very much like Rand seen her mother do, Sienna complied. She lay flat on her back and placed the doll beside her. He repeated his earlier instructions of watching the waves on the beach until he was satisfied that this time she was fully under hypnosis.

"Good," said Rand. "Now I'm going to ask you a few questions. When I snap my fingers, I want you to wake up. And when you wake up you won't remember any of this." He watched the little girl who, for all appearances, appeared to be sound asleep.

"If you understand, nod your head."

Again Sienna responded.

"All right," Rand said. "Now I want you to think back. Back as far as you can, to the first thing you can remember." He paused for a few seconds, waiting for an image to come to her. "What do you see?"

"It's a birthday party," Sienna said in wooden tones. "There is a big pink cake with purple frosting flowers all over."

"How many candles do you see on the cake?"

"Four."

"Is it your birthday cake?"

"I think so," Sienna said, in the same flat, matter of fact voice.

"Are there people with you?"

"Yes. There are four girls and my mom."

"Do you recognize any of the girls?"

A slight frown crossed Sienna's forehead. Then her face relaxed. "Their names are Kylie, Susan, Cathy and Lisa." She smiled. "Lisa's my best friend. She gave me Ballerina Barbie."

"That's nice," said Rand. "Now I want you to think ahead to a year later. What do you see now?"

Sienna's face crumpled into a pout. "Mommy and Daddy are fighting. They're yelling and it scares me."

"What are they fighting about?"

"I don't know. Mommy's yelling at my dad. She said, 'Tim, you're spoiling her.' I guess she means me."

Rand froze, unable to ask the questions he had ready. Tim? Surely she had that wrong or he must have misheard her. *Who was Tim?*

"Your mother and father are fighting," he said. "What are their names?"

"Mommy's name is Melanie," Sienna said. "Daddy's name is Tim."

"Are you sure?"

"Grandma calls him Timothy when she's mad at him. She lives with us."

For a moment Rand was taken aback. No grandparents had been mentioned before. He decided to prompt her further. "Can you see anything important that happens later on?"

"Lisa and I are walking to school. There are lots of flowers."

"Does that make you happy?"

Sienna nodded, then frowned.

"My arm hurts."

"Why does your arm hurt?"

"I broke it. Tomorrow the doctor is going to take my cast off."

"How did you break your arm?" Sienna didn't answer. A wave of terror flashed across her face. She sat up abruptly staring straight ahead, her vision unfocused.

"Lisa, look out!" she screamed. Her arms flew up to cover her face and her body shook from head to toe. Then she fell back limply against the couch.

"Sienna," said Rand, alarmed. "Sienna, can you hear me?" She gave no response. Rand's heart skipped a beat. He reached over, picked up her hand and felt for her pulse. It was racing. He had to bring her round. And fast.

"Sienna, you're going to wake up now." He snapped his fingers.

But she didn't appear to hear either his voice or the sound. Trying not to panic, he felt her pulse again. It had slowed so dramatically he could scarcely detect a beat. He raised her eyelids. Her pupils were rolled back in her head. And then he realized she had stopped breathing. Immediately he stood and leaned over her, pumping rhythmic compressions above her heart, not even considering what it would look like if Cantrell were to walk in.

She began to inhale in short, choking gasps, her arms thrashing in wild oblivion. He leaned over her and pinned her body with his own, clasping her hands together with his left hand. At first she fought against the pressure of him, then she appeared to yield and he could feel the tension in her releasing. He snapped his right fingers so loudly they hurt.

This time Sienna's eyes began to open, slowly at first as if the lids were weighted by miniature pulleys. He sat back in his chair, muscles quivering as the strain slipped from his body, his chest heaving from exertion.

Finally when he was able to breathe normally, he willed his voice to calmness and asked, "Did you have a good nap?"

"Uh, huh," she said groggily. Now she'd regained consciousness it was time to clarify what she'd said earlier. He put her to the test.

"Sienna, what is your mom's name?"

"Melanie," she answered without hesitating.

"How about your dad's?"

She paused for a moment. "John."

"Not Tim?"

She shook her head. "I don't know anyone named Tim," she said. "That's a dumb name."

"Do you know girls named Kylie or Susan?"

She shook her head.

"How about Lisa or Cathy?"

She shook her head again.

"Okay, Sienna." He stood and reached for her hand to help her down from the couch. "We've done enough work for today. You can go home and tell your grandma that you're doing fine."

She scowled. A puzzled expression crossed her face. "My grandma lives in Florida. I've never met her."

"What about your other grandma? Everyone gets two, you know."

"She's dead," she said. "Mommy told me she died before I was born."

At that moment there was a brief rap on the door and Cantrell entered. Sienna moved toward him with that strange, toed-out walk. It was disconcerting not to be able to explain the inconsistencies in her story. He decided not to relate Sienna's paroxysm to Cantrell, or what she had said under hypnosis. At least for now. First he needed to talk to Melanie and get the truth from her. Find the identity of her real father.

He watched Cantrell as he stiffly took his daughter's hand, noting how awkward the two seemed with each other. It was apparent they didn't spend much time together. They were almost out the door when suddenly Rand recalled something Cantrell had told him in a previous conversation.

He waited until Sienna was a few steps ahead so she wouldn't overhear them, then said, "You once told me Melanie had lost a child. When was that?"

Cantrell shrugged. "It happened around the time I took

over the company, about five years ago." He cleared his throat and his face reddened. "Melanie was married to another man at the time."

"Melanie was married before?"

Cantrell nodded, looking even more embarrassed.

"Any idea who the guy was?"

"A boy from high school from what I remember. Melanie got pregnant and he dropped out of school. Went to work in a mill. Kind of a deadbeat. Name of Tim, I think."

A strange feeling, like that of having all the hints to a cryptic crossword puzzle, but not knowing where to begin, came over Rand. Rather than try to solve it in Cantrell's presence, he shook the notion away. "What happened to the child?"

"She was on her way to school when she was hit by a car. She never regained consciousness. A persistent vegetative state, I think they called it." He looked down at his hands, turning them over as if scrutinizing them.

Rand's chest tightened. Poor little girl. Poor Melanie. Losing a child was the single most traumatic event in a parent's life. Why hadn't she mentioned it to him?

"How did Melanie handle it?"

"She fought with the father for a couple of months about not keeping her on life support. Finally they pulled the plug on the respirator and the child died. By then Melanie had given birth to Sienna." He glanced quizzically at Rand. "That's all I know. Really. She never speaks of the child."

It must have been a painful memory, Rand thought, for Melanie to have relinquished her past with such finality. He stole a look at Cantrell who seemed uncomfortable with how much information he'd divulged. At that moment Sienna came running back, body-checking her father and then tugging on his sleeve.

"Can we go now?" she whined. Rand winced at the sound, but patted Sienna on the head and shook Cantrell's hand.

"We're in agreement on keeping this between ourselves?"

he said as Cantrell steered Sienna out the door.

"You have my word on it," Cantrell assured him.

But later he pondered the events that had transpired under hypnosis. If case histories had taught him anything, Sienna might be suffering from multiple personality disorder. Except for one small detail. There didn't appear to be more than one personality. Just one version of Sienna, and another version of Sienna. How could that be? he wondered. And more importantly, was there a connection between Melanie's first child and her last?

Chapter Eleven

The Board Room of Excel Electronics was not the sort of place staff members found to be a relaxing sanctuary during the rigors of a work day. Melanie scanned the room, pleased with what she saw. Under her redecorating scheme, shiny geometric-shaped chrome and glass tables had replaced the heavy mahogany. The welcoming sumptuousness of the oversized, burgundy velvet wingbacks had disappeared. In their place were inexpensive black leather chairs that became uncomfortable if you sat for more than an hour. The coziness was gone and it was deliberate. Board meetings adjourned faster that way. Exactly the way she'd planned it.

Though John had approved the budget, she had been dismayed and disappointed that he hadn't been thrilled with her choices. Most of the departed furniture had consisted of antiques and collector pieces. John had no idea of what had become of it. But she did.

Not about to donate the old furnishings to Goodwill as John had suggested, she'd instead had them appraised by an antique furniture dealer who'd taken it all off her hands at a price that had amazed even her. And as John had given her a hundred grand to refurnish the office, between what she'd made on the sale of the old furniture and her savings on the new, she'd pocketed a hefty sum without his knowing. Actually, she'd invested it, but he didn't know that either.

A portion of the money had gone toward a down payment on a small but elegant condo in a neighborhood close to downtown that had become nouveau chic from the swell of baby boomer investments and remodels. The balance had gone into high yielding deposits that, though she'd be unable to touch for quite a number of years or lose equity, would pay off handsomely if she were ever to find herself suddenly single again.

And she was pragmatic enough to realize the possibility of that existed because John had been particularly secretive of late. It had been months since he'd shared information with her, whether it was to do with business or with Sienna, and that was disturbing. She needed to protect her assets; protect her daughter. Something had him so distracted that he didn't seem concerned that Sienna needed to see a psychiatrist or that her life appeared to be in jeopardy.

She dismissed thoughts of her uncommunicative, recalcitrant husband and let the image of a dark haired psychiatrist replace him. Despite the seriousness behind Sienna's psychiatric assessments, Melanie found herself looking forward to their visits with Dr. Morrissey. For a man closer to her own age than John, he was refreshingly innocent and untouched. Almost virginal. The way Tim had been when they first met. An innocence like that presented an unspoken challenge. It had been a long time since a man had paid attention to her other than just giving her the eye when she walked by. She sighed. She was too young to be feeling this old.

After making a final check of the room for water pitchers and drinking glasses, she left the Board Room, passing by several rows of employees' desks sitting out in the open. She'd had the decorators dispose of the removable wall partitions, those claustrophobic, artificial offices that created workers as tender, white and flaccid as veal destined for the slaughterhouse. Now the staff worked harder and made less personal phone calls when they thought they were being watched by management.

She headed to John's private office, a room as opulent as the old Board Room had been, and one he wouldn't let Melanie touch. Lean contemporary furniture from Milan and a Salvador Dali painting of melting watches hung ostentatiously on the wall behind his leather chair. But John was not there. This was his regular golf afternoon. He'd be gone for the rest of the day.

In the six years since John had taken control, profits at Excel Electronics had risen to an all-time high. With stock about to go public it was only a matter of time before it became a Fortune 500 company. Though he hadn't volunteered the information, Melanie knew he'd been talking merger with a corporate software giant. If she were to share that knowledge it could open a lot of doors for her; close them to John.

She poured herself a cup of strong black coffee from the high tech chrome coffee maker on the credenza, then sat at John's desk and worked the computer mouse until the monitor 'woke up.' With her left hand she reached over and hit the intercom switch to contact the front desk.

"Linda," she told John's assistant, "please see that I'm not disturbed for the next hour or so. I'm on a deadline and have to get these press packets drafted before the end of the day."

"Anything I can help with?" Linda asked.

"No," said Melanie. "I'll call you if I need you. Just keep everyone out."

"No problem," Linda replied obediently, though Melanie detected a sarcastic reluctance.

She knew she could count on Linda, who had been hired against her better judgement. She was too perky, too pretty and too peroxide. On principal, she didn't trust other blondes. But she'd trained Linda to be the perfect Administrative Assistant to John. And she knew Linda understood very well what would happen if Melanie's orders weren't followed closely. Her three predecessors hadn't realized the importance of following instructions. That's why the secretaries at Excel tended to have such a high turnover rate.

Melanie opened John's e-mail, which they'd set up together when he was transferred to Excel so she knew his password, and began composing a message. The letter was addressed to John's closest friend, the golf buddy he was with today, Eric Randolph. They'd known each other since their college days. John was even godfather to Eric's kids, a fact that always brought Melanie's blood pressure up a few notches because

Eric and his wife hadn't reciprocated with Sienna. They'd demurred that 'there must be someone they were closer to,' when she'd asked. If there had been anyone closer, she wouldn't have suggested it.

"Eric," she began to type, "what I'm going to tell you must be kept under the strictest confidentiality. I would have mentioned it today when we were golfing, but with others around it was impossible to talk. There's about to be a big change at Excel. So big that if anyone knew they'd want to pick up as much stock as they could right away. I can't go into details because Melanie isn't aware of it yet and I'd like to keep it like that. Don't mention this to anyone, or even respond to this message. See you next Tuesday. JC."

After carefully reading it over for accuracy, she mouthed the words, sotto voce, as if John were speaking them. Yes, it sounded as overbearing and arrogant as John. Very carefully, she pushed 'Send Later' under 'File' on the e-mail menu and read: "When you send an e-mail message, it will be placed in your 'Outbox' folder ready to be sent the next time you choose the 'Send and Receive' command." Then she turned off the computer and smiled to herself. She knew that in the morning Linda would turn on the computer and the message would be sent without anyone else's input.

She stared at the monitor for several moments. What she'd just done might completely remove John from her life. And Sienna's too. The Feds were pretty firm on the rules of insider trading before a merger was made public. And even if he managed to wiggle out of it, she had scaffolded several abuse stories to cement his sentence.

For a moment she wondered why she didn't feel guilt over what she was doing. After all, she was about to ruin an innocent man's life and reputation. Except he wasn't really so innocent. He wasn't guilty of what she was setting him up for, but he was guilty of many other things. Just thinking about him made her so angry she couldn't help but grit her teeth. She counted off on her fingers.

"Let me see," she said aloud. "He's a condescending,

anal-retentive asshole, but most importantly, an adulterer."

She stopped counting and frowned, angry with him all over again. Yes, he was an adulterer. Did he really think he could hide traces of another woman from her? She had seen the business expenses. It was stupid of him to have submitted so many that coincided, same time, same-place with a certain sales associate, Emily Watson. And unlike men, receipts didn't lie.

For reasons known only to himself, John had lost interest in her. Acknowledging that had tossed her world upside down. And it wasn't because she was still in love with John. But it was the reason she'd begun secreting away investments. For the first time in years she had reason to fear for her financial security. After being poor for the first twenty-plus years of her life, she'd vowed never to lack for money again. If this thing between John and Emily got serious, her marriage could be in jeopardy.

John's interest in Emily had not only affected the attention he gave her, but Sienna as well. Even with the onset of Sienna's sudden medical problems it seemed as if he hardly noticed her. And if he didn't recognize problems with their child, what would become of their marriage? Of her? Something had to be done. She couldn't just sit around waiting for the walls to close in around her.

She'd thought about fixing his girlfriend with a well-placed e-mail to her husband but had decided against it. She didn't have enough time or energy to destroy their relationship. If she was angry enough the next time they submitted their expense account for a nonexistent business trip, maybe she'd do it. She grudgingly admired Emily, whose modus operandi mirrored her own, though Emily lacked her own competitiveness. Her will to survive.

Melanie hadn't grown up in what she considered a normal family unit. She couldn't remember a time during her childhood when she'd seen her mother sober. The sting of humiliation she could still feel from the day her mother had come to get her from school and fallen down the steps, alcohol practically seeping from her pores. There had been an awful scene. Her teacher had refused to let Melanie get in the car if her mother drove. And as her friends watched the drama, she had almost died from embarrassment.

But more often she was on her own. There were days her mother would leave the house late at night in her 'going out dress,' revealing deep cleavage and more thigh than if she'd only worn panties. The 'going out dress' inevitably brought home a new stepfather. She'd come home reeking of booze, cigarette smoke and the pungent scent that Melanie thought of as 'morning smell.' The raw odor of sex emanating from her mother and the male stranger spooning her against the counter while she made coffee.

The series of stepfathers, or as she referred to them, child-molesting perverts, had been around sporadically while she was growing up, never providing a male role model, or at least one an adolescent girl would want to idolize. Each man had fathered at least one bastard apiece, none of whom her mother could afford or was capable of caring for, but who came to rely upon Melanie, the eldest, as their mother. That is until she became pregnant herself and left home to marry Tim. Then the state had taken her five siblings away from her mother and it was the last she'd seen of any of her family. Good riddance, too. Their presence in her life only dragged her down and ruined her plans for the future.

Without jobs or money, she and Tim had moved in with Tim's mother. She rolled her eyes at the memory. What a soul-sucking old hag she had been. She knew the woman had despised her on sight. Hated her for taking away Tim's future. But what his mother didn't realize was that Tim would have turned out the same, with or without her. No goals or dreams. Just take one day at a time, one bill at a time, one problem at a time.

His mother's dislike of Melanie was apparent in the way she would never make eye contact with her, and even when she spoke she never faced Melanie directly, almost as if she were trying to remove her from Tim's life through sheer will power. She'd hidden much of his mother's evilness from him. If there was a hereafter, she knew for a fact he and his mother were headed in two different directions.

Then John Cantrell had come into her life. In many ways he became the father figure and role model she'd never had. She'd absorbed his knowledge of people and business as if he were a beloved first grade teacher. Even before they became lovers, he'd seen the ambition in her, the overwhelming need to be cherished and admired.

"People are kind to you because they revere the status you've already achieved," she'd told him. "Me, I'm an open invitation for judgements from people who couldn't judge a demolition derby."

She hadn't meant to get pregnant again and apart from the annoyance of having another baby, giving birth to Sienna had turned out to be a very good thing. Through Sienna, John had given her everything she'd ever wanted and never dreamed she'd been able to have. But now with John's new girlfriend in the picture, and not knowing what was happening with Sienna, it was all in jeopardy.

Chapter Twelve

Kate Petroski's apartment was a renovated loft in an older neighborhood of northwest Portland, within walking distance of newly sprouted coffee shops and specialty clothing boutiques for the price unconscious. No garage sales or flea markets here. And no expense spared in the use of marble flooring or floor-to-ceiling glass. With that much glass, Rand surmised as he rang the brass doorbell beside the etched door, probably no children either.

Kate met him at the door with two glasses of Cabernet, smiling shyly as she handed one to him. He smiled back, raising the glass and taking a long sip. She was dressed casually in loose fitting grey sweat pants and a red T-shirt that hugged her slender frame. He noticed she was careful to always avert the side of her face with the port wine birthmark, as if she was ashamed of it. It was obviously something she was uncomfortable about and he could understand why. She'd probably had to deal with unkind classmates in the past; possibly even still had the occasional jerk who made hurtful comments.

He broke the awkwardness and glanced around her apartment. The angular lines of the cold Scandinavian decor, which to Rand seemed as if had been ordered straight out of Ikea, wasn't his style. It looked stark and unfriendly, and as much as said 'don't sit here.' He did anyhow.

"Guess what I learned today?" Without waiting for a response he proceeded to tell her about Melanie having had another child before Sienna.

"You've got to be kidding me!" she burst out. "What else did you learn from Cantrell?"

"Not much more," Rand admitted. "He hadn't been on

the scene very long before the kid's accident and never even met her, either before or after. It appears Melanie is not eager to let anyone know that she'd had another little girl from a previous marriage or she'd have told us."

"How did the girl die?" Kate asked, her voice softening.

"She was hit by a car. All that Cantrell could tell me was that it happened before Sienna was born."

"Why don't you ask Melanie about it?"

Rand pondered for a few moments, gnawing at the inside of his lip. "If I did that I'd have to divulge that her husband brought Sienna in for hypnosis without her permission. And I just know that would work against us.

"No," he continued, "I think I'll let things settle down. There's nothing more I can do for Sienna unless she or her mother choose to confide in us. I'd like to set up more sessions, as many as several a week if I can. And I haven't ruled out the possibility of more hypnosis. I made a lot of progress with her the day John Cantrell brought her in."

Kate let out a ripple of laughter. "That'll be the day Melanie Moran allows you to hypnotize her kid, especially if there's information she doesn't want you to have. I wouldn't hold my breath for that one."

"You may be right," Rand said slowly. "But if I can find out exactly what happened to the sister and any history of childhood illnesses or psychoses she may have had, it may shed some light on what's happening to Sienna."

"Can I help?"

Rand threw her a surprised glance at her. Despite her casual friendliness and that carefully maintained reserve, he sensed that she liked him. Maybe more than he realized. She'd removed her glasses and in her beautiful green eyes was a tentative, yet eager expression. He smiled, suddenly pleased at the turn of events.

"Of course," he said. "When do you want to start?"

* * * * *

Finding information on a dead child without help from the parents turned out to be more complex that Rand had thought. He didn't know the child's name. He didn't know if she had even lived in the Portland area. And he kept coming up against individuals who seemed to consider it their personal mission to make things difficult for him.

Having Kate accompanying him helped. Not only would she be able to extract information from people more effectively than he, she was also an attractive and entertaining companion. She had a quiet calm that made him feel as if he'd known her much longer than the few weeks they'd spent together. He couldn't help wondering if she looked forward to being with him as much he did her.

They shared a late breakfast together at a Starbucks, creating an action plan over lukewarm lattes, then headed back to Rand's office. It seemed logical to start with the person at the nucleus of everything. Melanie. Not having a lot of background on her slowed the process. But by deliberately breaking the HIPPAA laws they retrieved the medical insurance information that was on Sienna's file, and was able to get Melanie's social security number. Her maiden name was Demchuck. Once they had that, it was relatively easy research to learn that she'd gone to school at Madison High.

When they called, school officials refused to give out any records or information over the phone. So they drove to the school, thinking an in-person contact might be more effective. Ignoring the curious stares from the overly made-up, scantily dressed teenage girls and boys whose pants looked as if they'd drop off if they took one step forward, they made their way to the library.

The blue-haired librarian was friendlier than Rand remembered librarians being during his own school days. She pointed them in the direction of a shelf full of yearbooks dating back to the inception of the school. Knowing Melanie's maiden name helped only a little as they still had to pour over hundreds of photos of fresh-faced teenaged girls. Finally they found the only Melanie in that graduating class. It was without question the right person.

The yearbook painted a pictorial of the teenaged Melanie and yielded vague details of who might have been among her friends. One of the photos showed Melanie as a cheerleader. After making a note of several of the names, Rand and Kate were able to track down a few of the team members listed in the phone book. Most of them didn't remember her. But one did and she still lived in north Portland.

Allyson King had been the head cheerleader of the rally squad the one year Melanie had been on the team. She was happy to talk and invited them to stop by her well-kept ranch style bungalow. Long past cheerleading weight, the now plump, bleached blonde Allyson greeted them as if they were old friends.

"Melanie and I were both seniors together. A lot of the boys were infatuated with her. She dated most of the football team that year. Rumor had it she put out," she bubbled con-spiratorially. "She'd only date guys for a couple of weeks, then she'd dump them for the next conquest."

She went on to tell them that Melanie kept it up until she had such a reputation for heartbreak in the senior class that no one wanted to date her. It was then that she set her sights on the junior class. And one nerdy 16-year-old fell right into her trap.

Rand had been making notes. "Do you recall his name?" he said, not looking up from his pad. Allyson frowned, think-ing.

"Jim, maybe," she said. "No, wait. Tim. That was it. Tim Moran."

A big piece of the puzzle had finally dropped into place. Rand glanced at Kate who returned his look with a quizzical one. He hadn't told her what Sienna had said under hypnosis, only to deny it later. Tim, the name of her father. Only he wasn't her father. There was no way it could be coincidence. Rand set down his pad and paper.

"Tell me everything you can remember about him," he said.

Just then they heard a baby crying from upstairs. As Allyson rushed to her child, Rand filled Kate in on the results of the hypnosis. Allyson returned with a squalling, red-faced baby, with a thatch of dark hair on the top of his head that looked like an askew toupé. Without hesitation she flipped out a large white breast, stuck her nipple into the baby's mouth and proceeded to tell them about Melanie.

Although only a year older than Tim, Melanie was already worlds ahead in experience. According to Allyson, Tim became infatuated with her, and his former friends fell by the wayside as Melanie took over his life. He'd always been a shy boy, serious about his studies, but after Melanie came into the picture, his grades dropped and he isolated himself from everyone else. Soon it was only the two of them. That was how Allyson remembered them. Tim and Melanie, always together.

"Melanie graduated with our class, but everyone knew she was pregnant," Allyson said smugly. Rand detected a hint of satisfaction in her voice. "Tim dropped out of his junior year to support her and the baby. After that, I lost touch. We didn't exactly hang with the same crowd."

Suddenly she jumped up. There was an audible 'pop' as she forgot about the baby who began to yowl again as the nipple was ripped from his mouth. In one smooth motion she stuck the nipple back in and grabbed a large book from a bookshelf. It was a senior yearbook, the same one Rand and Kate had perused at the school.

"Here." She handed it to Kate. "This is Tim."

Rand and Kate examined the photo of a skinny, dark haired boy, attractive enough, but nothing that would make him stand out in a crowd. It felt strange to be looking at the father of Melanie's dead child. With this information to go on, they thanked Allyson and left. It wasn't much, but it provided a badly needed lead.

There was no listing for Tim Moran in any of the local phone books, but Allyson had written down the names of some of Tim's classmates. Rand placed a call to one fellow who remembered that Tim had gotten a job at a local sawmill.

After calling most of the mills in Oregon with no luck, then concentrating on southern Washington, they discovered he worked for Clarkson Sawmill in Longview. The Human Resources department would only confirm that he was still employed there.

Now they'd narrowed the search down to his workplace, finding where he lived was easier. Assuming he lived a commutable distance from work, they searched the phone books and eventually discovered that he had a listed number, with an address in Longview. He was also very friendly on the telephone until Rand mentioned his ex-wife.

"I don't want to talk about her," he said. "I have nothing to say." He slammed the phone down, jolting Rand's ear.

Though annoyed, Rand wasn't surprised at Tim's response. He'd counseled enough ex's to know that friendly divorces were rare. But Tim Moran was the only person who could give him any family history on their deceased daughter. It occurred to him that by appealing to his paternal nature perhaps Tim might speak with him. If he were to show up on Tim's doorstep would he turn him away?

Rand flipped his cell phone closed and turned to Kate. "Want to meet Melanie's childhood sweetheart?" He couldn't help but grin.

Kate sighed and grimaced. "I'd love to but I'm on call for emergency this week. Longview would be a heck of a commute if I got called in."

He felt a sudden rush of disappointment but managed to keep from showing it. He threw one arm around her and gave her a quick hug. Her hair smelled of flowers. Quickly he pulled away.

"I'll fill you in on the gory details when I get back," he said, giving her a wink.

"Take notes." Kate laughed, a light cheerful sound that made him smile. "I can't wait to hear."

Although Rand would have preferred to have company for the long drive, the solitude gave him time to mull over the questions he would pose to Tim. What sort of information he expected to gain he couldn't say. And how would he justify dredging up painful memories from a man who could probably provide no enlightenment on the medical condition of a child; although not related to Tim, a half-sister to his daughter?

As he crossed the bridge into Longview, the sweet and sour stench of wet wood coming from the sawmill told him he was in the right place long before he could see the steam from the smokestacks that clotted the air above them. He drove slowly along, squinting in vain for street signs. The neighborhood he'd ventured into deteriorated with each house he passed. Now the streets were fringed by dilapidated houses with doors hanging loose, fences entangled with weeds, and abandoned shopping carts on the front lawn.

He began checking for house numbers and finally spotted a modest duplex amidst a row of identical units. Ancient khaki-green paint hung from the exterior in peeling ringlets and the faded cedar shingles on the roof curled like potato chips. A couple of stunted pines and a rhododendron with a single pink blossom perched on a leafless stick was the only landscaping. If nothing else, it looked like a definite indication that there wasn't a woman currently in Tim's life. As Rand walked up to the front door he noticed that while all the other yards had bicycles and toys strewn about the lawns, Tim's was bare.

Rand walked up to the door and hesitated. The doorbell button had been pulled out and bare wires dangled loosely from the cavity. Rand banged hard on the door, wincing as a long sliver bit into his palm. After several minutes the door opened to reveal a middle-aged man with one of the worst haircuts Rand had ever seen. His dark brown hair was trimmed on the sides and long at the back; a full-blown mullet streaked with grey.

With a jolt of recognition, Rand realized that this was the boy from the yearbook photo. A year younger than Melanie would have put him at about thirty-one, but he could have been mistaken for fifty. The stub of a cigarette smouldered in yellowed fingers. He tossed it onto the sidewalk, narrowly missing Rand.

"I told you I don't have anything to say about Melanie." He glared at Rand with suspicion, perhaps wondering what kind of person would want to resurrect the most painful memories of his life.

"It's not Melanie I came to talk about," Rand said. "It's her five-year-old daughter, Sienna."

Tim's face turned white, then flushed a deep, spotty red. Rand took him by the arm and guided him into the house where they sat down on an old denim-covered sofa, so threadbare that springs poked through. Rand sat on a safe spot where he wouldn't get skewered and waited for Tim to compose himself.

A rampantly shedding marmalade cat came up to Rand, flexed, then began rubbing its fur off against his pant leg. Rand was about to shove it out of the way with his foot when it leaped upon the sofa and skittered behind him where it lay, purring and kneading its claws against the back of his neck. He tried to ignore it, though his nose and eyes itched desperately.

Tim stood up, grabbed the cat and carried it down the hallway. Rand heard a yowl and then a door slammed. He waited until Tim sat down again.

"I'm sorry. I thought you knew she had another child."

Tim shook his head, his face crinkled with consternation. "I knew she was pregnant, but the way she felt about having more kids, I just figured she'd have an abortion and get rid of it."

Tim glanced off toward the living room window and for a few moments Rand was able to study this anguished, prematurely-aged man. Once he had been a good-looking boy, his slender build promising to fill out as he matured, playing sports and sating the voracious appetite of a typical teenager. But years of stress combined with poverty, medical bills, poor eating and long term tobacco use had given a grey cast to his skin.

"How did you find me?" he asked. "Did Melanie send you?"

Rand shook his head. "She doesn't know I'm here. In

fact, she has never mentioned you. We only learned she'd been married before from her current husband, John Cantrell."

Tim looked as if he'd been punched in the stomach. Instantly Rand regretted his bluntness, but he couldn't think of anything to say that would soften the situation.

Finally Tim ventured, "Is he the father of this little girl?" His face flushed an even deeper mottled pink that traveled down his neck to his open shirt. His voice became so low Rand almost couldn't hear it. "Does he treat Melanie well?"

Rand shrugged. "I think so. From what I'm able to tell, anyhow."

Tim stared down at his hands. Rand noticed that he was missing two fingers. Tim saw him looking but made no attempt to hide them.

"Then that's the guy Melanie cheated on me with," he said, almost to himself. "He was her boss. Is still her boss, I guess." Suddenly he glared at Rand. "Why are you here? I can't tell you anything about the girl's family history that Melanie couldn't."

There was a kind of hedginess in his eyes that raised Rand's psychiatrist antennae. He briefly filled Tim in on Sienna and her mysterious bouts of unconsciousness. The various teams of doctors by whom she'd been examined; the lab tests she'd been put through. The brain scans. And the complete lack of any possible diagnosis thus far.

"I'd like to know about your daughter, the one you and Melanie had together. Not necessarily about the accident. I need access to her medical history to see if she'd ever experienced anything similar to what Sienna has gone through. Right now we've got nothing else to go on."

Tim shook his head. "I don't think you're going to get much from her records. She never had anything like what you're talking about. She was just a normal kid, with normal cuts and bruises, things like that, before the accident. Poor baby, she never had a chance to grow up."

"Would you be willing to sign a medical release giving me access to her records? It would really help Sienna if we could find a clue to what's going on with her. Maybe even save her life."

"Would Melanie know what you're doing?"

Rand's brow wrinkled. "Would that matter now?"

"If Melanie came back into our lives again, I don't know what I'd do. I don't ever want to encounter her again, not even for the sake of her child." Tim glanced away for a second, then back at Rand, his eyes starting to redden.

"What do you mean 'our' lives?" Rand asked, puzzled. "Have you remarried?" The condition of the yard, the house, was not the way most women would live.

"Mine and Chelsa's." Tim ducked his chin.

"Your daughter is still alive?" Rand's voice rose with excitement.

Tim nodded. "Very much alive. I guess there's a lot more that Melanie hasn't told you." There was no mistaking the heavy sarcasm in his voice.

Trying to mask the shock of this new discovery, Rand paused for breath, now so congested from the cat dander he was no longer able to breathe through his nose. He scratched his neck where the cat's claws had been. He could feel hives beginning to form. He fought the urge to scratch harder. In his mind's eye he could still recall Sienna's medical history and information release forms that Melanie had filled out. He'd gone over them several times. Melanie had deliberately left out any information about a sibling. Why would she do that?

"It was Cantrell who told me about Melanie's daughter. *Your* daughter," he corrected. "I don't think he knows she's alive. Does Melanie?"

Tim gave a snort of disgust. "Probably not. She hasn't even visited Chelsa since shortly after the accident. Her own daughter. How could she just leave her and forget about her." This came out as a statement, as if there was no point in asking because he already knew the answer.

"This isn't to help Melanie," Rand said. "It's for a little girl whose life is in jeopardy."

Tim was quiet for a few moments. "All right, but I don't

want Melanie to know about this, okay? Don't tell her you've seen me. And for God's sake, don't tell her about Chelsa."

Rand nodded. "You have my word on it."

"Do you want to see her now?" asked Tim. "Chelsa, I mean. She's in a long-term care nursing home a few minutes from here." He had the look of a new parent eager to show off the baby. If he'd handed him a cigar Rand wouldn't have been more amazed.

"Sure," Rand replied slowly. He hadn't expected the offer, but it might help. Anything was worth a shot.

Rand followed Tim's battered rusty green Taurus station wagon to the nursing home, maintaining several car lengths behind to avoid having the burned oil fumes come through the vents. Tim had been right about the distance. It took only ten minutes to get there from Tim's house. An easy commute for him after work each evening. They parked the cars side by side and walked together into the building. The receptionist smiled at Tim and nodded in recognition as they passed.

As they walked down the hall Rand tried to match his stride to Tim's but found he couldn't keep up, causing Tim to bound back toward him like an Irish Setter on a beach walk. Finally they stopped in front of a door marked Room 204.

"You don't have to be quiet," Tie explained unnecessarily as he pushed open the door to Chelsa's room. "We won't wake her."

Rand refrained from rolling his eyes. Considering the kid had been in a coma for five years, it seemed pretty unlikely that anything short of a plane crashing into the building would have awakened her.

Tim went in first, hurrying over to a crib-like bed. A skeletal form lay in a fetal position, covered up loosely with white blankets. As Rand approached, he saw tangled dark-blonde curls falling over the face of an emaciated pixie. He froze in his tracks. For a moment the floor seemed to move beneath him. Involuntarily he swayed, grasping for the wall behind him to prevent himself from falling. His stomach lurched, forcing a rush of bile to the back of his throat.

Carrie? Oh my God, it was Carrie! He shook his head violently to free the thought, allowing reason to take over. Of course not! It couldn't be. Carrie was dead. A sudden pain seared from behind his right eye all the way back to the top of his head, blinding him with its intensity. He noticed Tim frowning at him and forced himself to take a few steps toward the bed to stare down at the comatose girl. He heaved a sigh of relief. Really, she bore no resemblance to Carrie, his little sister. Then why had her memory surfaced with such numbing clarity after all these years?

He watched as Tim picked up the girl's limp hand. Although the limb was flaccid, the fingers were rigid in a permanent grasping claw, typical of many patients who'd lain in the same position for years. Physical therapy and constant manipulation of the digits could have helped relieve that, but it was a time-consuming and exhausting ritual. And without extra insurance coverage, long range therapy was probably too expensive for Tim.

"Daddy's here." Tim leaned over and kissed Chelsa's pallid cheek. Grabbing a tissue from the nightstand he dabbed at the drool that trickled out from the corner of her mouth onto her pillow. He rearranged her hair behind her ear so Rand could get a good view of her face and then pulled a couple of hard plastic chairs close to the bed. Rand noticed a CD player and a CD of the Dixie Chicks sat on top of a dog-eared issue of *Seventeen* magazine.

Rand inhaled deeply. He could feel a migraine coming on. He squeezed one eye shut to dispel the visual aura that would precede the blinding pain that always followed. "Tell me about Chelsa's life before the accident."

Tim sighed, massaging his daughter's fingers. "Like I said, she was just a regular kid, although she was pretty clumsy when she was younger." He flashed a glance at Rand. "Most little kids are accident prone, right? Broken arms, bruises, things like that?"

Tell him the truth, Daddy.

Rand studied him for a few moments. "They can be," he said slowly, "a few have help."

Tim frowned. "What do you mean?"

"Were Melanie and Chelsa close? Was Melanie overly strict with her?"

Tim shook his head. "I wouldn't say close. She was always closer to me than Melanie. They had the usual mother-daughter battles."

"How usual? Did she spank her? Punish her unnecessarily?"

"I don't think Melanie hurt her; Chelsa would have told me."

"Children most often *don't* tell," said Rand. "Either from misplaced loyalty or because of a threat that their lives will change for the worse. If they told, we'd have fewer child deaths at the hands of a parent."

Tim contemplated that for several minutes. Finally he said, "Her hospital visits are on record. It would be all right with me if you looked at the files. If you find anything strange I might be able to remember what had happened before she was hurt. But all I can recall anymore is the day of the accident."

Chapter Thirteen

After Dr. Morrissey left them, Tim sat down next to Chelsa's bed and watched her as she lay motionless, her breathing so shallow she scarcely seemed alive. But Tim knew she was, just as she'd been when everyone else considered her dead. He knew everything about her. He'd been the one who'd looked after her all these years and he could recognize even the subtlest of changes. He picked up a CD and popped it into the player, adjusting the volume high enough so Chelsa could hear the lyrics.

At first he'd thought God had failed him by not answering his prayers for Chelsa's recovery, but then he began to comprehend that each new idea he tried was a journey to his final goal. Trying to get Reverend Maloney to baptize Chelsa had been the first step and though the church could not help, it showed him which direction he needed to go to get Chelsa back. When he'd completed the entire length of his journey, God would let him know.

He leaned back in the chair and as the music played, he reveled in the warmth and sheer joy that passed over him. Yes, he had to keep faith. God would show him the way. The step he'd taken in hiring the psychic had seemed blasphemous at first, but it had proved useful. Surely the child's voice had been a warning to him. There was an evil force out there of which to be wary. From where it would come or when, he did not know. But he knew it was there.

This new medial nerve response therapy held the greatest chances for Chelsa's recovery so far. If the machine could stimulate her dormant brain to respond to the outside world, he knew God would provide her with the soul that had left her body when she'd been pronounced brain dead. Just because she was as dormant as a frog in a frozen pond didn't mean that she wouldn't recover one day. The doctors, with all their knowledge and years of medical training behind them, would never convince him of that.

His mind flickered back to the day of Chelsa's accident, the first horrific night at the hospital, and the war with Melanie. Over the years he'd managed to successfully extract Melanie from his conscious thoughts. She'd hurt and betrayed both of them so terribly, he'd preferred to think of her as dead. That is, she was dead to him until Dr. Morrissey unexpectedly resurrected her. Anger flared in him, as it always did when he thought of her. Then he dismissed it, just as quickly. It wasn't the doctor's fault. Melanie was a formidable force for anyone to have to contend with. He should know.

He still remembered the first time he'd seen her. It had been at a high school basketball game where she had been a cheerleader on the rally squad. She was popular and outgoing, everything he was not. She could have dated anyone, and pretty much had at one time, but in the end she'd chosen him. At the time he couldn't understand why. He'd preferred not to question his good fortune. But after nearly nine years of marriage and the years since their divorce to think about it, he knew. Melanie needed to be in control of something. She'd had little enough in her dysfunctional childhood, but she'd been determined to change all that. She'd chosen him like prey, weak and helpless, and she'd fed from him while they were together. How she managed with Cantrell, he couldn't say. Nor did he care anymore.

* * * * *

In that moment at Chelsa's bedside, Rand had been catapulted back in time nearly twenty years with the gut-wrenching force that accompanies dredged up memories that are best long forgotten. A late February afternoon in eastern Oregon, when dropping temperatures transformed the sickly pre-spring sun-

115

shine into a fading misty sunset that looked like melting orange sherbet.

That day, twelve-year-old Rand, his eight-year-old sister, Carrie, and their oversized mongrel Matt, had spent the day stomping through the semi-frozen marsh around Logan Lake. Matt was a useless, guilty-looking dog that had gotten his name from the coat that couldn't be completely brushed through. Not having mastered basic obedience training, he raced back and forth, usurping wild birds who protested with squawks of indignation.

As Rand and Carrie made their way home, the air crinkled with the beginning thaw, forcing the ice-encrusted branches to shed their casings. The lake was still frozen over, but when they stood very quietly they could hear the loud cracking of ice shifting uncomfortably in the warming sun.

Matt sprang ahead of them like a deer, all four feet together as he leaped through the muck. Carrie, who from infancy had worshiped her older brother, trudged behind him, stretching her legs to fit her tiny boots into his much larger footprints. But as she pulled her foot out to take the next step, her felt-lined duck boot stayed behind in the mud. Unbalanced, she teetered back and forth on one foot, then finally fell over on her side.

"Rand, stop!" she called.

Rand froze in his tracks and turned around. Laughing, Carrie held out her muddy gloved hands to him.

"You clumsy idiot," he scolded, but not unkindly. Even though he loved his little sister, his parents too often put him in the unasked-for position of protectorate. He walked back, picked up her boot and forced it on her sodden wool-socked foot. Then he pulled her to her feet and gave her a little push in the direction of the house.

"We should go back," he said. He wiped his gloves on a clump of dried grass. "The sun's starting to go down and it'll be dark soon." He started off again, heading toward home. Matt presumably was already there. The barking had stopped and he was nowhere to be seen.

"Can't we stay a little longer?" Carrie pleaded. "There's a patch of snow over there. We could make one last angel."

Rand glanced back to her, suddenly exasperated. His gloves were soaked through, numbing his fingers to the bone, and his nose was beginning to run. Still, when he looked into Carrie's bright blue eyes, their color heightened by the redness of her cheeks from the frosty winter air, he couldn't help but give in. She was a pretty good kid, he thought, not like some of the bratty younger siblings of his friends.

"Okay," he said reluctantly, because a forewarning told him they shouldn't linger. But he followed Carrie toward the beckoning patch of untouched snow-drift, shaded from the sun by a stand of firs. It stretched from the shore nearly to the center of the lake. Soon Rand was caught up in Carrie's enthusiasm and ran after her, feet crunching through the crusty snow. They fell simultaneously, giggling as they waved their arms and legs to make the snow angels.

Rand sat up and glanced around. It was as if they were all alone in a completely undiscovered world. The snow drift was like an island, sitting on top of the frozen lake. The oblique angle of the setting sun made the snow sparkle, blindingly bright like glittering pink diamonds.

"I dare you to grab a handful of those diamonds to take back to Mom," he said. "It's her birthday soon. She'd love pink diamonds." Carrie's eyes lit up.

"Really? Pink diamonds?" She followed his gaze to take in the beauty of the sunset. Leaping to her feet she ran off, plunging clumsily through the snow. Rand started to laugh. She was so gullible.

He watched her run until she reached the end of the snow-spit. Then she stumbled and fell headlong, her arms splayed before her. And then there was a sickening crack. Carrie's weight, combined with the heaviness of the melting snow, had broken through the ice. She disappeared into the water before she had a chance to scream.

But then just as suddenly, her head bobbed above the ice and she was able to lay her arms out in front of her along the jut of snow bank. Rand could see her eyes wide open in terror, her mouth working wordlessly as she struggled to call his name. He ran toward the broken ice, but as he neared he moved more slowly, stepping cautiously so he too, would not fall through. When he reached her, he lay on his stomach and stretched out his hands. Carrie's eyes were clouding with fear. She grasped his hands, too terrified to speak.

"I'm going to try and pull you out." He tried to sound confident. "I'm going to inch backwards on the snow."

Carrie nodded, her eyes riveted on his face. But as Rand tried to wriggle backward, he heard an ominous crunch. He froze for a moment, then closed his eyes, took a deep breath and ignored the sound. He drew one knee back and tried to feel around for some leverage. Then an icy cold wetness soaked the knee of his snow pants. He'd broken through the ice. He stopped moving. He knew what he had to do, he just didn't know if he could do it.

Taking a deep breath he said, "I have to go for help, Carrie. If you lie really still and don't move, you'll be okay until I come back." But he was lying to them both, because he wasn't sure of that himself.

Carrie started to whimper. Her hands were slippery and purple now, her lips turning blue. Rand squeezed his eyes shut and forced himself to stay calm. When he opened them he felt as if the coldness was starting to make him lose touch with reality. The setting sun had created a shimmering golden aura around Carrie's head. He shook his head violently and began once again to inch backwards across the ice.

"Don't leave me," she pleaded. Her teeth chattered to the point where she couldn't control them. It was so loud they sounded as if they were going to break and it scared the hell out of him. Then he had a glimmer of hope.

"Matt!" he said. "Matt went home. When Mom and Dad see that Matt has come home without us, they'll start looking."

Carrie's blue eyes, the only familial trait they shared, brightened with love and trust. And that look frightened Rand more than the ice and snow and the freezing water. Because it was his fault that she was in this mess. If only he hadn't dared her…

Chapter Fourteen

Once Rand had the signed Consent Forms to release Chelsa's medical records he had no trouble accessing her medical history. He'd had the attending clerk at the nursing home make copies for his own files, then headed home to examine them. He dropped the papers onto the kitchen table and grabbed a beer from the fridge. Flopping onto a chair, he began leafing through the documents.

Chelsa's birth records were the first papers he came to, then carbon copies from multiple admissions to St. Augustus Emergency for minor childhood injuries. At the age of five, a broken ankle from falling down the basement stairs. A year later when Chelsa was six, she'd sustained a sprained wrist from a 'twist' injury. A 'playground mishap' at the age of seven, noted bruising on legs and buttocks—all explained away with notes saying 'Parents interviewed—no charges or other reports filed.'

Eight weeks prior to the car accident she had broken her arm, again without an explanation noted. Then finally there was the accident report filled out by the neurology resident who had admitted Chelsa the day she'd been brought into Emergency. All in all, it was a thick file for a girl who'd only been eight at the time of the accident.

And then something extraordinary caught Rand's attention. He made a mental math calculation and wondered at the coincidence of it. It was a simple thing, really, and probably held no significance to either girl. Chelsa had been struck by the car and pronounced brain dead exactly nine months before Sienna was born.

He noted the name of the attending doctor who'd been

on duty the day Chelsa had been brought into emergency. A Dr. J. Elias, Neurology Resident. Rand didn't recognize the name, but then he wasn't familiar with many of the medical population at St. Augustus unless he'd been called to consult on one of their patients. He soon discovered that Dr. Elias was no longer on staff at St. Augustus. But reaching a doctor of any specialty was relatively easy; most were listed in the phone books or on the internet. He'd find him eventually.

But when he Googled Dr. Elias on the internet, he could not find any doctor whose medical time-line matched. There was no listing in the local telephone directories and Rand could not verify that he was in any medical practice in Portland or the surrounding area. He'd even asked Kate, who was in the same specialty. She'd never heard of him. He began to think that Elias must have moved out of state and then he got an idea to contact the Alumni Association of the hospital where he'd trained.

Of course, no one would give Rand any direct information as to the doctor's whereabouts, though they did offer to pass on a message. So it was much to Rand's amazement when he received a call back within a couple of days. Dr. Elias was still in Portland and he'd changed his specialty from neurology to pathology. He seemed reluctant to meet Rand privately, although he finally offered to have Rand meet him at his place of work.

Though pleased to be back on track with Chelsa's medical history and that he would be able to have his questions about her early hospital stays answered, Rand was secretly alarmed at the thought of visiting the pathologist. There was only one place he disliked more than an active treatment hospital—the morgue.

At the Medical Examiner's office, Rand was shown into a room where he was to put a gown and booties over his clothing and cover his face with a mask. He left the mask hanging down until he was about to enter the room, though he came to wish he hadn't. He had a strong aversion to the smell of blood. And the sight of it. Not that his patients weren't mentally hemorrhaging. Occasionally you could almost smell it on them—the walking wounded. But at least psychiatrists didn't need to use disinfectant.

Once he'd managed to bluff his way through the requirements of his medical residency, he'd only had one other occasion to visit the morgue. Until passing through those icy steel doors, he'd managed to repress that memory. But along with the unforgettable odor of formaldehyde, it now came rushing back.

Several years earlier he'd counseled a middle-aged woman named Nancy who'd survived breast cancer and was well on the road to recovery. Physical recovery, that was. Her mental state was in a shambles. Even the reconstructive surgery of her breasts that yielded as near to perfect results as nature had made them failed to lift her depression. At the heart of the problem was her husband, whose lack of moral support and rejection of her earlier disfigurement had thrown her into a downward spiral.

Rand had brought the two of them in for counseling without making much progress. Then one day Nancy came in alone. She'd arrived home to find her husband had moved out without a word. She was still taking the strong antidepressants he'd prescribed. So severely depressed she couldn't even get out of bed in the morning, he eventually increased her medication to an even more potent dosage. After she failed to show for her weekly appointment, something she'd never done before, he became alarmed. He called her home number and cell phone without getting a response.

Later that day he received a call from the Medical Examiner's office to come and identify her body. She'd been found in a motel room, dead for three days with no identification on her but for the empty bottle of pills with both their names on it. With the husband out of the picture and no other next of kin, he was the only one able to come down to the morgue to identify her.

Forcing the painful memory aside, he pushed open the doors to the autopsy room. Row upon row of metal coolers lined one wall, but another contained a display of jars filled with formaldehyde-preserved specimens from past autopsies. The room was so cold you could almost see your breath. A pervasive damp seemed to trap the odor of decaying tissue, blood and body fluids.

A doctor performing an autopsy leaned over a whitish-green body, the chest cavity flailed open. He had an oscillating fan blowing the smell away from him, but rather than dissipating the odor, as it headed in Rand's direction it seemed only to intensify it. The stench of formaldehyde and putrefaction brought Rand's breakfast dangerously close to his esophagus. He swallowed hard, hoping he wouldn't embarrass himself, and forced himself to grin. It suppressed the gag reflex. As he walked over to the table Dr. Elias looked up from his work.

"You must be Morrissey." His voice had a soft sibilant 's' lisp to it. "Good thing you gowned up. I hope you don't mind if I don't shake your hand; you wouldn't want any of Mr. Stinky to get on you. There's some Vick's Vaporub on the counter if you need it."

He turned his attention back to the cadaver. "I'm on a deadline to deliver the cause of death on this one, and the next room is stacked up with even more. We're pretty shorthanded with all the cutbacks. I guess they figured this was a place they could reduce funding."

Rand nodded, exhaling deeply through his nose, inhaling as shallowly as he dared through his mouth. With only the opening of his mask exposing his face, all Rand could see of Dr. Elias were dark, deeply set eyes, one of which had a streak of blood from straining. A stubby man, his elbows barely came up to the edges of the steel table. He didn't seem to notice when his sleeve inadvertently dipped into the rivulet of greenish fluid that seeped from the body. Diverted by the flanged edges of the table it trickled in a slow stream toward the drain and into a catch basin.

The doctor cleared his throat and the unexpected gurgling sound nearly caused Rand to vomit. Though it was an admirable vocation, he couldn't understand why anyone would want to enter this facet of medicine. He shuddered, trying not to see Dr. Elias's object of attention.

"What did you want to talk to me about?" Dr. Elias's eyes searched Rand's covered face. Rand could see them crinkle at the corners above his mask. No doubt he realized Rand was having difficulties and found it amusing. He resolved to make an effort not to show his weakness.

"About five years ago when you were a neurology resident at St. Augustus, you admitted an eight-year-old girl who'd been struck by a car. She had severe head trauma and showed no signs of life. The recommendation was to turn off life support, but the father resisted. Her name was Chelsa Moran. Do you remember seeing her?"

Dr. Elias halted mid-cut to stare directly at Rand.

"Of course I do. She's the reason I went into pathology." He paused and glanced at the wall clock, shifting uncomfortably. It was obvious that Dr. Elias recalling the event was painful at the least, but possibly even more. Professionally humiliating, maybe?

"It was one of my first trauma cases," he continued. "And it was tough. Made even tougher because it was a child. I don't think I'll ever forget that." He set the scalpel down on the steel table.

"When the child was first brought in she wasn't breathing. I happened to be nearby, checking on a patient in the next ward. I got there before the team with the crash cart." Distractedly he began peeling off his rubber gloves. He reached for the disinfectant and began to slather it on, rubbing vigorously as if he were trying to erase away the memory. Finally he stopped, gazing at his hands somewhat embarrassed. He turned to Rand.

"What I'm going to tell you is to remain between us. Do you understand? Off the record, as they say."

Rand nodded, puzzled.

"I'm not a religious man, you see, and as a young med student I was even less back then, so I can't explain what I witnessed." He hesitated for several seconds. "As I entered the room I saw what looked like vapor above the child's body. A gauzy white, shapeless mass. It seemed to emanate from within her. It hovered about two feet above her for a moment and then dissipated. At first I thought it was steam. A cold room and a feverish, perspiring child can produce steam when the covers are removed. I've seen that before. But the room was around 70 degrees and the child was neither flushed nor feverish. I couldn't explain it."

Elias shivered. "The vision was so surreal that even now it makes me shudder. The vapor disappeared so quickly I wasn't even sure it actually happened. I rushed over and began attempting resuscitation. She wasn't responding. There was no pulse, no heartbeat, no breathing. I started working harder, and called in a Code Blue. Then the team with the crash cart showed up."

He glanced away quickly and Rand saw the red streak in his eye spread outward, filling the entire sclera. He blinked hard and glanced down at his hands.

"And then the strangest thing happened," he said. "It turned out the crash cart wasn't needed. Although Chelsa was still comatose and needed the respirator to breathe for her, her heart began beating on its own. To this day I don't know what I saw, but if I was religious, I'd be tempted to say that what I'd seen was her soul leaving her body." He gave a derisive snort.

"After that I had the grim task of having to tell the parents that their kid was brain dead and the best thing to do would be to discontinue life support."

"I take it they didn't want to do it?" Rand said.

Dr. Elias shook his head. "As I recall the mother eventually realized nothing more could be done for the child. She seemed to be the brains of the two. But the father refused because of religious convictions. We adhered to the parents' wishes and kept the machines on. A lot of times the patient dies anyway, so the feeling was that it was just a matter of time."

"But that didn't happen?"

Elias sighed. "No, it didn't. Anyhow, that was enough for

me. The next day I put in a request to switch my specialty to pathology."

After his conversation with Dr. Elias, Rand was so unsettled he could scarcely concentrate on his drive home. It was difficult to believe that what Dr. Elias claimed to have witnessed had shaken him profoundly enough that he no longer wanted to work with living patients. He was a man of science. He should have been able to come up with a logical explanation for what he saw. And it was too dismissive to assume Dr. Elias only imagined it.

He drove the Volvo onto the carport of his floating home and then headed into the kitchen where he was greeted by the frantic Goldie. He let Goldie onto the floating home's deck to relieve himself then headed back to the front entrance, reached outside to the mailbox and retrieved his mail. He began sorting the junk catalogs and credit card offers from the bills. An invitation to join the AARP bearing the former homeowner's name got thrown across the room in the general direction of the paper shredder. Then he slipped into the den and switched on his laptop.

He searched various web pages on death, dying, and spiritual planes, all the while trying to visualize what it was Dr. Elias thought he had seen. If he suspended his disbelief of things theological, then he could envision Chelsa's soul leaving her body. But from nearly everyone's perspective, if the soul leaves the body, then technically the person is dead.

Tim had told him that Chelsa had never been baptized. He had heard that some religions believe the souls of unbaptized children go into Limbo, a purgatory of sorts. If her soul was in Limbo, then it was free to go elsewhere. But if that were true, where did it go?

He shook his head. To an agnostic like himself, it was incomprehensible. There was not enough evidence to support a theory like that. He couldn't explain a persons' faith in God. He didn't believe in reincarnation. He didn't believe in organized religion. He didn't go to church. He wasn't even sure if he believed in God. Yet, from a scientific perspective there were too many aspects to this case that defied explanation. So, given all that, he could scarcely believe what he was beginning to consider. He needed an authority on the subject. And as luck would have it, he knew where to find one.

That night he sent an email to Angela to have her reschedule his first few morning patients. Then early in the morning he took a drive to the outskirts of town. On the south end of the city, not far off the freeway, was a Buddhist temple. The resident monk, Mr. Suchit Chhim, was a former patient he had treated for an allergic reaction when Rand was still an intern. Perhaps Mr. Chhim had sensed Rand to be a lost soul or maybe he was just attempting to make a convert, but when he was about to leave the monk had urged him to one day visit his temple. Rand couldn't deny that in the man's presence he had felt an inexplicable and overwhelming calm.

The temple itself nestled in the center of a fir grove on a small acreage, incongruous to the large suburban neighborhood encroaching it. A low, wrought-iron fence that had been recently gilded enclosed the delicate landscaping of miniature sculptured evergreens. The temple's architecture was a faithful reproduction of ancient Cambodian temples of centuries ago, with its curving roof structure and gold and red embossed exterior.

As Rand entered through the vestibule he removed his shoes and placed them on a mat inside the doorway. He immediately realized he must be in the shrine room. The far wall was covered by a mural of a vast forest, with pink-blossomed cherry trees and a brook so realistic he could almost hear the trickle of water. A life-sized golden Buddha squatted beside it, surrounded by enormous porcelain vases filled with white daisies and yellow and purple snapdragons. Incense and candles burned at the Buddha's feet. Glittering lights from a large crystal chandelier reflected off it, bathing the entire room in a golden glow.

Mr. Chhim came to greet him, wearing the traditional attire of flowing orange robes and leather sandals. A diminutive man with a shaved head, his smile of welcome transcended any religious beliefs. He held out his hand in welcome.

"So, finally you come to see," he said with a slight smile. He offered a very small nodding bow. Rand, unsure of protocol, did the same.

Mr. Chhim took Rand's arm and showed him to a small room, apparently used as an office, off the main temple room. It was meagerly furnished with a fake oak desk and aged, wobbling chairs. Wood plank shelves packed with layers of books stacked haphazardly lined both walls. A small window behind the desk gave a view of the monastery garden where several other monks, their orange robes tied above their knees, weeded and hoed the dark rich soil.

"Is there a special reason for the visit?" Mr. Chhim asked, giving Rand a kind look that made him feel as if the man could read his thoughts.

"What are your beliefs on reincarnation?" Rand said.

Mr. Chhim blinked in surprise. "Mine in particular, or are you asking if it exists?"

Rand thought for a moment. "Both, I guess. I have a patient whose behavior cannot be explained from a medical or even psychological standpoint. I've begun to suspect reincarnation."

"I see," said Mr. Chhim. He pressed both index fingers alongside his chin. "According to Buddha, the spirit of someone who dies is continuously reborn until that person reaches their ultimate enlightenment."

"Does that mean they don't go to Heaven or Hell?" Rand contemplated for a second. "Or even into Limbo, if the person was not baptized?"

"There is no Heaven or Hell in Buddhism," said Mr. Chhim. "Or even Limbo. There is only your Karma that dictates how you will be reborn."

"Could a person be reborn without being completely dead?"

Mr. Chhim looked surprised. "I don't understand."

"The patients I'm talking about are two sisters. Half-sisters, actually. One is in a deep coma, a persistent vegetative state, basically brain dead. At the exact time of the accident that caused this her sister was conceived." He knew it sounded ridiculous, even to someone whose beliefs were unconventional from his own and most of his contemporaries. "Could this embryo have received the soul of her brain dead sister? Received it prematurely?"

Mr. Chhim rubbed his shaved head for a moment and stared out the window at the gardeners, lost in thought. His face was inscrutable. Rand half-expected him to answer 'don't be ridiculous' to his question. Then he realized he was only projecting his own doubts. He gazed reverently at Mr. Chhim, who could have made a fortune at playing poker and could scarcely believe his ears when the monk finally said, "I believe it could."

After his visit to the temple, Rand's mood was oddly elevated. Mr. Chhim had spoken of reincarnation as if it were a perfectly natural occurrence, as inevitable as birth and death. Yet somewhere between Chelsa dying and Sienna being conceived was a soul caught, suspended between two girls, both of whom appeared to be fighting for it. It was a form of Limbo, all right, though not the one he'd considered before.

He didn't have all the answers yet, but Mr. Chhim's explanation reinforced his theory. If putting aside his doubts, believing in what he couldn't see or explain away would save Sienna, maybe he could suspend his disbelief for once. And helping one child might somehow make up for the one he hadn't been able to. His own sister.

Though he'd initially dreaded a consult with Sienna he now found himself strangely elated, as if a window had been opened and now he had an opportunity to see farther into the distance. In spite of himself, he wasn't sorry he'd agreed to see her. This soul rightly belonged to Chelsa, but through a quirk of time and fate, almost as though God had blinked, it had inadvertently gone to Sienna. There was only one problem, if his theory was correct. Losing the soul completely would kill either child. Or if one came out the victor, the other's death was inevitable.

Chapter Fifteen

Despite the best possible care and Rand's family praying day and night, his sister Carrie never regained consciousness. Suffering from hypothermia, she remained in hospital for two weeks, during which Rand rarely saw his mother and father as they alternated shifts at her bedside. Because he was only twelve he was not allowed into the Intensive Care Unit. And though she'd been technically dead since his father had dragged her icy blue body out of the frozen lake, they hadn't let him see her until just before they officially pronounced her dead. It was the day before his mother's birthday.

They'd accepted his explanation. Of how they were playing and Carrie had gone one step further. She was always going one step further, they knew that. She was a daredevil, a risk taker, but when she died the entire life went out of the family. His mother was in tears all the time and his father rarely smiled. He knew they didn't blame him, but it seemed now as if no one ever talked to him. And finally he stopped talking at all. At the time it seemed as if he couldn't open his mouth because if he did nothing would emerge. Or if his voice came, it might inadvertently spill the truth about Carrie's accident.

For a while no one really noticed. The emotional disappearing act he'd pulled. He refused to leave his room. He began to skip classes and eventually got suspended. After that his mother hired tutors for him. He'd done all right with the written work, but there had been no verbal communication with his parents, no interaction with classmates, no social life.

It wasn't until one of his teachers sent home a note asking to speak with his parents that they suspected there was something profoundly wrong. They'd been so enveloped in their own grief that they hadn't realized he'd been withdrawing from them and everything around him. But even when his parents began to pay attention to him and try to bring him out, it hadn't worked. Finally, despairing of losing another child, Rand's mother took him to a child psychiatrist and Rand's life began to turn around.

For an adult, Rand thought Dr. Irving Silverstein was the funniest man he had ever met. He was as brown as a chestnut with the luxurious snow-white mane of a symphony maestro. In spite of the year-round, dark tan that made him look like a photograph negative, his face was unlined from the sun. A young man with white hair. If Rand had been any less angry, he would have found this hilarious. But he hadn't laughed in a long time and he wasn't going to now.

On that first visit Dr. Silverstein showed him around the office, told him to sit down and get comfortable, then he ushered Rand's fidgeting mother back to the waiting room. He'd sat across from Rand on an uncomfortable wingback chair in a tiny cubicle of a room, unlike anything Rand believed he'd known about a psychiatrist's office. For a long time no one said anything. Rand shifted uncomfortably in his chair. Would Dr. Silverstein just sit there until he spoke first? Well, that wouldn't happen. He wasn't going first, that was for damn sure. But Dr. Silverstein picked up an ancient copy of *National Geographic* and began reading, ignoring him completely. Finally he couldn't stand it anymore.

"Don't you even want to know why I'm here?" he blurted. Dr. Silverstein set the magazine down upon the coffee table.

"If you want to tell me, Randall."

"Only my mother calls me Randall," he snorted. "My aunts call me Randy. But I won't answer if you call me any of those. My name is Rand."

"Fair enough."

"Why aren't you taking notes?"

"It's distracting. For both of us."

It occurred to Rand then that Dr. Silverstein was probably

pretty good at this. He'd had no intention of talking and now here he was doing it. Damn. He scowled at the floor.

"Do you report what I say back to my parents?"

"Only if you want me to. Otherwise it's just between us."

For reasons he couldn't explain, Rand knew he was telling the truth.

"I killed my sister." He stared at Dr. Silverstein, hoping to have shocked him. He hadn't.

"What makes you think you killed her? Your parents said her death was accidental."

"It wasn't," Rand said defiantly. "I dared her to go out on the ice. I knew it could break."

"Did you want her to get hurt?"

"No!" It came out more forcefully than he'd wanted. "No," he repeated quietly. "That part was an accident." He examined his fingernails for a minute then gnawed at a cuticle.

"I wanted to scare her a little, get her to scream when the ice cracked. I didn't think it was so melted she'd fall through. Otherwise I'd never have done it."

"Did your parents know about this?"

Rand shook his head. "They thought it was an accident. That it was just bad luck that Carrie had fallen through and not me."

"Did they ever ask why Carrie was in the middle of the pond on the rotten ice while you were on the safer, firm ice?"

"Never did. No."

"Do you think they might have suspected it and just never mentioned it to you, knowing how terrible you felt?"

Rand shrugged. "Maybe. But the newspapers and my family all said I'd done the right thing staying there instead of abandoning her." Tears started to roll down his cheeks. Dr. Silverstein passed a box of tissues. Rand blew his nose.

"You know that she would have slipped under and died before you got back?" the doctor said gently.

Rand didn't answer. He stared down at the floor again.

"I should have risked it. If I'd run really fast I think I could have made it."

"Then why didn't you?"

Rand continued to stare at the floor.

"Rand, why didn't you go for help?"

Rand hesitated. He'd been holding this in for such a long time it had made him sick to his stomach. "I knew if I told I'd get in really bad trouble. They'd punish me. But if I got her out myself I'd be a hero. I'd be the favorite one again."

"I don't believe you. I think you're making that up to punish yourself."

Rand's eyes widened in anger. "Okay, I'll tell you. She begged me not to leave her. She made me promise. I couldn't just leave her there." He looked up at Dr. Silverstein. "My parents don't know about this. It would kill them if they knew what I'd done. Please don't say anything."

Dr. Silverstein shook his head and smiled sadly. "Rand, our sessions are completely confidential. No one will ever know what we've discussed here." Rand had no choice but to believe him.

Six months later his father passed away. The doctor said the heart attack was from stress. Rand knew better. He had died of a broken heart. Carrie had been his dad's favorite. His face used to glow whenever she would bounce into the room. But he hadn't smiled again after she died, not even when Rand told him a funny story to cheer him up. And if his father had died because Rand had let Carrie die, then he'd been responsible for his father's death, too.

Nearly a year of therapy went by and little by little, Rand opened up to Dr. Silverstein. Then one day it happened. They were nearing the end of their session when Dr. Silverstein mentioned that he was leaving town for the winter as he always did, for his condo in Mexico. Rand felt the blood drain from his cheeks and his heart began to race. He was afraid the doctor would realize he felt trapped, incapable of functioning in the real world. He clammed up and refused to say anything more. And then Dr. Silverstein said the most amazing thing.

"It wasn't your fault, you know. No matter what happened out there, and only you and I know what that was, no one is blaming you." With that, Rand's resolve broke and he began to cry for the first time since his sister's death. Dr. Silverstein, who stood several inches shorter than the growing teenaged boy, went over and cradled him in his arms.

"Let it out," he said. "It's been eating at you too long. You must let it out." And he did. But after he'd finished drying his tears and his mother had come to get him, he was ashamed and scared. Ashamed that he'd let his guard down and scared that he'd one day have to tell his parents the truth about the accident.

So in an abrupt tour de force, as if to put it at the back of his mind, he became a model student. Eschewing friends, he put all his energy and waking time into studying, to the point where his mother again worried and sent him back to Dr. Silverstein.

But this time the doctor told her that Rand just needed time to adjust. Eventually he'd become interested in playing sports again, start discovering girls, get his driver's license. The things regular boys do. Once again, Dr. Silverstein's advice proved right. Rand slowly came back to life. A fact he owed to the bronzed little psychiatrist. Though there was still a part of his life missing that was too elusive for him to identify yet.

Chapter Sixteen

Over the past few days Rand had uncovered enough information, which he'd promised to share with Kate, that he decided not only would it be beneficial if she could see Chelsa's condition for herself, it might also help alleviate an immediate disbelief of what he was about to tell her. Chelsa's suspicious medical records, the strange revelation from Dr. Elias, and the disturbing, though enlightening, visit to Mr. Chhim.

He arrived at Chelsa's nursing home room a half-hour before Kate arrived. Tim had already been for his daily visit and left. Rand took the opportunity to study the child in the bed and observe her emaciated, contorted body. She was still being fed through a nasogastric tube, which was all that was keeping her alive. He had a hard time understanding Tim's assertions that she would awaken from this state. Rarely did that happen, and even at that, the brain damage would be incalculable.

As Kate approached him where he stood at the bedside in Chelsa's room, she gazed at him with concern. He knew he looked ill. The mind-numbing migraine that had begun after mistaking the comatose Chelsa for his long dead sister was still present. No amount of Aspirin seemed to alleviate it.

He closed his eyes tightly shut for a moment as if trying to block out the white noise hum of the fluorescent lights in the hospital room. But when he reopened them it hadn't made a difference. The room was still tinged a sallow pink, making Chelsa, who lay there in the chipped enamel-framed crib, look like a grotesque waxen doll.

"Have you ever heard of Limbo?" Rand asked.

"The only Limbo I know is the name of a dance from the sixties," Kate replied, bending her head and shoulders backward in mimicry of the dance. A flush of embarrassment moved up her throat, splashed up her cheeks. "Of course, I'm not old enough to..."

Rand didn't appear to notice. He took a shallow breath and exhaled deeply as he tried to dispel the hospital stench combination of disinfectant, overcooked broccoli and vomit. The smell was making his headache worse. His aversion to hospitals had been the decision-maker in his entering clinical psychiatry instead of an active medical or surgical career. There was a certain irony at having chosen a profession in which he'd be dissecting the psyches of others when his own was so ravaged.

"Limbo is a term from Christian theology, a nether land suspended between Heaven and Hell, where the souls of unbaptized children spend eternity. It's reportedly where the Prophets of the Old Testament dwelt. It was first used in that sense by Thomas Aquinas in the 13th century. It's the only explanation I can come up with for what's happening to Sienna. Her soul is in Limbo."

Kate let one finger slowly stroke the sunken cheek of Sienna's half-sister, lying in the bed. She stared back at him, nonplused. "Are you saying that what makes her a distinct human personality is now gone? Because if you are, the Theologians would eat you alive. Heck, the majority of the hospital staff would do it."

Rand reached down and picked up a small valise he'd brought with him. He flipped it open and pulled out a file that contained copies of Sienna's medical records. Thumbing through the contents of the file, he glanced briefly at the test results and page upon page of notes. The neurologists with all their CT Scans and EKG monitors could not render a physical explanation to the intermittent periods of unconsciousness Sienna was experiencing. The internists had run batteries of tests and all the lab results couldn't explain it. Neither could he. Except for this new notion, controversial though it might be.

Wearily he brushed a lock of dark hair off his forehead and rubbed his eyes. For a moment he considered what he had just said to Kate.

"Until we come up with another theory to explain what's going on here it's the best I can offer." He sighed. "I told you what Dr. Elias said he witnessed the night Chelsa was brought in."

She nodded, though he could see from her face she wasn't following his line of thinking completely.

"For a moment imagine that reincarnation exists," he continued. "I think that when Chelsa was hit by the car and died her soul passed on and it became available to a baby that was being conceived. A baby conceived at the exact moment that Chelsa's soul left her body."

"And...?" said Kate.

"And I think that the newly conceived Sienna was that child. The new recipient of Chelsa's soul."

"What does Chelsa have now?"

"She's in a vegetative state. Technically dead."

"So the reason Chelsa has never been able to awaken from the coma is because of Sienna?"

"Possibly. I think what's been happening with Sienna is that her supposed subconscious memories are really Chelsa's, from Chelsa's childhood. And now that Chelsa has shown signs of regaining consciousness, she's fighting to get her soul back."

"So neither girls have a soul?"

"Sienna does. Chelsa does. They're sharing it. It's caught in Limbo between the two girls. Whoever is stronger and wins, lives."

"That's too fantastic to be believed," said Kate. She gave a scornful laugh.

Rand shrugged. "Thanks. That's probably the same reaction I'll get from everyone else."

Kate looked as if she'd regretted her comment. "What can we do?" she asked, her voice softening. "If there is only one soul between two girls, they have to get another from somewhere."

Rand stared at her for a moment and their eyes caught.

"Oh, you're not thinking what I think you're thinking," she said.

"Exorcism?"

She nodded.

"But who should be exorcized?" Rand asked, almost to himself. "Who is the legitimate owner of that soul?" He shook his head. "Anyhow, exorcism is out of the question. It's too dangerous. Even for an unbeliever there are too many unknown factors. Not to mention that at least a couple of the parents have psychoses."

"Which two?" Kate replied with a sarcastic laugh.

Rand flashed her a lukewarm smile but didn't respond. He rubbed his chin, lost in thought. "Sienna is being discharged this morning?"

Kate nodded. "There's no reason to keep her here." She waited for him to respond. "What do you want to do?" she said finally.

"I'd like to put the girls together in the same room. See what happens."

"What could possibly happen?"

"With these girls and their disjointed family threesome, there are any number of possibilities." His brow furrowed for a moment as he began to formulate a plan. "How hard would it be to get unsupervised access to Sienna so I can hypnotize her again?" He glanced at Kate and was dumbfounded by her scowl of disapproval.

"Rand, I could lose my hospital privileges. My job. Hell, I could lose my license to practice medicine, going behind the parents' backs."

He dropped heavily onto a chair, shuffling his weight as he tried to get comfortable on the hard surface. Finally he looked back up at her. She hadn't moved. Her hands were still on her hips, waiting for him to come up with a better idea. He shook his head.

"No, that's what I have to do. I have to hypnotize her again and see what else she will tell me."

Kate frowned once more. "And you're going to accomplish this how? Without me, that's certain."

Rand gave her a persuasive grin and put his hand against her cheek. "Please? You can be there the whole time."

She shook her head in exasperation. "I still don't see how you're going to do it."

Rand smile became smug. "You leave that to me. I'll get as much information from Sienna while I have the chance. I want to know what sort of things happened to her sister before the accident."

Kate sighed and shrugged. "Okay, you win. What's the plan?"

Rand's plan, as it turned out, hadn't gone far past the premise of isolating Sienna from her parents for further questioning. He and Kate sat parked in her poison-green Volkswagen beetle on the boulevard a couple of houses away from the Cantrell's home. It was, in Rand's opinion, an ostentatious structure of no particular architectural style that he could discern. Enormous, just to keep up with the neighbors.

The hamlet of Oracle Lake was built around a man-made water feature that supported a hybrid selection of exotic waterfowl not indigenous to the area, much like the transplanted residents who lived there. Even the used car lots, crowded with used Mercedes, Jaguars, Lexuses and BMW's never hosted anything lowlier than a grandmother-driven Cadillac.

The developers, in order to maximize their profits, had built the new homes so tightly together that a housekeeper vacuuming too close to an open window could put someone's eye out in the next house. In fact, the neighborhoods had become so crowded that the only thing that distinguished them from row housing was a glimpse of the lake between each, hence the determination to shoehorn in as many high end homes as possible.

The incongruity of the artificial country setting contrasted sharply with the incessant hum of lawnmowers, whining leaf blowers and the chatter *en espanol* of the landscaping service workers. You couldn't hear birds chirping or the chatter of a squirrel. You couldn't smell the freshly cut grass and shrubs over the exhaust of the machines that kept them looking like an estate featured in a *Better Homes & Garden* magazine. There was a certain pointlessness to it all, Rand thought. Fertilize the grass just to have to mow it. Not for the first time he was glad he lived in a floating home with no yardwork to accompany it.

As he and Kate sat and waited in the car, a forty-something expressionless blonde in a black Spandex outfit that could have been painted on loped past, not seeming to notice them. Her perfectly sculpted hair and meticulously made-up features scarcely jiggled as she ran. Rand was close enough to see that her face was so rigid with Botox injections it was actually incapable of movement. After she'd passed, Kate's eyes met his and they burst out laughing.

She turned her attention back to their mutual purpose. "What makes you think they're going out tonight? Or that they won't have Sienna with them?"

Rand had brought a small, hand-held tape recorder in case they managed to get inside to see Sienna. He had also brought a pair of field glasses. He raised them and squinted toward the house, trying to catch a movement. He watched for a few moments then lowered them onto his lap, rolling his eyes to relax the strained muscles.

"Just a hunch."

"I know a good plastic surgeon who can correct that," she said, her eyes sparkling.

"Droll, very droll," he replied, though he couldn't keep from laughing. He peeked at his watch and his stomach growled automatically in response. It was nearly 7 p.m. They'd been so involved in his scheme they hadn't had a chance to eat. He glanced at Kate.

"You hungry?"

"Starved."

"Me too. It'll have to wait."

"Thanks," she said drily.

But when his stomach growled again he began to wonder if maybe he'd miscalculated a young couples' desire to go out on a Friday night. Then a decade-old blue Toyota Camry, with dents on every possible surface, pulled into the Cantrell's driveway and a teenaged girl got out.

"The babysitter?" Kate surmised. Rand nodded.

At that moment an enormous chocolate Labrador made his way down the street, scarcely missing a vertical obstacle as he marked his vast territory. As he lifted his leg beside a mailbox, he revealed the fact that he was an unneutered male.

"Looks like he's smuggling kiwis," Rand remarked.

Then, apparently unaware there were people in the car, he stopped and sniffed at the front wheel. Kate tried to shoo him away, without success. Hastily she rolled up her window. He was nearly as tall as the car and overshot her tires completely.

"Ohhh, no!" she moaned. "Now I've got to wash the car." She saw Rand's body shaking with laughter and gave him a punch in the arm. "If you think it's so damned funny, you wash it."

"Ouch!" He rubbed his arm. Then he remembered the babysitter and redirected his attention back to the Cantrell house. His instincts had been right on target. Within ten minutes the Cantrell's garage door retracted and a white Mercedes backed slowly out and onto the street.

"Duck!" Rand hissed. They hunched down below the dash together as the Mercedes passed, waiting for a couple of minutes to be safe before they raised their heads. Rand sat up first.

"Coast is clear," he said with a laugh.

"Jesus!" Kate pulled down the visor mirror and smoothed her hair. "I feel like a P.I." Rand was already opening his door.

"Where are you going?" she called out, scrambling to lock the car doors.

"Follow my lead," he said. "I have a plan."

"Right," she muttered under her breath, trotting to catch up.

He walked up to the front door and pressed the doorbell. The first few notes of Beethoven's Ninth Symphony rang out.

"Maybe she's been instructed not to answer the door,"

Kate suggested. He shrugged and pushed the doorbell again.

After a few minutes a young woman's voice came over the intercom. Good girl, he thought. That's how you keep safe in a crazy world.

"Who is it?"

"It's Kathy and Randy Morris, friends of John and Melanie. We're here for the dinner party." Kate raised her eyes toward the ceiling at the audacity of his fib. There was dead silence for a few moments.

"There's no dinner party tonight." The girl's voice was heavy with suspicion.

"Oh my god!" Kate said, loud enough for her voice to carry over the intercom. She punched Rand in the arm. "I knew it was next week, but you just had to be right again!" She made a clucking sound, winking at Rand as he rubbed his bruised arm. "I'm so embarrassed. Sorry to have bothered you. Don't let Melanie know how scatterbrained we are, okay?"

They heard the babysitter give a cautious laugh and then the door opened to a narrow crack. He caught a glimpse of a sweet looking girl with bright green eyes, a carrot-orange ponytail and the fresh clear complexion of a healthy teenager.

"Did you want to leave a message?" She still sounded skeptical. At that moment Sienna poked her head from behind the babysitter.

"Hi, Dr. Morrissey," she said. "Why are you here?"

The teenager scowled, took a step forward and began to close the door, "I thought you said your name was..."

Rand reformed his plan and hurriedly explained to Sienna, "We came to visit your parents but it seems that they've gone out."

Sienna turned her attention to the babysitter. "Jen, can we invite them in for dinner?"

Jen widened her eyes and glared at Sienna as if to say 'shut up.' She heaved a melodramatic sigh. "We were just going to order pizza."

Rand would have killed for pizza right about then. He took out his wallet. "Why don't you let me buy it?" Jen stepped back with a grumpy expression, though she allowed both of them to enter.

He wished he didn't have to do this. They'd compromised her effectiveness and safety as a babysitter. She might even lose her job if the Cantrells found out. It made him feel guilty as hell. Out of principle he almost turned and left the Cantrell house. Almost. He must not forget why he was here.

Once he and Kate were inside Rand suggested, "Why don't you order whatever you usually get?" Jen nodded, picked up a portable phone from the kitchen, speed dialed and placed the order. She cradled the receiver over her shoulder and glanced at Rand.

"An hour and a half for delivery," she stated. He shook his head.

"We'll pick it up," she said into the phone. After she'd hung up he handed her two twenties.

"It dawned on me that I don't know my way around town," he lied. "You're going to have to get it while we stay here with Sienna." The girl frowned hard.

"I don't think..." Then Sienna piped up.

"It'll be okay, Jen, they're my doctors."

Jen heaved another sigh that only a teenaged girl could do that effectively and grabbed her purse. "It's all the way across town," she muttered. "That's why I wanted delivery." Then she stomped out the door.

Kate looked at Rand and raised her eyebrows. She mouthed the words, "How much time?"

"Twenty minutes each way, possibly three-quarters of an hour round trip," he answered. "I know where she's going. Not a lot of time, but enough." He took Sienna's hand, led her to the family room and sat down on the largest hunter-green leather sectional sofa he'd ever seen. He placed Sienna beside him while Kate perched on a matching rose and green uphol-stered chair across from them.

"Do you want to play hide and seek while we wait for Jen to come back with the pizza?"

Sienna nodded, excited.

"Kate will hide first. You have to close your eyes and pretend to be asleep. I'm going to count backwards from twenty. Then we'll go find her, okay?"

Sienna squeezed her eyes tightly shut but Rand could see her eyelashes fluttering.

"No peeking." He placed his fingers on her eyelids, forcing them closed with a gentle pressure. She giggled. Kate tiptoed a short distance away and hid behind a wall from where she could watch them. Rand nodded to her then turned back to Sienna.

"While I'm counting you're going to go to sleep for a while until Kate finds a really good spot. When I snap my fingers you'll wake up and you won't even remember that we were here. Do you understand?"

Sienna slowly raised and lowered her chin in agreement. As he began counting, Sienna appeared to be falling asleep. A lock of dark, curly hair fell across her cheek. Kate stepped forward as if to smooth it back but Rand shook his head abruptly. She understood. They didn't have much time to do this. She couldn't risk waking her. She slipped back to her former position on the chair and waited, her hands folded in her lap. Rand reached into his pocket, pulled out the tape recorder and switched it on.

"I want you to think back to your earliest memory and remember whatever you can."

Sienna's little face crinkled in concentration, though her eyes remained closed.

"Do you remember anything yet?"

She nodded slowly.

"Can you tell me what it is?" He glanced at Kate, then back to Sienna.

"My arm hurts," she said. Kate started to get up again to reposition Sienna. Rand reached out, pulled her back down and gave her a stern shake of his head. "No," he mouthed, "it's not her."

"Why does your arm hurt?"

"Mommy grabbed it."

"How old are you? Hold up your fingers."

Sienna held up seven fingers. "I'm eight," she said.

"How old?" he repeated.

"I told you. I'm eight!"

Kate pressed her hand to her mouth to keep from laughing. But then her expression sobered because Sienna had tears running down her cheeks.

"Why are you crying?" Rand asked.

"My arm hurts," she whined. "Daddy's home now and he's real mad at mommy. He says he's going to take me to the hospital."

"Sienna, what did your mommy do to your arm?" Sienna frowned.

"My name's not Sienna. It's Chelsa. I don't know who Sienna is." Kate and Rand exchanged an alarmed glance.

"Chelsa, has your mommy ever hurt you before?" There was a few minutes of silence and when it appeared she wasn't going to answer, Rand prompted her again. "Chelsa, you need to tell me if your mommy or daddy has ever hurt you."

"Not daddy," she said slowly. "Daddy makes it better. But mommy gets mad when I do bad stuff."

"What do you do that's bad?"

"Not eat my dinner or do my homework. Sometimes I make a fuss about going to bed." She contemplated for a moment, and then as if justifying it said, "It's only when I'm really bad, though."

"What does she do when you're bad?"

"She grabs my arm too hard. That's why it hurts."

"Did you ever tell anyone?" Sienna shook her head.

"Not even your daddy?"

"Mommy said if I ever told anyone something bad would happen to daddy. He'd lose his job and they'd get a divorce and I'd never see him again."

Rand sighed. He was about to prompt her again when the front doorbell rang. Kate shot Rand a look of sheer panic.

"Take Sienna into another room and come right back," he whispered.

Thinking rapidly, he watched Kate pick Sienna up in her arms and head toward the living room where she placed her gently on a sofa. Then she returned to the family room. The doorbell rang again. Rand's mind raced. Just as he had decided to ignore the caller, Jen walked in from the garage entrance, her arms akimbo with pizza boxes. She walked to the front door and juggling the boxes, reached out to open it. Standing there was a tall, handsome teenaged boy with an Oracle Lake High School letterman jacket.

Everyone froze as they drank in the situation. The guilt on Jen's face at the presence of her boyfriend, who was probably not allowed there when she was babysitting. The wariness on the face of the boy at being caught off-guard. The consternation in Kate's and Rand's eyes at having yet another witness to their unannounced visit.

Jen stomped past them and into the kitchen, the aroma of pepperoni and tomato sauce invading the room. Rand, Kate and the boyfriend stood motionless, staring at anything except each other. Jen set the pizzas on the counter and returned, looking very uncomfortable.

"Where's Sienna?" she asked, suddenly remembering her babysitting responsibilities.

"She's having a nap in the living room," Kate assured her. "We were playing hide and seek and she got really tired."

Rand stole a glance at her and from the tension on her face could tell she was regretting her decision to accompany him. Guilt washed over him. Then he got an idea of how to extricate themselves from the awkward situation. He turned to Kate and ran his fingers through his hair. "Oh my god. I completely forgot that I'm scheduled to meet a patient at the office for a late appointment."

He looked at his watch and snapped his fingers loud enough for Sienna to hear from the next room and wake up from her trance. "They'll be there any minute."

"We have to leave now," he said to Kate.

"Sorry we can't stay," he said to Jen. "But you three enjoy the pizza." Then he heard Sienna call out from the living room.

"Jennifer, where are you?"

Jen eyes widened at Rand, pleading for his silence about the boyfriend. "You won't tell...?"

"No," he said, "but we really have to leave now."

He grabbed Kate's arm and steered her through the door before Sienna could see them. Once outside they raced to the car and hugged each other, laughing.

"That was close," breathed Rand.

Kate snorted. "I must be out of my mind, letting you get me into this mess."

"If you are," he said, laughing, "I know a good shrink I can refer you to." He reached into his jacket pocket, produced the tape recorder and switched it off.

"This is what it was all about," he said. "And we still didn't get any of that damned pizza!"

Chapter Seventeen

Rand had just finished seeing his last patient of the day, a 37-year-old woman who was having difficulty coping with the aftermath of her husband's affair. He'd counseled both of the Daltons individually in the past and was on the verge of referring them to a marriage counselor. It was too draining acting as confidant and father confessor to both. And it would not serve either of them well for him to be caught between two warring factions.

He set their files on the corner of his desk to remind himself to make the call in the morning. He was just about to lock up for the night when he heard his door squeak. He glanced up to see Angela. She gave him an apologetic smile and twitched her head slightly to the side to indicate there was a person behind her and she didn't want that person to see her.

"Melanie Cantrell's here," she said. "She'd like to talk with you for a minute—says it's very important." She rolled her eyes as if she didn't believe that for a moment.

"Did she call ahead?" Rand asked, but he already knew the answer. He grimaced. It had been almost a week since he and Kate had interviewed Sienna under hypnosis at her house. There had been no time to evaluate what Sienna had told him. He had to be careful because anything he divulged would mean confessing to Melanie that he'd hypnotized Sienna without her permission. Not to mention, he'd practically broken into her house. He was too exhausted and in no mood to talk to her right now, no matter what she had to say.

He gave Angela a pleading look. "Can you tell her I've gone for the day? Tell her I got called away to another patient. Set up an appointment for next week. Anything."

Angela's shoulders fell wearily. She shook her head as she backed out of the room. "I'll do what I can, but you owe me."

Grateful for her loyalty, no matter what the motive, Rand vowed to make it up to her. As soon as the door closed, he stood up, locked his desk drawers and pulled on his sweater. He always used the back door to the office to get to the parking garage, so it was unlikely he'd run into Melanie on the way out. He sprinted down the three flights of stairs, opened the door to the second level where he'd parked the Volvo and headed over. Then he hesitated. Despite his plan to go straight home from the office, the stress from Melanie's surprise visit and dealing with the draining, dueling Daltons before that had taken its toll.

He re-clicked the remote locks on the Volvo and suddenly froze. For a moment he had the overwhelming impression that someone was watching him. When he scanned the parking lot there was no one to be seen. He took a few steps, then stopped, certain he could hear approaching footsteps behind him. But again when he checked there was no one. He shook his head at his paranoia. Then he headed across the street to the Aquarius, a local karaoke bar with friendly staff and a clientele among which he could disappear.

Above the entrance door to the Aquarius, a glowing neon water bearer poured a never-ending stream of amber liquid from an urn into a beer stein. Rand stepped beneath it and into the darkened depths of the bar which filled with greasy smoke from grilled foods. Someone singing a horrible karaoke version of "I Will Survive" filled the air. After his eyes adjusted to the light he found his way to the back and sat at a small table with one chair and an upholstered bench. The cocktail waitress was over before he had a chance to look around.

"Heineken, please." He placed a ten dollar bill on the table. His eyes grazed the room. Several faces from neighboring offices were familiar, but no one he knew on a first name basis. There were a few couples at secluded tables, nothing unusual or remarkable. He began to relax.

A new, would-be singer, a tall, slender black woman

stepped up to the microphone. Rand closed his eyes, praying that this singer would be better than the last and as the woman began a Whitney Houston song in low, husky tones, Rand felt the tension in his ears slacken. Then he heard someone say, "What a coincidence seeing you here!"

He opened his eyes to see Melanie Cantrell. His heart sank. He tried not to let the dismay show on his face and forced a smile.

"All the tables are filled," she said. "Do you mind if I share yours?"

How could he say no to her request? he wondered. Had she deliberately followed him here to meet up with him? That was too bizarre a notion. If it was, as Melanie said, a coincidence, then he should be gracious. But her presence still bothered him. A bar was not the place to be, or be seen with, the mother of one of his patients. Especially a married one. He suppressed a sigh.

"I'm sorry," he said. "Where are my manners? Of course you can sit here." He stood up quickly and pulled the chair out for her and then he sat on the upholstered bench seat across from her. Melanie smiled disarmingly at him. There was awkward silence for a few minutes. Rand took a guilty sip of his drink because Melanie had not yet been served. In fact, the cocktail waitress, who formerly had been so hospitable, now seemed to have disappeared.

Finally to break the awkwardness, Rand stood up. "I'll get you a drink from the bar. What's your poison?"

Melanie started in surprise, then apparently got the joke.

"Scotch. Straight up, please."

She peeled off her black leather jacket. Underneath she wore a clinging, sleeveless black sweater with a deep V-neck trimmed with gold braid. She leaned forward and handed Rand the jacket, revealing a glimpse of her round firm breasts. Then she sat back, smoothed the crinkles out of her cream colored slacks and relaxed into her chair.

Rand slung the jacket over the back of his seat, catching the scent of her perfume. It was a strong citrus that was almost masculine, but suited her. His heart rate sped up a little. He turned and quickly headed for the bar. He could feel her eyes on him as he walked away. It was rather unnerving. A few minutes later he returned with her drink and a napkin, which he placed in front of her.

"Thanks." She took a long swallow of the drink that was almost the same color as her eyes. Rand noticed she didn't even wince at the strength of the liquor. Stronger man than he.

"I didn't think I'd see you here since you had that last minute emergency patient," Melanie said without sarcasm, not letting on whether or not she thought Angela had lied to her. She reached for the napkin and patted her lips, leaving coral lipstick imprints on it.

Rand shrugged and took a long sip of gin. He wasn't going to be forced to apologize for skipping out on her. But she didn't seem to want that.

"I'm sorry if I inconvenienced you by showing up without an appointment," she continued. "I need to share something with you before I go to the police."

Rand sat up in alarm. "What are you talking about?"

Melanie glanced around the room and then leaned forward conspiratorially. "I think John has been abusing Sienna," she whispered.

Rand, mid-swallow, choked and almost dropped his drink. "Do you mean sexually? Because we never found any evidence of that."

"No, no." Melanie hastily shook her head. "I know John would never do that." She stared at her glass, swirling the amber contents in contemplation. "He can be very strict and rough. I think he might have inadvertently given her a hard shake once or twice." She paused for a moment. "There's been times when we've had arguments that I see a side of him, well, I'm a little afraid of what he'd do to me."

"Has he ever actually hit you?"

"Not yet, but he's come close. He brought his fist up near my face one time. That's what I mean. It's the threat I feel." Her face crumpled. She glanced away, averting her face, so he couldn't witness her emotions.

"I wish you'd told me this before," Rand said. "Although Sienna doesn't seem to be afraid of her father, I'd have used a different line of questioning if I'd known."

"Do you remember how she said 'don't' in her sleep? I think she was referring to something John might have done."

Rand stared thoughtfully at Melanie, and frowned. "If you don't have any evidence, and I couldn't see any physical signs of abuse on her, than this is a pretty severe accusation. Before you say anything to the police we'll have to question Sienna and perform another examination." Suddenly he recalled his interview with Cantrell several weeks ago, how he'd said he'd smacked Sienna and then gotten defensive when Rand had questioned him further on it.

Melanie breathed a huge sigh of relief, and her shoulders relaxed. "I'm so glad I told you. I've been holding it in for days. I couldn't bring myself to believe he might be capable of abusing his little girl."

Rand scanned the room, caught the waitress's eye and ordered another round for both of them. His stomach was rather unsettled. Maybe two drinks on an empty stomach wasn't a good idea, but he definitely needed another now. He stood up and dropped a twenty on the table.

"Have to use the men's room," he apologized as he hurried off.

He used the urinal, then washed his hands and threw cold water on his face, toweling dry with rough paper towels. He didn't want to go back out there. The drinks were paid for. Couldn't he just slip away without Melanie seeing him? But he knew he couldn't. For a variety of reasons. Taking a deep breath, he opened the men's room door and headed back to the table. Maybe if he got drunk enough...

When he reached the table he saw that Melanie had applied fresh coral lipstick and her eyes were brighter, shinier, possibly due to the Scotch. He flashed a brief smile and sat down. Then he took a long drink of his beer. Melanie smiled back at him and made a mock toast with her drink.

"*Salut*," she said. "To whatever happens tonight."

Whatever happens tonight, he thought. He watched Melanie calmly sipping her drink and noticed for the first time that she had the most incredible lips. For a moment he envisioned them moving along his body. His gaze jerked upward to her eyes and he caught her watching him. She reminded him of a cat watching sparrows at a bird feeder. He tried to think of her child, husband, but like an itch he couldn't reach, it wouldn't subside.

He felt her foot move up to the inside of one calf. She ran her fingernails lightly along the inseam of his trousers, stopping when she came to his groin. She jiggled her chair closer, leaned near to him and began to nuzzle his neck. Her breath was so hot it seemed to sear his skin. Enveloped in her perfume, he was having difficulty breathing and the pressure in his pants was becoming unbearable. He shifted to redistribute the chaos Melanie had created.

"Let's go somewhere," she breathed into his ear. He couldn't summon the will to resist.

"I'm feeling rather ill," he muttered. He glanced at Melanie and noticed the room behind her had begun to sway and blur like an abstract painting. Maybe it was only a migraine from the alcohol and not having eaten anything. "I need to get home. If I can walk out of here."

Chapter Eighteen

Around 11:00 p.m. Melanie slid her gold BMW convertible down the driveway of her three story house on the shores of Oracle Lake. In this nouveau-riche neighborhood, her contemporary home looked as if it had been constructed from sandstone building blocks. Except for the street lamps that lined the boulevard, the rest of neighborhood of mini-mansions was dark. Then she noticed that a light was on in the kitchen and her stomach gave a nervous lurch. John was still awake. She hadn't expected that. And as he was the soundest sleeper she had ever met that didn't bode well for her.

Melanie pressed the garage door opener hidden in the console of the car and the garage door lifted without making a sound. She let the car roll inside. Then she turned off the engine and stepped out. Taking a deep breath to steady herself, she felt her footsteps dragging as she entered the house to face the music.

She passed through the mud room that led into the kitchen and saw John standing in the kitchen near the sink, his back to her. Even from that distance she could smell the cup of coffee he held in his hand. For both of their sakes she hoped it was decaf. Although he must have heard her footsteps, he didn't turn to greet her when she entered the kitchen. She dropped her purse onto the center island beside the stove top and paused, waiting for him to speak.

When he still hadn't acknowledged her presence, she walked past him and headed upstairs toward the bedroom, the exhaustion and strain of the last few hours finally hitting her. As she was half-way up the stairs, John finally turned and called up to her.

"Don't you even want to know how your kid is?"

She stiffened and froze in her tracks, not comprehending what he meant. Had something happened to Sienna while she'd been gone? Her hands shook as she groped for the bannister; she turned and headed back into the kitchen. This time he faced her. The coffee mug paused dramatically at chest level. The cold glare she knew so well, colder than she'd ever seen it.

"What's wrong?" she demanded. "What's happened?"

John gave a short humorless laugh. "What the hell do you care? You never even called to let me know where you were. I've been worried sick." He examined her carefully, as if searching for evidence he might be able to use against her.

"Relax. Sienna's fine. I put her to bed at her regular bedtime."

Melanie expelled a sigh. But her relief was only temporary because he still hadn't asked why she'd been gone all evening. She had to come up with a quick explanation.

"I left you a note," she said. Her mouth went dry as it always did when she lied. She swallowed hard. "Didn't you see it? I went over to Karen's to watch a movie. We were drinking wine and stayed up late to see the end. Both of us passed out. I thought it was best to wait until I was sober enough to drive. She was still sleeping when I left."

Karen was someone she considered her best friend, in fact, essentially her only female friend, and John knew it. Although she was married to a friend of John's, Peter Stewart, she was certain Karen would vouch for her. As soon as she got out of the hot seat with John, she'd call Karen to prepare her.

John shook his head and shrugged. "I must have missed it. You'd better get to sleep or you'll end up sick. Have you forgotten we're invited to dinner at the Stewarts' house tomorrow. Didn't Karen mention it?"

Melanie's fingers flew to her temples. The blood vessels behind her eyes felt as if they would burst. She struggled for a logical response, but her tired brain wasn't giving her much help. Still, she was Melanie Cantrell and she could think on her feet faster than anyone she knew.

"We talked about it," she said, "and decided that with Peter not getting home until later in the afternoon, that maybe we should postpone it until next weekend." She walked back toward the stairs and then turned to him with a cool, appraising glance.

"I'm exhausted. Just let me have a good night's sleep and I'll get it reorganized." She took the stairs two at a time to get into the bedroom before John could respond. At their bedroom door she hesitated. John hadn't followed her. Instead of entering the master bedroom they shared together she opened the door to Sienna's room and stepped inside.

As she gazed down at her perfect, dark-haired daughter, she thought, there is nothing so beautiful as the sight of a sleeping child. It was unbelievable how at a moment like this they could be so angelic you couldn't help but love them, yet when they got cranky and defiant, sometimes you just wanted to smack the hell out of them.

Sienna had reached that age where she thought she knew it all. That sassy attitude that kids get once they start kindergarten and suddenly the parents they'd idolized have become idiots. It drove her nuts. Chelsa had been that way when she turned five. But she'd had even more attitude than Sienna. She attributed that to Tim's influence. He'd always taken Chelsa's side in everything. But John left all the parenting to her, rarely interfering. Or helping, for that matter. Though when he did, he sided with her, which was just how it should be.

The pink comforter covering Sienna had slipped part way off the bed. She pulled it up and tucked it around her to seal in the warmth, her hands lingering for a moment on the child's neck. Sienna moaned and wriggled a little in her sleep. Melanie leaned down and kissed her on the cheek, then tiptoed out of the room.

Outside in the darkened hallway she stopped again and made the decision not to sleep in the master bedroom with John. She walked further down past Sienna's door to the room at the very end. The bedroom they kept made up for any out of town guests who might be staying with them. Quietly she closed the door behind her and groped for the light switch. The sudden brightness flooding the room caught her off guard. She squeezed her eyes shut until they could get accustomed to the light.

As she peeled off clothes that seemed to reek of the bar, even though they no longer allowed smoking, she caught a glimpse of herself in the mirror and shuddered. God, she looked awful lately. It wasn't just because she'd been awake half the night. Her hair was as dry as straw and her normally good complexion was bumpy and sallow. She felt awful, too. In fact, she hadn't felt and looked this bad since...and then she recognized what was happening to her.

"Oh, *no, no, no,*" she moaned. "Oh god. I have to be the most unlucky woman in the history of the universe." She grabbed the sides of her hair with both hands and suppressed a scream of anguish. She knew it. It had to be that. It couldn't be anything else. She was pregnant again.

Childless women all over the world yearned to have children, paid thousands of dollars for infertility treatments, and she, Christ, she couldn't even think about a penis without getting pregnant. It was an accident that she'd gotten pregnant with Chelsa and as religious as Tim was, he wouldn't hear of an abortion. To prevent another pregnancy she had managed to talk him into having a vasectomy. She was adamant there would be no more babies.

Then she'd had an affair with John, who obviously had not had a vasectomy, and she'd gotten pregnant with Sienna. Though she loved Sienna, at the time she would have aborted the fetus or given her up for adoption. Except that John had been thrilled to be having a child and wanted to marry her. But after that, she'd used a diaphragm because John flatly refused to have a vasectomy.

She knew this was John's child. She'd gotten what she'd been after and had never cheated on John. He wasn't the fool Tim had been. And he also wasn't easily put off with headaches and menstrual flow. If John wanted sex, well, John got what he wanted. He was the one who controlled the relation-ship.

She'd always thought that marriage was a union of ideal-ists. Initially, when she and John had been consumed in mutual adoration, she'd promised to love, honor and obey. Sometimes it was all she could do just to be a decent person. Long after the love had gone, all that was left was honor and obey. And in every union that has endured nearly a half dozen years, there was only one person in the union who honored and one in the union who obeyed.

John's assertiveness had attracted her at first. But after a couple of years the novelty had worn off and she'd yearned to gain control of her life. And his too, if the truth be told. If he learned of this new baby, he'd give her no alternatives. He'd been hinting at having more children and she knew he'd be ecstatic about it. That is if he believed it was his. He'd convince her to go through with the pregnancy. She had no choice but to get an abortion. Without him knowing about it, of course.

By the next morning, after spending a sleepless night mulling it over, she'd changed her mind. As long as they were both healthy she'd keep the baby. It was a trump card she could use if their marriage broke up and he tried to cheat her out of what was rightfully hers. Maybe this time she'd get a nanny. She certainly didn't want to raise a kid by herself. But there were a few other hurdles she'd have to clear first, starting with John. She began to formulate a plan.

When he came down for breakfast, she greeted him smil-ing, moving toward him with an offered cup of coffee. He shook his head and sat at the kitchen table with his back to her, burying his face in the morning paper. She realized instantly that the atmosphere between them was still cool. She was about to change that. She set the coffee cup within reach of his fingers.

"We need to talk," she said. She pulled out a chair and de-liberately let it scrape across the floor as she sat across from him.

John reached for the coffee and took a sip without looking up from the newspaper.

"I've said everything I need to."

She sighed heavily. "John, listen to me." She hesitated long enough that he finally stared at her, setting his coffee cup down.

"What?"

She closed her eyes for dramatic effect. "I didn't tell you the truth about last night."

"You think?"

"Let me explain, okay? I went to Dr. Morrissey's office to discuss Sienna's progress. He had just seen his last patient and didn't want to take the time to talk to me."

She saw she'd finally gotten his attention. She began to warm to her topic. "The receptionist refused to let me in so I left. Then when I was going to my car I saw him heading toward this bar down the street from his office. I followed him there."

John was frowning now. Not necessarily a bad sign, but she had to be careful.

"I went in and sat at his table. I told him I wanted to discuss Sienna. He offered to buy me a drink, which I saw no harm in at the time."

Cantrell's eyebrows raised, but he remained silent.

"He wouldn't say much, as usual, other than the bar was an inappropriate place to discuss a patient. I agreed. Then he said, 'maybe we should go back to my office.' I said okay. He paid the bill and we left together. When we got back to his office it happened."

"*What* happened?"

Melanie exhaled raggedly. "He began accusing me of terrible things. Of deliberately hurting Sienna. He said I must be abusing her to bring on the fainting spells."

"Why would he say that?" John's face darkened and his eyes narrowed to angry slits. "There's no truth to it, is there?"

Melanie stared down at her hands and took another deep breath. "Of course not! What kind of mother would deliberately harm her child?" *Good, Melanie,* she thought. Answer a question with a question.

"So what did you say?"

"I told him he was full of shit and I was going to file a complaint with the Psychiatric Association." John was watching her a little too closely. It made her nervous.

"Maybe it was the alcohol that made him do it but then he grabbed my arm and started to shout at me. I panicked and scratched his face. He released my arm and I ran out of his office." She dropped her face into her hands and started to cry.

"Jesus Christ!" John roared. "And you've been letting that quack treat our daughter?"

Melanie shrank back against her chair, intimidated by his anger.

"You get the police on the phone right now and file an assault charge against him." He slammed his hands on the table and glared close to her face. "He's not going to practice psychiatry anywhere except in prison showers."

He glowered at her until she moved away from the table and pretended to search for a phone book. Finally John resumed reading the newspaper. Apparently unable to concentrate, he stood up and threw the newspaper against the wall. Then he stormed out of the room without another word.

Melanie watched him go, relief flowing through her until she realized she'd forgotten to tell him about the pregnancy. Despite her previous resolve to go through with it she was still having problems rationalizing her decision. Or sharing the news with John. She gnawed at a fingernail, pondering the unlikelihood of an appropriate moment in the near future to share her news.

Chapter Nineteen

Rand awoke with the most excruciating hangover of his life. A relentless banging resounded through his aching head, made worse when Goldie began to bark. The stench of old alcohol and a nauseatingly familiar perfume seemed to ooze from his clothes. He tried to take a deep cleansing breath but only managed a short, winded cough. Just getting air in his lungs was a challenge. He wasn't a smoker, wasn't much of a drinker, and did not believe in the value of alcohol as a problem solver, but last night, well...

He stood up, his head reeling. An overwhelming wave of nausea struck him. He made it to his bathroom just in time to lose everything in his stomach, which was nothing at all, only bile. That was the problem. He hadn't eaten last night. Just beer on an empty stomach.

He made his way to the kitchen, took a glass from out of the cupboard and then went to the refrigerator to get ice. As he dropped the ice into the empty glass, it cracked along the side and split, slicing the back of his index finger.

"Damn!" he said. He grabbed another glass, reached in for more ice then filled the glass to the top with water. He took a long swallow, feeling the bottom of his stomach settling a bit. Then he reached for the dust pan and broom and began sweeping up the chunks of broken glass.

The dog was still barking in the living room. "Shut up!" he shouted, every word bringing new pain.

What had happened last night? He groped his way back to the bathroom sink and stared at himself in the mirror. As his bloodshot eyes took in the ravages of the night before, he almost got sick again. There was a sight he had not expected:

four long scratches down his right cheek. They had to be fingernail scratches. He touched the wounds and winced in pain. They burned like hell. How was he going to cover them? And more importantly, how had they gotten there?

The clanging noise in his head began again. He tried to ignore it as he attempted to retrace last night's chain of events, from the time he'd slipped out the back door of his office, to going to the Aquarius. But he couldn't remember anything past that. He glanced down at his shirt, the only thing he still had on from the night before. It was streaked in blood from his cut finger, or perhaps even the scratches. There wasn't a lot of blood, but enough to make him suspicious about where it came from. He ripped off the shirt and on a whim, sniffed it. Then he remembered why he recognized the citrusy perfume. It belonged to Melanie Cantrell. He thrust the shirt into his laundry hamper and slammed the lid.

The banging continued to increase in volume. It was only then Rand realized it was coming from his front door. Hastily he retrieved his pants from the floor and pulled them on, grabbing a dirty T-shirt from the hamper. He headed over to answer the door and grabbed Goldie's collar to hold him back. A loud voice from the other side made him jump.

"Dr. Morrissey, Portland Police."

He opened the door to see two plain-clothed officers. A tall officer with gelled, spiky-blond hair asked, "Are you Rand Morrissey?"

"Yes," he answered, bewildered. "What the hell's going on?"

"I'm Detective Dixon and this is Detective Vasquez from the Portland Police Department. May we come in?"

As Rand nodded assent, completely perplexed, the shorter Vasquez said, "We have a warrant for your arrest. You'll have to come with us." He proceeded to recite Rand his rights.

"What am I being charged with?" He fought another wave of nausea, the bile threating to bubble up in his throat.

"A complaint has been filed against you by Melanie Cantrell. You're being charged with third degree assault," said

Detective Dixon. "Come on, psycho-doc, we'll have a whole list made out for you by the time your attorney arrives."

"I don't have a lawyer," Rand said. "I haven't had to use one since I set up my practice."

Detective Dixon pulled Rand's arms behind his back and cuffed his hands together.

"Well then," said Detective Vasquez who had begun to search him. "You'll remember from the rights we just read that you can have one appointed to you."

"I've never touched Mrs. Cantrell," Rand said. "Why would she charge me with assault?" He'd never been this confused or nauseated before. If the officer had let go of his arm, he was certain he would have fallen.

"I'm sure it'll come back to you," said the cop, "once your DNA has been matched with the skin under Mrs. Cantrell's fingernails."

Rand was hustled into the back of a squad car and then taken to the official prisoner intake, a few miles to the south. He recognized the correctional facility from having once visited a patient there. It was a sprawling labyrinthine structure constructed of nondescript concrete. It also doubled as the county jail and intake center for criminals from all over the state.

Once inside the building he was seated before a desk where he was booked on the charges Melanie had filed. Another officer searched him once more. After he had relinquished everything in his pockets into a tray on the desk, he was fingerprinted, photographed and shown to a holding cell.

"You're allowed to make one phone call." The desk sergeant pushed the telephone across the desk. Rand shook his head. At that moment he was still in shock, unable to conjure any images other than that of the police coming through his front door.

He was taken to his cell, a tiny concrete room with a vinyl covered pad on a cot suspended from the wall. An orange plastic chair with duct-tape covering a crack along the seat was shoved against a wood-grained Formica table. A rust-stained sink and toilet crowded together in the corner of the room. Above the sink was a rectangle of burnished aluminum that served as a mirror.

Rand staggered over to the cot and sat down heavily, closing his eyes to shut out the glare from the only light in the room, a single throbbing fluorescent tube. If his head would stop aching for a second he might be able to figure out what had happened last night.

As he sat alone in the holding cell watching the prison personnel come and go, he pondered over who would be best to call. He rarely spoke to his mother, and besides, she was in Arizona for another month. He was thankful for that. At the moment he didn't have an attorney. If he was going to need one he wanted time to investigate a person with experience defending this type of situation. Perhaps he could call Kate. Kate would understand, wouldn't she?

But his one phone call was wasted. He couldn't reach Kate, only her voice mail. What kind of message could he leave? he wondered. Hi, Kate, I'm here in jail for assaulting a woman, a patient's mother actually, in a bar last night. Can you bail me out? Without mentioning he was in prison he left a careful message saying he'd been called out of town on an emergency and would be out of touch for several days, and could she please let Angela know. She might wonder why he couldn't call her himself but he'd deal with that explanation later.

He sat quietly on the cot in his cell, hoping Kate would get his message before things began to get out of hand. He had a full day of patients booked in his office. Without knowing his whereabouts, Angela would be frantically trying to cancel and reschedule his patients. Any of his other patients who might try to reach him would get only his answering machine, but no referral to another psychiatrist in case of an emergency. That could pose a serious problem for his more dependent patients.

As he waited he had time to ponder what might have happened with Melanie last evening in the bar. He remembered his disgruntlement at seeing her at the Aquarius, remembered buying drinks, and getting up to use the men's room. But he was damned if he could remember anything after that. He wasn't used to drinking much, and maybe he'd had a couple too many that night. But he'd had hangovers before. By comparison, this one made the others seem insignificant.

And then there was the question of the scratches on his face. Gingerly he reached up to touch the right side of his cheek and withdrew his hand immediately. It was crusted with dried blood and stung as if it had been burned. He tried to see his reflection in the burnished tin, but couldn't make out any details. The effort of struggling to examine his injuries made him dizzy again. He dropped quickly down onto the cot before his legs gave way.

Dinner time came and went with a tray of tepid, pasty macaroni and cheese, an oatmeal cookie and an overripe banana. Listlessly he picked at the food, not hungry enough to worry about being hungry later. He tried to doze to ward off the recurring nausea that threatened to reverse the tiny portion of the meal he'd eaten. But the noise from the adjoining cells, the constant clanging of the doors as prisoners came and went, and the incessant telephone ringing was too distracting. Eventually he gave up. Then just as he dozed off the jangle of keys in the cell door jarred him awake.

"Get up," said the guard. "You're getting out."

Rand struggled to sit up, fought with a rush of nausea and vertigo, then stood, cautiously grasping the edge of the wall.

"Must have been a rough night," the guard said unsympathetically as he stepped back for Rand to pass.

"If I could remember I'd share it with you," Rand responded drily. The guard led him back to the booking office where his personal effects were returned to him.

As he signed the receipt for his belongings he asked, "Who posted my bail?"

"No one posted bail," the desk sergeant replied. "The charges were dropped so we have no reason to hold you. You're free to go."

He looked Rand over from top to bottom. "If I were you,

I'd go home, get cleaned up and try to stay out of trouble. Next time you might not be so lucky."

Rand had to agree with him. The guard escorted him through the locked doors and into the main lobby. He used the pay phone to call a taxi then waited outside the compound for it to arrive. Ignoring the curious stares from people in passing cars, he prayed no one would recognize him.

When he got home he wasn't surprised to see his message machine flashing frantically. The message bank was full. Most of them were from Angela, ranging from 'Where the Hell are you?' to 'If I don't hear from you in 24 hours, I'm quitting.' He didn't know where to begin. He'd shower first, then deal with the mess later.

In the bathroom he was finally able to assess the damage to his face. He had four long scratches starting on the right side of his lower jaw and then extending downward along his neck. They weren't very deep, and although there would be scarring for a while, a few weeks with disinfectant and Aloe lotion applied should restore the skin to normalcy. The problem was, how did he get them? Had Melanie done it? He simply had no memory of the incident.

After he got out of the shower and made a sandwich, he called Angela. He placated her with promises of time off and a raise, and managed to get her to rescind her threat to quit. He was beginning to feel better. There had been no catastrophes with vulnerable patients. No unanswered calls with threats of suicide. Things could have been much worse.

And speaking of things unanswered. Could he really have hurt Melanie? He'd been brought up to respect women. Hadn't even had much time to touch them on a friendly level, let alone in anger. Violence wasn't in his nature, though the nagging thought that remained was that under the right circumstances, anyone can be capable of violence. As a psychiatrist he knew that better than most people.

He wondered if Kate had gotten his message. If she learned of the arrest she'd be devastated at the very least and probably would avoid speaking to him in the future. And who could blame her? Would she believe the charges against him? Could there ever be a relationship, professional or otherwise, between them after this?

Late that evening when he was certain the rest of his office building would be deserted, he headed to his office to take care of any pressing patient business that couldn't wait until Monday. As he'd expected, he met no one he knew in the parking lot; only heard the cleaning staff's cart at the far end of the corridor. After sorting through the neat stacks of files the efficient Angela had set out for him, he finished by making a few notes and prioritized patients for Angela to reschedule.

Just as he was about to lock up for the night an abrupt knock at the door startled him. He hesitated. The cleaning staff had keys and he never consulted with patients in the evening. If it was Kate he didn't want her to see the marks on his face. But he needn't have worried. When he opened the door he was stunned to see John Cantrell. He tried to steady his breathing but found himself visibly shaking. After all, this was the man whose wife he was accused of assaulting. For a moment the two men locked gazes, each waiting for the other to speak.

Cantrell spoke first. "I know what happened between you and Melanie." He pushed past Rand into the room and dropped down into a chair without waiting for an invitation. Rand had no choice but to follow. He sat opposite Cantrell, rather than behind his desk. Obviously this was to be a man-to-man conversation, not a doctor/patient interview. At least he hoped it would be a conversation, not an interrogation. Or a beating.

"I was able to piece together what went on last night," he said. "Melanie set you up."

"What do you mean?" Rand demanded.

"When she got home so late I asked for an explanation as to where she'd been. She made up a story of spending the evening with a girlfriend. But I'd already checked that out earlier and knew it was a lie, in spite of her friend trying to cover for her. So I called her on it. She fed me a story about how the two of you had come back here to your office. How you'd accused her of deliberately hurting Sienna."

Rand's mouth dropped open. "That's what she told you?"

John nodded. "She also said she'd scratched you." He paused and almost smiled. "I see she wasn't lying about that."

"How did you know she lied about the assault?"

"Let's just say it's easier to know when Melanie's telling the truth. It's less frequent. Besides, there wasn't a mark on her."

"So you were okay with her having me arrested?"

John gave a short laugh. "It took me a while to connect the holes in her story until the whole thing fell apart. Be grateful. I did have her drop the charges against you."

Thanks for your prompt attention, Rand thought, unable to think of anything else to say to the man. Cantrell took care of that for him.

"That doesn't mean that you're off the hook," he warned. "Melanie is up to something. We should both be on our guard."

Rand contemplated that advice, wondering what Cantrell would have to fear from Melanie. Rather abruptly he asked, "How is your marriage?"

For a moment Cantrell looked as if he were about to slug him. Then his face took on a softer, pensive expression, almost one of regret, Rand thought.

"Even a stranger could tell we're not getting along," he answered.

"Are either of you seeing other people?"

John plucked at a piece of lint on the chair. "What's said here is between us? I can't have this getting back to Melanie."

"It stays in this room."

John inclined his head, a sad resignation crossing his face. "I've been dating a woman from my office. I can't speak for Melanie's social life. Apart from the office we rarely see each other."

Rand was dumbfounded. Wouldn't Melanie be enough for most men? But of course, that wasn't the issue. Melanie was a beautiful woman. It wouldn't have surprised Rand if she was seeing someone outside the marriage. He'd just assumed Sienna's health issues were contributing to their problems.

"Has this been going on for a while?"

John scrunched his face, reflecting. "A few months, maybe. It's not serious for either one of us. Neither wants out of our marriages. It's just a diversion."

A diversion that's detrimental to your family, thought Rand. But it wasn't for him to pass judgment. "Do you think Melanie knows?"

John shook his head. "I don't see how. We've made every attempt to be very discreet and we don't call each other at home. We made a rule. We only meet when we go out of town on business. I've always traveled a lot. It's part of my job."

Rand considered the timing of John's extramarital dalliance with the onset of Sienna's fainting spells. "Have you ever thought that maybe Sienna has picked up on your affair, acting out to gain attention and keep you at home?"

Cantrell stared thoughtfully at him for a moment.

"I don't think so. My relationship with Sienna has been the constant in the family, even though Melanie and I argue from time to time. No one suffers."

That, thought Rand, was the most naive misconception he'd ever heard. He'd been brought up to believe that love and honesty were synonymous in a relationship. Was there no sanctity to marriage anymore? Ultimately someone always suffered or was hurt by an extramarital affair. In the case of John and Melanie Cantrell, it was most likely Sienna.

After Cantrell had gone Rand considered the ludicrousness of what had just happened. That Melanie had dropped the assault charges should have been enough for him to forget the whole mess. But what bothered him even more than Melanie's lie was the sequence of events that had landed him in jail. He still could not recall leaving the bar, or anything until the police arrived to arrest him. Had she slipped something in his drink? And if she had, how could he prove it?

Before leaving the office he decided to take the medical

files of Melanie's two daughters home to study. He walked over to the file cabinet and thumbed through the 'M's,' searching for the small file he'd created for Chelsa, who was not technically his patient. It wasn't there. Then he went to the front of the file cabinet and searched the 'Cs' for Cantrell, thinking it had been misplaced with Sienna's. But Sienna's file wasn't there either. And a search of Angela's tidy desk produced nothing.

Puzzled, he went back to his desk and pulled open the drawer where he kept the tapes he'd made of Sienna's hypnosis session. And then he knew why Melanie had come to the Aquarius that night. Why she'd set him up on fake assault charges. The tape and the files were gone.

Chapter Twenty

That night, Rand lay in bed awake, thinking back over the events of the previous two days. Melanie had been a very busy lady. Now he knew she'd manipulated and probably drugged him so they'd go back to his office, and she'd be free to search for the tape he'd made of Sienna's hypnosis.

He wondered how she'd learned about it. Sienna couldn't have told her. He was certain she was well hypnotized before the interview. And they had been completely finished by the time the boyfriend and Jen had arrived. He couldn't figure it out. Not to mention, why would she even be concerned with what was on the tape? What did she have to hide?

He felt uneasy calling Kate to tell her about the theft. She would have gotten his voice message and he'd have to explain that. And then it occurred to him that if he just told her the truth she would understand. At least he could hope she would.

When he finally got up enough nerve to call he was relieved that she didn't mention his message. It was possible she hadn't received it. But if she had it apparently didn't concern her enough to question him as she extended an impromptu invitation for him to come over.

"I'm glad to see you," she said, when he arrived at her apartment. "I thought you'd be out of town for a while."

He gave her a quick hug. Avoiding her eyes, he made his way to what had become his favorite chair, an angular 'S' shaped contraption of leather and chrome, and settled down. He sighed, feeling a nervous flutter start up in his stomach. So she *had* gotten it.

"I'll explain later," he said. "Right now we've got more pressing issues. The tape I recorded of Sienna's hypnosis was stolen from my office."

"How did anyone know of its existence? And who would steal it?" Kate asked, puzzled. "How could someone have gotten access to your office?"

"I think Melanie took it. Maybe she's afraid something on the tape would incriminate her."

"How did she gain access to your office?" she repeated, scrutinizing him closely as if she were trying to read his thoughts. It made him uncomfortable. He glanced away, picking up a magazine to busy himself and didn't answer.

"I don't understand how she could have even have known about it," Kate persisted.

Rand didn't look at her. "Neither do I. None of the three people at the house that night could have been aware of it."

Suddenly Kate laughed out loud.

"What's so funny?" Her infectious laugh brought a smile to his face.

"Nanny cam," she said. "I'll bet Melanie's got the place rigged with a Nanny cam to keep an eye on who might be coming to visit Jen. That's how she knew."

"But why didn't she say anything to me about it?"

"So you wouldn't know she knew. Everything that's on that tape will be on the Nanny cam tape. In fact, there'll be even more on the Nanny cam. Everything we said."

Rand groaned. "Oh, boy. Do you think we're in trouble?"

"No. I think we'll be fine."

Rand stared at her. She appeared unbelievably smug for someone whose career might be in jeopardy. "You seem rather optimistic for a person who was afraid to do the interview in the first place. How can we fight Melanie if she has all the evidence against us illegally hypnotizing her child?"

"Oh ye of little faith." Kate grinned. She reached into her pocket and pulled out a clone of the tape that had been stolen. "Voila!" She popped it into a voice recorder and turned it on.

As Rand's recorded interview with Sienna/Chelsa filled the room they exchanged disturbed looks. They played it back twice more then finally turned it off, both of them sickened by what they'd heard.

"That was pretty clever of you to have made a copy for yourself," Rand said. "Apart from my computerized notes, with the tapes and the files on the girls missing we'd have no evidence." He leaned back and stretched his arms toward the ceiling.

Kate winked. "Two steps ahead of you."

"So what do you make of it?"

"Sounds to me like the kid, whoever she is, or thinks she is, is being abused." She stood up. "Can I get you something to eat? We keep missing out on pizza." She laughed heartily at the memory. Rand grinned at her.

"I kind of lost my appetite for a while there, but it's starting to come back now." He followed her into the tiny galley kitchen.

"How about a sandwich?" she said. But he was turning her around from the counter and encircling her in his arms. She stiffened. He dropped his arms to his sides. Her lips opened, but no words came out.

"I'm sorry," he said. "I didn't mean to startle you." She shook her head, turned back to the counter and began buttering slices of bread.

He watched her, a little hurt by the rebuff. Was it him? What had he done to put her off? Maybe it was the whole subterfuge of the visit to Sienna. His experience with women was limited enough that he really couldn't tell.

His first shutdown had come in his senior year of high school. His psychiatric appointments with Dr. Silverstein had come to an end. At school he'd gotten the impression he was thought of as odd; not considered boyfriend material, though no one at the school knew of his breakdown. He had discovered that sometimes being a little odd can be an exotic elixir to the opposite sex, potentially even cool. And though he was clever enough to realize that it would probably be a turn-off to be really odd, with graduation coming up and no prom date in sight, he decided to try for the really cool.

One day in Health class during a discussion of mental

health, he made an offhand comment about what it was like to visit a shrink. There was a girl named Sara he'd had a crush on for months. She wasn't one of the snotty popular girls, but just a nice, tanned and athletic member of the basketball team whose eyes had occasionally met his and held.

Unfortunately Rand's admission had the opposite effect he'd desired. Wherever he went after that, his classmates whispered and giggled behind him, the guys occasionally going so far as to mimic how they interpreted a mental patient to look and behave. Needless to say, when he asked Sara out she stared at him in total disbelief, as if to say, 'are you kidding me?' And though she tried to soften the blow immediately after by telling him she had other plans, her initial reaction shattered his confidence completely. Recalling that moment of rejection, he turned to leave the kitchen but Kate grabbed his arm.

"It's not you," she said. "I'm just not ready yet." She gave him a hug with the one arm that was free from the butter knife. It warmed him all the way through.

"I keep forgetting to thank you." Rand was unable to look at her in case she met his gaze.

"For what?" She appeared to be uncomfortable because she kept her back to him while busying herself with retrieving plates for the sandwiches.

"For breaking your rules. For coming with me to the Cantrell house." It was too awkward and embarrassing to spit the whole thing out. She still hadn't questioned him about his call from the jail and he couldn't understand why. There was the possibility that she didn't consider the message to be of any importance. She really was too inscrutable to read. He had to know. "And for not asking about the call I made to your cell phone."

"Don't mention it," she replied as she walked away toward the dining room with the plates in her hands. As he watched her go a hollow spot seemed to form in his chest, as if he'd lost something. He touched her arm and a jolt of static electricity shot through them both. She turned around, confused and appearing a little annoyed.

"Would you like to have dinner sometime?" He held his breath, bracing himself if she turned him down.

"I'm steering clear of relationships right now."

"I'm not asking you to marry me, I'm asking you to have a meal with me."

She turned her head to one side and squinted, scrutinizing him the way one might inspect an amoeba under a microscope. "What's wrong with you?"

"Wrong? With me?" Rand was at a loss. Did she mean there something had to be wrong with him if he asked a girl out on a date?

"I don't mean it the way you're thinking." She sounded apologetic. "But I never once met a psychiatrist who didn't need to spend as much time on the couch as beside it. I think it's part of what attracts them to the profession. If anything is profoundly wrong with you I want to know what it is before we go out."

Rand nodded like a robot. She was right. Could she see right through him? Or was he being paranoid? He almost laughed because it wasn't the first time he'd felt that way recently. Perhaps he shouldn't be diagnosing himself.

He sighed. "I work too much, don't get out enough, and eat poorly. But I don't have any psychoses or mental hang-ups, if that's what you mean."

Kate smiled. "Go on."

"On the plus side, I'm good to my mother, haven't dated much, despite my obvious good looks and I'm financially solvent."

Her grin broadened. She glanced at him from under her eyelashes as she took a sip of her drink. "So you've never been in analysis?"

His stomach lurched. Was she joking or was this a planned attempt to derail him? Did she already know? Then he chided himself. There was no way she could know about his breakdown.

He decided to try a glib approach. "Hasn't everyone?" His laugh belied the anxiety her questions aroused.

"You're probably right." She raised her chin until her gaze held his.

Uncomfortable, he glanced away. "So, dinner or not?" he asked.

Her grey-green eyes lit up in a way that made Rand's heart jump.

"Sure," she said. "What have I got to lose?"

It turned out neither of them had anything pressing to take care of the next evening after work. Once Kate had made her final rounds of the pediatric ward she called Rand and arranged to meet him at a quiet French bistro in downtown Portland.

"I could have picked you up," he said, as she approached his table.

As he stood and pulled her chair out for her to sit, she waved her hand and shrugged. "Easier this way." But he knew she'd done it to eliminate the awkwardness of traveling in a car together at night. The inevitable 'what do we do now' feeling when you pull up to her house at the end of the evening.

A server materialized, filling their glasses with ice water containing paper-thin lemon slices. He offered Rand a wine list and handed dinner menus to each of them.

"Would you like wine with dinner?" Rand asked. She nodded.

"We'll have the Adelsheim Chardonnay," he said. The waiter nodded as if pleased with the selection. He returned with the bottle, uncorked it and filled their glasses. After Rand gave his approval of the wine he ordered the Wild Salmon with chanterelle sauce for both of them, then returned the menus to the waiter. Kate watched him leave. She turned her attention to Rand, giving him a quiet smile.

"Cheers." He lifted his glass to Kate's.

"Cheers to you, too." She took a sip, then set the glass down. "Have you gotten any additional information on our little coma patient?"

He shook his head and groaned. "I interviewed the half-sister's father several days ago. He thinks he's God's instrument and that the ultimate plan for Chelsa will show itself soon. How that affects Sienna, I have no idea. It's alarming how devout this guy is."

The silence that followed was oddly comfortable, Rand thought, as if they'd been together before, unlike most first dates where any lapses in conversation can be disconcerting. When you start saying anything just to break the silence and the next thing you know you're babbling about an embarrassing childhood mishap. But not so with Kate.

The waiter arrived with their food and refilled their glasses. They waited until he left again. Kate smiled at Rand.

"What are you going to do with the tape?"

"I haven't decided yet." He took a bite and chewed for a few moments, thinking. "I've considered taking it to the police, which would mean it might be admissible evidence for Melanie to be charged with child abuse. Or it might be inadmissible given the circumstances under which it was made."

"You know what else it would mean?" Kate sounded concerned. He noticed she hadn't started to eat yet. He swallowed a mouthful of the salmon and stared at his plate for a moment.

"That's what's been on my mind all night," he said. "Sienna would lose a mother and Melanie would probably go to jail."

"And you'd be testifying in court for a long time," said Kate.

He sighed. "Yes, I'd be in court a long time." He thought about the tape for a few minutes, wondering who could be attributed to speaking during the session, Chelsa or Sienna. There must be some way he could bring the girls together physically, while separating them forever spiritually. It would be like separating Siamese twins. The dangers were just as real.

"Let's put them in the same room together," he suggested.

"What?" Kate sputtered, her mouth full.

"We could try putting the girls together and see what happens."

Kate rolled her eyes. "You really do want a malpractice suit, don't you?"

"Not me." He grinned. "I'm just trying to drum up a little excitement."

Then a question came to him that he'd been meaning to ask for a while. "You never told me how you know Dr. Silverstein."

Kate was in the middle of chewing her salad and it seemed to Rand that she took an inordinate amount of time doing so before she swallowed. Finally she set her fork down and stared directly into his eyes.

"He was my therapist when I was going through a tough time several years ago."

"Oh," said Rand, regretting that he'd asked. It should have been obvious. He'd just assumed they'd crossed paths in a professional capacity.

"Don't you want to know why?" She gave him a look that had a hard edge, one he hadn't seen before. He didn't like it. He became uncomfortable and squirmed under her gaze.

"If you'd rather not...," he began. The truth was, he really didn't want to know. Because if things started out like this then sooner or later he'd have to divulge how Dr. Silverstein knew him. And he couldn't do that. Not ever.

But Kate seemed determined that she share the information of her therapy. "I was raped."

She focused on an unseen object past his right shoulder, avoiding eye contact. "During my first year at college I was on my way back to my dorm from the library. Three guys jumped me. I never knew who they were, but they each took a turn at me." Her hands flew involuntarily to the port wine birthmark on her face. "One of them had a knife. After they finished with me he offered to remove my birthmark so I wouldn't be so ugly..." Her voice trailed off.

Rand reached out as if to touch her hand in comfort but she snatched it away as if he were on fire.

"I'm so sorry," he said. "Did they catch them?"

She shook her head. "No, they covered my eyes with a

tied sweatshirt so I wouldn't be able to identify them. From time to time I recognize the aftershave of one of them because it was on the shirt. When I smell it I want to throw up because all the horrific memories come rushing back. But I'm working through it."

She looked up at him, her face illuminating with a forced brightness. "It's okay." She laughed softly. "I still like men."

Rand forced a sympathetic smile that helped break the tension, but it didn't dispel the pervasive disgust and shame he felt on behalf of men in general.

"I've even consulted a plastic surgeon here at St. Augustus, Dr. Thea Donovan, to see if she can do something about my birthmark." Her words emerged in a rush, as if she were self-conscious. "Maybe you've heard of her?"

Rand shook his head. "I don't know many of the surgical staff at the hospital." He reached out and smoothed her hair away from the mark. It was a part of her and it no longer shocked him. "You should leave it the way it is. I like it."

Kate blushed, the warmth from her face magically blending into the mark.

Adroitly Rand changed the subject to alleviate further embarrassment to either of them.

"What made you decide to go into pediatrics?"

He took a mouthful of wine, unaware that the smile had frozen on her face. And then he knew why she'd chosen the specialty before she answered.

"As it turned out," she said, trying to keep her tone light, "one of the bastards impregnated me. My family all agreed the best thing to do would be for me to have an abortion."

He watched her closely, noticing how her voice had taken on a cynical tone when she said 'my family.'

"And was it the best thing?"

She shot him a troubled look. "Am I in therapy here?"

He winced. "Sorry."

"No, *I'm* sorry. I shouldn't have brought it up. I don't know if it was the right thing to do, but it feels like I'm inadvertently atoning for my sin of aborting the baby." She sighed and took a sip of wine. "Anyhow, that's why I went into pedi-atrics. You see, the operation had an inadvertent side effect and I got an infection. I can't ever have children."

Rand was at a loss for words. He wanted to go over and put his arms around her, but he knew their relationship hadn't progressed to the point where she'd feel comfortable. Instead he reached over and squeezed her hand to reassure her it was okay with him. This time she didn't pull away. *Kate* was im-portant to him, not her uterus. She lifted her glass with her free hand and took a sip of wine.

"So how do you know Dr. Silverstein?" she said.

Chapter Twenty-one

It took several days before Rand was ready to divulge his plan to the girls' parents, that of putting Chelsa and Sienna together in a room. He had Angela call and arrange an appointment for John and Melanie Cantrell; Tim Moran was to be included. He'd had some trepidation about having the three of them in the same room, but he only wanted to do it once. He wasn't about to tip his hand by giving them any information before the meeting, either. Finally he decided they should all be adult enough to be together when he relayed his findings, though given what he knew, it still sounded improbable even to him. At the last minute the decision proved not to be his.

"You'll have to talk to Mr. Moran yourself," Angela reported. "He won't discuss his daughter with me." But when Rand called, Tim flatly refused to be in the same room with Melanie.

"You can't be serious," Tim said. "Chelsa's starting to show signs of improvement and you want to throw her back into our lives?" The pitch of his voice escalated with each word, making him sound as if he were about to scream by the end of the sentence. Rand wished he could rewind the entire phone call and start again.

"You're right," he demurred. "I didn't think it through. But you need to understand this is something that could improve Chelsa's chance of recovery as well. I wouldn't involve her if it was just for Sienna." A dead silence followed until Rand spoke again. "Tim?" He heard a grunt of acknowledgment. "Maybe we should talk about it in person. Can you come to my office on Tuesday?"

"I'd rather meet you at Chelsa's room," Tim said. "I want

you to see the progress she's making and what we stand to lose if you mess things up."

"All right," agreed Rand, trying not to sound exasperated. "I'll be there tomorrow night around seven during visiting hours. In the meantime I'm meeting with the Cantrells to discuss what we hope to accomplish with both girls in the same room."

He understood Tim's resistance. Though he kept it hidden from Tim, he had a strong feeling of foreboding as well. He didn't have to be clairvoyant to know that major obstacles lay ahead, and the possibility of real danger existed for both girls.

Melanie and John proved easier to coordinate, although the situation was just as awkward. When they arrived for their scheduled appointment, Melanie was dressed in a cobalt blue, designer workout suit, as if she'd just come from the gym. John wasn't dressed much more formally, wearing a faded pair of jeans and sweatshirt. They walked in together without speaking, as if an invisible partition existed between them, neither acknowledging the other. And when they sat down in his office you could have set up a string quartet between them.

As Melanie sat there, as calm and controlled as ever, it was difficult to believe that she'd actually had him charged with assault. Or that she'd stolen the tape from his office. It was as if she were two different people for she gave no indication that there had been anything other than a professional relationship between them.

John consulted his watch as soon as he was seated, as if he had more important places to be than discussing his daughter's health. He looked as if his mind was on anything else but Sienna. His cell phone beeped with a text message. He pulled it out of his shirt pocket and glanced at it briefly before punching a couple of keys and reinserting it in his pocket.

"How long is this going to take?"

Melanie's face tightened. She gnawed on the inside of her lip to keep from making a retort. A dangerous glint in her eye filled Rand with trepidation. He released a small sigh of relief when she managed to stay silent. He'd prepared himself for a confrontation.

"You've had Sienna in for several counseling sessions now, haven't you found anything?" Cantrell continued.

Rand took a breath and bought time before answering by opening Sienna's new file he'd created after the original went missing. He pretended to glance through it while mulling over how to explain his theory. When he looked up he saw them both staring at him as if they were cannibals and he the only meat they'd seen in months. Melanie, in particular, looked as agitated as a cat at a dog show when she saw the file. He caught her staring at it, as if wondering how it could be that another file had materialized. She quickly averted her gaze when he gave her a knowing smile.

"First I have to ask how open-minded you are to the arcane," he said. "All I have is a theory, not documented in medical or psychological textbooks. A theological explanation."

Melanie's face clouded. "Religious mumbo-jumbo? This must have something to do with Tim."

Cantrell reached over and placed his hand on her arm. "Melanie, let's hear him out. We have nothing to lose." Without looking at him she jerked her arm away and sat with them folded across her chest.

"Not religious, really." Rand tried to keep his tone and the content sounding logical. "But Eastern philosophies have written about such things."

"What's this theory?" asked Melanie. A scowl crept across her face.

"It's rather delicate." Rand was confident enough in what he was about to explain to make eye contact with them. "And personal." He had their attention now. He addressed Melanie.

"To understand what I'm about to tell you, we have to go back to the history of your other daughter, Chelsa."

Except for the carefully applied blush that remained on her cheeks, Melanie's face lost all its color. Two pink splashes, as bright as if she'd been slapped, appeared on her face underneath the makeup. She swallowed hard several times before she was able to speak.

"What kind of garbage is this?" she shrilled. John reached for her arm again, this time clasping her hand. Rand saw the rigidity of her body soften as she squeezed back. He wasn't sure if he preferred them as allies or adversaries. He waited while they both regained their composure.

"I went back to Chelsa's medical records and the accident report on the day she was hit by the car. According to the most reliable eyewitness, Chelsa was struck at approximately 8:15 a.m. on May 23rd. Almost exactly nine months later, Sienna was born." He waited for what he thought would be the obvious to sink in, but he was disappointed. Both Melanie and Cantrell only appeared confused. Finally he said, "Do you believe in reincarnation?"

Cantrell shook his head slowly from side to side in disbelief. He consulted his watch again then pulled his cell phone out of his pocket and switched it off.

Melanie made a sort of 'hmmmph' sound. "Is that what this is about?" She cast him a scathing look of incredulity. "You think there's a connection between Chelsa and Sienna. Well, there isn't. Chelsa was removed from life support long before Sienna was born."

"I'm aware of that." Rand deliberately lowered his voice to keep things under control. "I'm a skeptic, too. But I've been studying old texts on reincarnation, conception and the like. I've even spoken with an expert on the subject, a Buddhist monk. Although I'm not a religious person, I believe that life begins at conception, not at birth. To extend that then, I think we have a soul from the time of conception. And when we die, or our heart stops beating, or brain activity ceases, our soul leaves the body.

"If I suspend my disbelief for a moment I can imagine Chelsa's soul leaving her body, and what if at the very same time, another baby was being conceived..." His voice trailed off because Melanie had leapt up from her chair and headed for the door.

"Please listen to me." Rand stood as if to stop her, though oddly, John remained seated, taking in the drama. "I'm not passing judgment. This has nothing to do with anything other than the two girls."

Melanie stopped but didn't turn around.

"Please come back," he urged. "Let me explain."

Melanie sat back down in the chair, arms folded again in contempt.

"I think that Chelsa's soul was reincarnated into Sienna's body. In a comatose, persistent vegetative state since the accident, Chelsa has never been in a position to need it. Even before life support had been disconnected she was considered to be brain dead by the doctors who examined her."

"You mean she's not dead?" Melanie asked, her voice quavering with emotion. It was only then that Rand realized she'd been kept in the dark about her first daughter's condition. A look of wonderment and curiosity had appeared on her face. And sadness. Rand wished he knew what was going on in her mind at that moment.

"No, she's not," he replied.

"Where is she? Where's Tim kept her all these years?" she demanded.

"She's in a private nursing facility undergoing a new treatment."

"Is she still in a coma?"

"A coma so deep that it fooled nature into relinquishing her soul so another human could take it. Premature reincarnation, I guess you could say." Both Sienna's parents fixated on him with blank stares.

"Why Sienna?" she persisted. "Why now? If Sienna has a reincarnated soul, why would she get Chelsa's? Why not another kid's? Or a dog's? Or a butterfly's?"

"I can't answer that. But think about it for a minute," Rand continued. "Think back to Sienna's uncharacteristic behavior, acting out in class, her knowledge of Chelsa's friends, teacher." He hesitated. "Her father's name."

"Chelsa never behaved that way," Melanie protested.

"Unless she's trying to tell us something," Rand said.

Melanie became subdued, keeping her eyes downcast as she straightened her skirt.

"How does that tie in with the fainting spells?" Cantrell said.

Melanie was watching him, then suddenly turned to Rand.

"That's right. Chelsa never had anything like that."

"It's not only Chelsa's past medical history that's affecting Sienna," Rand explained. "It's her present."

Melanie heaved a huge sigh. "If she's still in a deep coma then she's a vegetable. She hasn't moved or eaten on her own for six years. There's been no improvement, right?"

"You're wrong," corrected Rand. The change that traveled across Melanie's face was perplexing, a strange mixture of fear and doubt. "She's been in a new treatment called Median Nerve Stimulation. She's shown several signs of progress, potentially even awakening from the coma."

Melanie stared down at her hands, at a loss for words. She was visibly shaking. John placed his arm protectively around her shoulders. Rand fiddled with a pen, taking it apart and screwing it back together while he waited for them to digest the news.

"Is she going to recover?" Melanie's voice was so quiet Rand had to strain to hear.

"I don't know what the chances are for recovery. It would be difficult for even the doctor doing the procedure to make any predictions. She may regain consciousness, but whether there is any brain function or motor skills left remains to be seen."

"If this theory of yours is correct, then she's definitely returning to some kind of life, whatever that may be, and now needs that soul back," Cantrell interjected. "I can't speak for Melanie, but I'm having a difficult time swallowing all this."

Melanie began biting at her exquisitely manicured fingernails.

Several long moments of silence ensued, the room becoming so quiet that the large brass clock in the bookshelf seemed to overpower the room with its persistent tick... tick... tick...

"What do we do now?" Melanie asked finally.

John watched her face for a moment and then turned his attention to Rand. "Yes, what do we do now?"

Rand sighed and placed his palms face up on his desk. "I'd like to see what happens if we put both Sienna and Chelsa in the same room. We will have to wait until Sienna has another one of her 'episodes' before even considering it, though."

He watched the parents' faces for any kind of emotion. They said nothing, just glanced at each other almost involuntarily until Melanie looked away. Too quickly, he thought. She couldn't meet his eyes, either. And that concerned him.

Chapter Twenty-two

Rand arrived at Chelsa's nursing home to find Tim already there. He wasn't surprised. Apart from going to work each day he was quite certain Tim spent the majority of his waking hours at Chelsa's bedside. He was on his knees praying when Rand entered the room.

"She's in God's hands," said Tim, standing.

Rand stiffened. He'd heard people say that before; heard it when Carrie was dying. That idiom along with 'they're in a better place' were trite phrases he'd never believed, or at least, hadn't believed since before conscious memory. And every time he heard it he wanted to smack common sense into the speaker.

Although not devoutly religious, his parents had taken him to their Presbyterian church and he could still remember Sunday school lessons. He could even recall the words to hymns. But he'd lost his faith when Carrie died. He'd refused to go to church afterward, and in fact, even his parents stopped attending. Well, his father had. His mother, he knew, had eventually gone back.

He felt bad about it now although he wouldn't have done anything differently. He didn't blame his mother for her continuing faith. She'd needed a sympathetic ear to talk to after Carrie; even more so after his father died.

"I don't think God's been listening to your prayers, Tim," Rand said. Suddenly aware of how cynical he sounded, he smiled apologetically. Tim didn't seem to take offense.

"I can understand how people might think that when they see Chelsa for the first time," Tim countered. "But there's something I haven't told you. Haven't told anyone, not even my pastor." Then he became very quiet and Rand had the feeling he'd divulged more than he'd intended.

"And what's that?"

Tim shook his head. "I've already told you too much. I should talk to my pastor first."

"In a way doctors are not so different from ministers. We have to abide by the same rules of confidentiality. Everything the patient or confessor tells us only helps us get closer to solving the problem."

Tim considered this for a moment. "Maybe you're right."

Rand waited, wondering what secret he'd been keeping. Tim was as uncomplicated as anyone could possibly be. But he couldn't be as insipid as he appeared. He was devoutly religious and that alone gave him the courage that had guided him through the past six years. But as much as he empathized with the man, he could not relate to him. All his energy was dedicated to and believing in that intangible being that Rand did not. God.

Finally Tim said, "It's about the night of Chelsa's accident." He stopped, swallowing hard. "Late one night after visiting hours I'd gone to the hospital chapel to pray. I asked God to show me a miracle. Even if he couldn't heal Chelsa right away. I asked him to give me a sign that if we had faith she would make it.

"As I knelt there, I felt a hand on my shoulder. It turned me around and pushed me gently out the door. The pressure on my arm continued until I got to Chelsa's room. I went inside and saw her lying there, hooked up to all kinds of machines. It made her look like a robot. I felt my arm being pushed again and then I found myself at Chelsa's side." He stopped and cradled his head in his hands. When he looked up at Rand his eyes were glistening.

"I don't remember doing it," he said slowly, "but I know I must have, because I saw that the machines were unplugged. They were plugged in when I got there so it must have been me. Right?" He sighed. "Then everything got crazy. The machines started to beep and the light above her bed began flashing. There was nothing I could do for her. I just ran out of the room."

Rand stood and walked over to him. "You were the one who disconnected Chelsa's life support?" His voice was full of wonderment and disbelief. Tim was sobbing so hard he couldn't answer.

"Get hold of yourself." Rand shook Tim's shoulder. "She lived, didn't she? You did the right thing. Somehow you knew."

Tim pulled away from his grasp. "God knew," he said. "I tried to kill my own daughter, but God kept her alive. I was just His instrument."

Rand waited for Tim to compose himself. Eventually Tim's sobs dissipated into sniffling gulps. Rand offered him a tissue and he took it with a nod of thanks, blowing his nose loudly. When Rand thought Tim was calm enough, in as simple terms as possible he explained his theory about Limbo and the experiment he wanted to perform by putting the girls together in one room.

Melanie and John Cantrell's reaction to his theory had been predictable, Tim's definitely was not.

"I won't let you do it." He glared at Rand, then turned and began pacing, stopped, rubbed his hands together and shook his head. "I can't. Not now."

"There wouldn't be any danger to Chelsa," Rand began, but Tim cut him off.

"How can you guarantee that?" he argued. "You have no way of knowing what could happen. She's starting to get better with the nerve stimulation treatments. This could reverse all the progress we've made."

Rand sighed. "She appeared to be making progress, Tim. You thought you saw her leg move a tiny fraction. That doesn't mean she'll regain consciousness. Or even function normally again."

"What good would it do to put them together?"

Rand was quiet for a moment. He'd had an idea, yet not a fully formulated plan. In truth he had no concept of what the outcome could or would be, but he needed to see it through.

"Call it an experiment. You've experimented over the years with different treatments for Chelsa."

Tim's whole body seemed to untighten. Finally he said, "All right. But I want to be there when it happens."

After Dr. Morrissey left, Tim had more time to consider the implications of the proposed experiment. If what the doctor suggested was true, that Chelsa's soul had been snapped up by Melanie's other daughter at conception, then she was preventing Chelsa from emerging from the coma. The solution was that Chelsa must either get a new soul or regain the one she lost. And he could see two problems with that.

The first was the problem of introducing a soul into Chelsa, who was now a young adult. If he were trying to exorcize a demon or spirit from a person, then a psychic could be called in. His mind flashed back to Madame Noella. Perhaps it was possible to draw the soul of an unbaptized child, like that of Chelsa herself, back into a body. But would Madame Noella have the power to do such a thing? She'd made an impression on him before. Though it was hard to fully believe in the abilities she claimed, there had been several moments in that room that he'd never been able to explain away.

The second problem was Melanie. Although he had no feelings left for her one way or the other, he still had no desire to see her again. She'd betrayed both Chelsa and him. There was no doubt in his mind she was in some way betraying her new family. And if her young daughter was having problems, then most certainly Melanie was behind them.

If Sienna had Chelsa's soul, he saw only one solution. He had to get it back for her. He found it increasingly difficult to conquer the feelings of jealousy he had over Melanie's other child. Yes, she was currently having fainting spells, but how dare she be so healthy? How dare Melanie have a perfect child after she'd thrown the last one away? He forced the thoughts from his mind and decided to focus all his energy upon Chelsa. Sienna was only a child, young and innocent of all the subterfuge around them. It was Melanie he should be blaming.

Chapter Twenty-three

Nearly a week passed before Rand heard anything more from either of the girls' families. He hadn't expected Tim to call about a change in Chelsa, but this was the longest Sienna had gone without a fainting episode. He'd already made arrangements with the staff at Chelsa's nursing facility to bring Sienna in when she was ready. At the beginning of his office day Cantrell called and said he was prepared. Rand had asked Angela to interrupt him should she hear from any one of them.

"Sienna is on her way to emergency," John reported. "A teacher at her school called. She's been unconscious for nearly ten minutes now."

"I'll meet you at the hospital," Rand said. "I need to finish up with my current patients." Fortunately he was near the end of his session with the Daltons, who were now holding hands during their visits. After they'd gone he told Angela to reschedule the rest of his patients. Instead she held the phone out to him.

"It's Mr. Moran. Something's going on with Chelsa."

Rand exhaled in a low whistle at the coincidence. This was the first time there was any evidence of a connection between Sienna and Chelsa, with both of them experiencing changes at the same time. He took the phone from Angela. She waited, listening intently.

"What's happened?"

Tim's voice on the other end was breathless with excitement. "She moved!" He choked a little with emotion. "I really saw her move this time. She even mumbled a little bit in her sleep."

"Did the doctors or nurses witness any of this?" Rand

asked, rolling his eyes at Angela, who blushed.

"No. But I'm not imagining it. It happened." He paused, sounding as if he'd stopped to breathe. Finally he said, "Are you coming over?"

Rand's mind raced. He didn't believe that Tim could have known about Sienna. And he wasn't going to tell him until they were all present at the nursing home.

"Yes," he said. "Sienna has been rushed to emergency at St. Augustus so I have to check on her first, then I'll be on my way."

He called Kate to alert her, sneaked out the back door to avoid any patients, and headed to the hospital. When he arrived Kate was waiting for him.

"We've already taken care of the blood work and urinalysis to rule out anything else," she told him. "But Rand, I found something in the tests I think we should talk about."

Rand looked at her quizzically, then noticed John Cantrell pacing in the waiting room.

"Can it wait?"

"I guess it'll have to." She sounded a little annoyed. They walked over to Cantrell.

"Where's Melanie?" Rand asked.

Cantrell frowned. "Haven't been able to reach her. She left early this morning for a doctor appointment." He stared at Rand. "What's the plan for Sienna now?"

"I've already made arrangements. I figured it's easier to move a healthy five-year-old than it is to have Chelsa's nursing home send her over. Not to mention the red tape involved in moving a comatose patient to active care. We'll take Sienna to Chelsa."

Cantrell didn't appeared thrilled at the idea and began to protest.

Rand ignored him, turning to Kate. "Are we ready?"

"I think so. Tim Moran's at Chelsa's care facility as we speak. We can follow the ambulance there."

They arrived at the nursing home to find Tim waiting for them in the parking lot, perched on the hood of the rusted Taurus. He stood up and walked over to them, shaking each of their hands in turn, even John Cantrell's, though he eyed Cantrell with distrust. As the paramedics transferred the still-sleeping Sienna into the nursing facility to Chelsa's room, the four of them headed into the building together without speaking. Outside the door of Chelsa's room they stopped when Cantrell grabbed the door handle first and turned to face them.

"Can we get some kind of partition? I think it would be too traumatizing to put Sienna next to the dead girl."

"Hey, wait a minute," objected Tim, a flush of red flooding up his neck.

"I didn't mean that the way it sounded," Cantrell apologized.

Rand waved his hand. "We know what you meant. We'll take turns monitoring Sienna so she's not alone when she wakes up. One day she'll be told that's her half-sister in there. Then there'll be other ramifications to deal with."

He turned to Cantrell. "Ready?"

"As ready as I'll ever be." He glanced at Tim. Rand watched the two men for a second and saw that, because they were now together in this life and death situation with their daughters, an unspoken truce had passed between them.

"Sure."

Rand opened the door. Kate rushed over to Sienna who had already been placed on a hospital bed that had been set up alongside Chelsa's. She checked her vital signs while Rand examined Chelsa. After Kate had finished examining Sienna, she folded up the side of the bed and covered her with a blanket. Having finished his examination, Rand moved away from Chelsa. He took Cantrell and Tim each by the arm and led them outside the door where they could talk without disturbing the girls.

"If either of you need food or coffee you should probably go now. I'll wait inside and we can alternate breaks. Kate will stay as long as she can, but she may have to leave as she's on call for Pediatric Emergency at St. Augustus. She couldn't find anyone to cover for her." He took a deep breath. "It might be a long night."

Cantrell nodded and walked toward the vending machines at the end of the hall. Rand watched him go then turned back to Tim.

"You want anything now?" Tim shook his head.

When they reentered the girls' room Kate waved to them from a chair at the back where she'd placed three more. There did not appear to have been any change at all in either of the girls' demeanor. Both lay completely silent. Chelsa in her six-year coma and Sienna in whatever state she was in.

Tim sighed and sat to the left of Kate where he had a clear view of Chelsa and only a slightly lesser view of Sienna. Rand sat beside him so that Kate would be between Tim and Cantrell when he came back. At that moment Cantrell pushed the door open with his hip because his hands were full with submarine sandwiches and Cokes. Rand jumped up to help him and together they passed the refreshments out to the group, then sat down to join them in the vigil.

Throughout the evening the four of them took turns getting up and leaving the room to stretch their legs, always maintaining the quietude inside the room. Never, it seemed, were John Cantrell and Tim Moran outside together, though. Near 2 a.m. Cantrell joined Rand outside in the hall.

"What exactly is it we're waiting for?" he demanded, sounding grumpy. He stretched his arms above his head and bent over from the waist to remove the kinks.

"If I knew it would be a lot easier," Rand admitted. "We won't know until it happens. Or even if it doesn't."

Cantrell rolled his eyes and went back into the room whereupon Tim emerged, reaching into his pocket for a smoke. He caught Rand's head-shake and slipped it back into his shirt pocket.

"What did he have to say?" He inclined his head toward the closed door.

Rand started to say something just as Kate leaned through the door.

"I think you should get in here now." Exchanging alarmed glances, Tim and Rand rushed back into the room. Almost involuntarily Rand grabbed Tim by the arm lest he make a move.

Chelsa was sitting up in bed, her rigored, twisted body bent like a wire-limbed doll. Her eyes were still closed but she swayed from side to side as if tugged by unseen hands. Tim tried to pull away from Rand's grasp.

"No," Rand whispered. "Leave her. She's not in danger of falling out because the bed rails are up and she doesn't have the strength to stand."

Tim relaxed, but now Cantrell was the problem.

Sienna had begun to thrash around under the covers until she had herself knotted in the sheets. Then she began kicking and flailing, which only bound the sheets more tightly around her.

Cantrell rushed over to Sienna's bed and begun jerking at the lever to drop the side. He reeled back as Sienna's hand inadvertently smacked his cheek. Rand came up behind him and pulled him away.

"She can't hurt herself," he said. In fact, Sienna's thrashing had slowed almost to a writhe. She fell back against the sheets, flaccid and perspiring from her exertion. Rand loosened the bedding that bound her and covered her with the blanket. Then they all sat back on the chairs to catch their breath.

But no sooner had they moved to the back of the room than Sienna jerked to attention, sitting up as if she was a puppet held aloft by strings. Though her expression was blank her eyes were open and wide with terror.

"Lisa!" she screamed. "Look out. There's a car!" She screamed again and it cut through Rand like no sound had ever done before. Then she fell back upon the bed, appearing to be fully conscious, her eyes gazing blankly at the ceiling. Kate rushed to the bed and took her pulse. Then she checked her pupils.

"She's okay," she reassured them. Quickly she examined Chelsa who also was now completely still. Kate shrugged and held up her hands. "She's fine, too."

"What the hell was that?" said Cantrell, shaking. This time he made no attempt to move toward his daughter, seemingly as paralyzed as the rest of them. Rand glanced quickly from one to the other, taking in the frozen, shocked faces that looked as if they'd just seen a ghost. And maybe they had.

Chapter Twenty-four

It had been a long night and while on vigil no one got any rest. In agreement that the girls should remain together for as long as it took to see results, they created an informal shift consisting of six hours apiece. John, unused to staying awake all night, was exhausted and the first to acquiesce and leave for home. Tim, who routinely worked night and graveyard shifts, seemed to be taking it in stride, but gratefully left when it appeared the situation was under control. Kate, used to being on call for hours on end, volunteered to take the first shift. Because it was his idea in the first place, Rand made the decision, against her protests, to stay with her.

Near dawn, with no apparent change in the girls' condition, Rand slipped home for some much needed sleep. He opened his kitchen door to step in a deposit his spaniel had left out of revenge for lack of attention. He didn't have the heart to reprimand the poor dog. It wasn't his fault.

He sighed, picked up the squirming dog and plopped him outside until he had a chance to clean up the mess. Kicking off his shoes he padded into the kitchen for some paper towels and discovered that the cleaning company he hired to come in once a week had left a note on the counter top. It read:

"Dr. Morrissey, we found one of your shirts behind the sofa. We put it on top of the washer. Just to remind you: we don't do laundry. Or clean up after pets."

Yeah, yeah, thought Rand, so he didn't pick up after himself. Still, it was unlike him to leave clothes lying around. He walked into the tiny laundry room and saw the offending shirt lying on the washing machine. Suddenly he remembered where he had worn it last. He couldn't believe he'd forgotten about it.

He raised it high above his head and examined it. There was blood smeared on the front and a hard object in the pocket. It was a cardboard coaster from the Aquarius. He turned it over. There was nothing unusual other than Melanie had written her name and cell phone number on it.

Rand was about to toss it out and then thought better of it. Although it made a lousy souvenir, perhaps it could provide a clue as to what had happened at the bar that night. He'd have the medical lab in his office building test the blood on his shirt and run any tests they could on the coaster.

He made a call to Kate to see how the girls were doing but she said there had been no change with either of them. After dropping the coaster off at the lab he headed to his office to see his morning appointments. He had Angela reschedule the rest of the day's patients. When he'd seen all his remaining morning patients he walked down the hall to the lab to pick up the paperwork from the tests. The lab tech pulled out the results from the file behind her and handed it back to him in a sealed plastic bag. He nodded his thanks and headed home to inspect the report.

He changed quickly, microwaved a frozen chow mein dinner, and popped open a beer. Then he sat down at the kitchen table. As Goldie tried to coax a taste, he took a mouthful of the chow mein and allowed his eyes to scan the results of the report. At first he couldn't quite understand what he read, it seemed so implausible. Then the information registered as he reread the test results and the report: 'trace of gamma-hydroxy butyrate (GHB) found in blood on shirt. Trace of gamma-hydroxy butyrate (GHB) found on coaster.'

GHB? A sinking feeling started to develop in the pit of his stomach. He pushed his dinner away. GHB was the once popular, banned, and very dangerous date-rape drug. But why would anyone slip him a date-rape drug? Could it have been accidently ingested? But even as he pondered it, he knew it wasn't accidental. Someone had developed a careful plan to incapacitate him to gain access to his office. And now he had the proof of who that someone was.

Everything about that night slowly came into focus. The blackout, the nausea, the loss of any memory. Melanie must have slipped it to him when he'd gone to the restroom. Or maybe even when he'd gone to the bar to get her a drink. Then they'd gone back to his office. And that was when she'd stolen the files on Sienna and Chelsa. Taken the tape of the hypnosis sessions.

He marveled at how diabolical she could be. Where had she gotten the stuff? he wondered. But he knew it wasn't difficult to obtain if you knew who to ask. Dealers hung around nightclubs, and it was known to be used as a synthetic steroid at fitness centers and gyms, which Melanie frequented. Other than that, he really didn't know much about it.

He switched on his laptop and began a search for GHB on the medical sites. Used prevalently in clubs and on college campuses, there was no shortage of information and dire warnings about possible seizures and nausea caused by it. But then a significant notation caught Rand's attention. And now the pieces of the amazing puzzle that was Melanie Cantrell were beginning to drop into place, all on their own. Three little words that described a possible side effect of GHB. Loss of consciousness.

He picked up the phone and dialed Kate's number, but only got her voice mail. The shift with the girls would have changed. By now either John or Tim would be holding vigil. He left a message for Kate to call him and then grabbed his jacket. He needed to get back to his office. In his computer files were results of the blood work that had been done on Sienna during her multiple admissions to hospital.

He unlocked the door to his office and switched on the computer. It took only a few seconds to bring up Sienna's records from St. Augustus' central hospital files. He scanned the results and saw the initials KP on a lot of the notes. Kate had done the entries. But to his dismay found no mention of GHB. And he'd been so sure.

He was going over them one more time to make certain he hadn't missed anything and then he saw the results from the blood work they'd done before placing Sienna in Chelsa's room. It read, 'Tests positive for gamma-hydroxy butyrate.' His cell phone rang. He jumped. It was Kate returning his call.

"I think I may have solved the mystery of Sienna's fainting spells," he announced.

"And that is...?"

"GHB."

"The date rape drug? That's what I wanted to talk to you about the night we placed the girls together but I forgot about it because we were so busy getting them ready. I didn't know what it meant then. I figured the lab must have made a mistake. How did you know?"

Rand wanted to laugh but found he couldn't because it wasn't funny at all. "Let's just say that Sienna and I have the same connection."

"Oh?"

"It's not what you think," he said. "We have to talk to the police. But I need to get to Melanie first."

Chapter Twenty-five

Melanie sidestepped across the office foyer at Excel Electronics and hesitated for a moment at the desk of John's assistant, Linda. Where was the girl? Then she saw her come out of the board room, an odd expression crossing her face when she noticed Melanie. Guilty. Embarrassed even. As if she'd been seen with her skirt tucked into her panties. Melanie waited until she sat back down at her desk.

"Is the board room ready for the meeting at two?"

Linda nodded. "I have water pitchers and glasses set up and I've ordered an urn of coffee."

Melanie paused, frowning. She could hear voices coming from the board room. She inclined her head.

"Who's in there?"

Linda turned pale. "Mr. Cantrell and a man. I don't know who it is," she stammered.

Melanie's eyes narrowed. She stared hard at Linda.

"I really don't know," insisted Linda plaintively.

Melanie turned from her and stomped toward the board room. Only one way to find out.

She paused before she entered the room, straightening her skirt and adjusting her cleavage to its best advantage. Then she put on an electric smile and stepped inside.

Cantrell and a short, bald man in a ratty tweed sports coat were standing next to the Dali. They appeared surprised to see her.

"Melanie," said John. "I'm glad you're here. This is Max Radner, he's an art appraiser. Max, this is my wife, Melanie."

Melanie held out her hand and shook his sweaty one, as cold and limp as wet sweat socks. She dropped his hand quickly, resisting the urge to wipe her palm on her skirt.

"What's going on?" she asked her husband.

"Max is appraising the Dali for me. I decided that with your recent renovations to the room it was out of place. I thought I'd sell it and invest in a lower end piece, maybe by an unknown artist."

He was staring at her now. She could feel cold perspiration breaking out on her brow. She turned toward the painting.

"But John, you love that painting. You wanted it for years and said you'd never part with it." Her heart pounded and her stomach was queasy. She wondered how long Radner had been there. What if he found out? Maybe he already knew.

Cantrell stole a glance at his watch. "Christ," he said. "It's almost two." He grabbed Radner by the shoulder and led him out. "I'm sorry, I've got the Board of Directors meeting here any minute."

Radner shook his head. "That's no problem, Mr. Cantrell. I can come back or I can take the painting with me."

Melanie clutched John's arm in alarm. "No," she insisted so vehemently she startled both men. "There's probably a faded spot underneath and with the Directors coming the wall will look terrible. It would be better if you came back."

Cantrell glanced at Radner who shrugged. "Fine," he said. "I'll arrange to pick it up tomorrow."

Inwardly Melanie heaved a sigh of relief. She wasn't off the hook yet. She had to convince John not to sell the painting or have it appraised. But how? She thought rapidly, forming a plan.

John turned to the art dealer. "I'll be in touch." They shook hands and Radner gathered up his papers, getting ready to leave.

"I'll see you out." Melanie smiled at Radner. She moved closer to her husband. "You go in and get set up. I'll be back in a minute." She led Radner to the elevator.

As he moved to press the down button she grabbed Radner's arm. "What did my husband tell you about the painting?" she demanded, her voice hushed. She didn't want Linda or some other passing employee to overhear.

Radner frowned. "Just that he felt it was a good time to sell. He's right."

"It's not a good time," said Melanie. "It's a fake."

"I didn't have time to examine it," Radner began, looking as if he were afraid she doubted his integrity.

"I tell you, it's a fake," Melanie insisted. "But I have to appeal to you not to tell my husband." When Radner started to protest, she reached into her jacket pocket and brought out a couple of hundred dollar bills. She extended her hand, showing a glimpse of the cash.

"There's a simple explanation. When I decorated the office the first time, John gave me a budget. I went over budget on imported furniture and ended up spending most of it there instead of on artwork." She watched his face carefully to see if he believed her. So far, so good.

"I couldn't see the point in spending five figures on a numbered reproduction when it's only hanging on a Board Room wall so I bought a good quality poster." Radner scowled. She had to be careful. Art was his life and livelihood.

"I now realize my error," she breathed. "It would have appreciated in value had I invested in numbered originals, while the furniture only got old." She saw that Radner appeared to be taken in. "If John found out, I'd be in terrible trouble. Maybe even danger." She dropped her eyelids and glanced up at him with appeal in her eyes.

"What should I tell Mr. Cantrell?" he asked, frowning. "He paid me to consult with him about the work, so he's my client. I can't back out without a credible explanation."

"Just don't return his calls," she said. "I'll convince him to keep the painting." She clasped Radner's hand and pressed the money into his palm. "I can't thank you enough." Then she gave him that special smile that meant she'd won.

But a few days later her subterfuge was riddled with bullet holes.

"What the *fuck*, Melanie?" John exploded. "The painting is a fake?"

She started to tremble and the inside of her mouth dried up. "I thought we decided...how do you...what makes you think that?" She was caught completely off-guard.

John was livid. His face was scarlet and one of the veins that stood out on his temple began to pulsate. "That dipshit Radner has been avoiding my calls but I finally convinced him to come in and appraise it."

The traitor, thought Melanie. She caught John staring at her, but in an odd way, not what she'd expected.

"I think it's an inside job." His voice was heavy with threat. "And when I find out who it is, they're dead."

She exhaled, and her stomach flipped as if she were about to lose her breakfast. She was quite certain she'd made the sale untraceable, but you could never be too sure.

"I'll get right on it." She backed out of the room, carefully keeping her face averted so he couldn't read anything there. Closing the door, she turned and headed toward her office, not noticing the bright, knowing smile Linda gave her as she passed.

Chapter Twenty-six

It was near midnight, yet Rand still sat at his office desk, pouring over the results of the blood work in Sienna's chart. A little smile formed on his lips. He stared unseeing at the metronome on his desk, not even hearing it's rhythmic tick-tick as a new realization spread over him.

"MSBP," he said aloud. "Oh my God, why didn't I see it?" Munchausen's Syndrome by Proxy. It hadn't occurred to him before. Melanie had told him John had been abusing Sienna. But it was Melanie herself. The intermittent fainting spells had been induced by her own mother. She'd been giving her GHB to promote hours of unconsciousness.

He thought back over the times he'd seen Sienna in the hospital. How she'd told him of things only Chelsa could have known. Chelsa or Melanie. Melanie must have told her about Chelsa. But then why hadn't it come out when Sienna was awake? Could she only recall it subconsciously? Had the information been planted by power of suggestion during her bouts of unconsciousness? And what would motivate Melanie to do that? Was it an attention-getting device from a neurotic, control freak of a mother? Or was it from a woman desperate to maintain her status quo in a quality of lifestyle she'd become accustomed to and fought so hard for?

But if Sienna's condition was precipitated by her own mother, what about Chelsa's? She'd had no contact with Melanie for over five years. *Or had she?* Melanie had made it appear that she was unaware Chelsa was still alive, but that could have been a ruse. He hadn't asked the care facility staff if Chelsa had ever had visitors other than her father. He shook his head. He didn't think it was likely, but it was possible. What could Melanie gain from it? A smug satisfaction at having one over on Tim?

He needed to talk with Melanie on a doctor/patient level. After considering Sienna's lab tests, he was quite certain now that Melanie had Munchausen's Syndrome by Proxy, the strange condition in which mothers harm their children to gain attention for themselves. He'd missed the signs when he'd read Chelsa's medical records because they stated that child abuse had been ruled out. That was because Melanie was adept at subterfuge and manipulating people into seeing only what she wanted them to. So subtle and insidious was the condition of MSBP that it was possible she was not even aware she was harming her child.

But he had a problem. Given their history of her having charged him with assault, it wasn't safe or ethical for him to treat or even be alone with Melanie. He should refer her to another psychiatrist, a doctor who had no prior involvement with the case and no predisposition to assuming his preliminary diagnosis was correct. But he couldn't bring himself to refer her on. Besides, she'd never consent to a psychiatric consult. He had too much invested in the lives of these young girls. Because of him a little girl, his sister, had died. He could never let that happen again.

The next day he had Angela call Melanie on the pretext of discussing Sienna. Then he went over how he was going to extract information from her. And suddenly he knew how he was going to do it. He would play a psychological mind game with a woman he believed was possibly an undiagnosed sociopath. When Melanie entered his office she appeared justifiably wary. And angry.

"I got a message that you wanted to see me," she said. "You'd think after the other night..." She threw him a meaningful glare. "You were damned lucky I dropped the charges."

But Rand was already calling Angela to come into the office. Melanie pouted like a teenager, plunking noisily into a chair. Angela came in carrying a notepad and sat down opposite Rand. She showed Melanie enough teeth to produce a power outage, but Melanie pretended to ignore her.

"What's the big mystery? And when are you going to allow Sienna to come home?"

Melanie wasn't her usual devastating self today. Rand took in her disheveled appearance that looked as if she'd dropped everything when she'd been called. She had dark circles under her eyes and her hair was tied back in a loose ponytail. The sweatshirt, jeans and sneakers were the type of clothes he wasn't even aware she owned. She couldn't have been at work like that. Briefly he wondered what had been happening in her home life.

"Dr. Petroski and I, with your husband's approval, have decided that it's in Sienna's best interest to keep her under observation alongside her sister."

"Half-sister," Melanie corrected. For no apparent reason she cast a sideways look of disapproval at Angela then turned her attention back to Rand. "I take it I don't get to have any say in this?"

"If we don't see any noticeable change in either girl in the next couple of days, we'll release her. Until then, we're doing our best to get to the bottom of Sienna's syncope."

Melanie shifted and moved around in her chair as if she was having difficulty getting comfortable. Finally she sat back and sighed like a recalcitrant child.

"I asked Angela to sit in with us because I've got a baffling case I haven't been able to work out. I have no background on motherhood so I thought you two women, having had children of your own, might be able to give me some insight." Melanie appeared annoyed. Was it because he thought of her as a mother rather than as a beautiful woman? he wondered.

"Angela's familiar with the case," he continued, "but here's the facts I have, although I'll only be able to use generalities because of patient confidentiality.

"There's a young mother who has a three-year-old boy. He had been severely malnourished and was finally brought into hospital. She claims he won't eat anything she prepares, that he's a picky eater. But for the week that he was in hospital the doctors noticed no problem with his appetite. They boosted him with vitamins that he was lacking and sent him home with a prescription to keep up where the hospital had left off.

"Within a week the boy was back in with the same symptoms. Again the mother claimed the boy wouldn't eat, so she gave him more of the vitamins than was prescribed to try and keep him from getting too weak. Then the doctors limited her visiting time with him at no more than every few days.

"When she was away the child would eat and gained strength, but when she'd take him home the symptoms would start all over again." Rand paused, shuffling papers around on his desk. Melanie was scraping at her nail polish, apparently disinterested. Angela pretended to take notes but Rand could see she was secretly watching Melanie.

"What do you think?" he asked, startling both women. Angela hesitated, glancing at Melanie.

Melanie pulled a face. "I don't know why you can't see it. Obviously the mother's doing it," she observed.

Rand frowned. "Why would a mother do that to her own child?"

"Yes, that's just sick," piped in Angela.

Melanie glared at her. "I think they suspect the wrong person," she said flatly. "It's not the little boy who's sick. It's the mother."

"You're right," Rand agreed. "She *is* sick. She has Munchausen's Syndrome by Proxy. Whenever her life gets out of control she deliberately harms her child to draw attention to herself."

Melanie was staring out the window, apparently lost in thought.

"There's something I want you to listen to," Rand continued. He reached into his desk drawer and produced the duplicate tape Kate had made of his hypnosis session with Sienna.

Melanie's eyes opened wide in fear. He saw immediately that she knew what it was. After all, she had the original. She'd stolen it. Rand locked eyes with hers and he gave her a tight smile. He wasn't going to take it any further and he wasn't going to resort to blackmail to get her to stop, if she was indeed harming Sienna. Melanie was extremely intelligent. Now she knew he was on to her, more than likely that would be enough. At least he could hope that it would work.

Chapter Twenty-seven

In her office the next morning, Melanie worked on eliminating any trail from the sale of the expensive furniture and the Dali that would lead back to her. She'd opened a new bank account under a business name, purchased a lock box and stored in it any incriminating information. The conversation yesterday in Dr. Morrissey's office had been excruciatingly painful to her. That Dr. Morrissey would insinuate what had happened to Sienna was her fault mortified her. As soon as she had enough financial security she was taking Sienna and leaving town.

Hearing a commotion outside her office door, Melanie stepped outside to find the place in a complete uproar. File drawers hung open like stairs to nowhere, their contents strewn around the room. Linda was running around as if the place were on fire and she was in search of an extinguisher.

"What the hell's going on?" Melanie demanded as she stopped at the reception desk for her messages.

Linda's mouth turned down at the corners and she looked as if she were on the verge of tears. "The FBI are in Mr. Cantrell's office," she said. "They've taken computers and a whole bunch of files."

The room seemed to sway for a moment. Melanie swallowed hard and took a deep breath. "Did they say why?"

Linda began to tremble so hard Melanie actually felt sorry for her. "I didn't want to ask. Mr. Cantrell's in a terrible mood, if you know what I mean."

Melanie did know. And though she had little use for Linda and her sneaky ways, she almost felt sorry for her. As John's hire, her days were numbered. The shit was about to hit the fan. Flushed with confidence, she strode off in search of him.

Linda hadn't exaggerated. John's face was purple. The little vein on the side of his neck pulsated. He looked as if he were about to have a stroke.

"Can you believe it?" he roared. "I'm being investigated for insider trading. The stock won't even go public until next week and they're already trying to shut me down."

Melanie backed up a step. "Why would they think that?" she asked, wide-eyed with innocence.

"Seems my good friend Eric Randolph turned me in. Said I sent him an e-mail telling him to invest in Excel stock now." He glared at her.

"The strange thing, Melanie," his voice grew toward a dangerous snarl, "is that the message to Eric came from my personal computer. Here in this office." He peered closely at her. "Only two people in this firm know my password. And I keep asking myself, if I didn't do it, who did?"

Melanie glanced surreptitiously around the office and let her gaze rest upon Linda.

Cantrell tilted his head and gave her the side eye. "Not Linda."

She raised her eyebrows.

"I don't believe it," he said. "What would she stand to gain?"

"Maybe someone's paying her for the information. Your competition, perhaps? Or maybe someone's husband?" She waited for the pointed remark to sink in.

Cantrell frowned, considering the possibility but not catching the innuendo.

"Did you ever find out who was behind the fake painting?" she asked.

He stared at Linda again. "You don't think she...?"

Melanie shook her head. "I'm just saying, anything's possible." She waited while Cantrell appeared to consider the notion. He'd hired Linda away from a competitor because her experience was valuable to him. She'd really only worked for him about two years. There was no way to tell where her loyalties lay. Which made her a perfectly acceptable scapegoat.

Melanie heaved an exhausted sigh. She was quite certain she'd managed to divert John's suspicions about her in Linda's direction. With that fire at least temporarily extinguished she was able to give more thought to the unpleasant encounter she'd had in Dr. Morrissey's office.

If she'd only paid more attention to what had been going on with Chelsa over the years. Maybe she should have kept in touch with Tim. She hadn't for one minute believed Dr. Morrissey's story of reincarnation between her two daughters. If Chelsa was allowed to return to a normal existence then she would have to get involved in her life again. And she couldn't do that.

Letting go of Chelsa had been difficult for her the first time around, no matter what Tim thought. Until Rand Morrissey had shown up, she hadn't even known Chelsa was still alive. Tim hated her enough that he wouldn't have let her know Chelsa had died, let alone tell her about a funeral. But how anyone could feel that the child in that bed was living was beyond her comprehension. Now they wanted a second chance for Chelsa, but at what cost? Even if she came out of the coma, she'd probably be severely disabled. With no hope of a future. Something had to be done.

After yesterday in Dr. Morrissey's office she knew he suspected she'd been harming either one or both of her daughters. But he was wrong. There had been the random occasion that she may have been too rough in disciplining them. If anything, it had not been abuse but neglect. Not paying enough attention to them when they needed her. But physically hurting either of them? Never.

She didn't know what evidence Dr. Morrissey thought he had on her. Those files and tapes she'd taken from his office the night she'd given him GHB had nothing in them that would incriminate her. It was only the one time that Sienna had accidentally ingested her GHB instead of the cold medicine, though she knew she'd never be able to prove that one way or the other.

Just as they'd never been able to pin any of Chelsa's unexplained injuries on her, though hospital personnel had always given her the third degree. Their pointed questions were designed for her to inadvertently incriminate herself. Except that no matter what any of them thought, she wasn't guilty.

She'd had to be on her guard constantly during those horrible years when she, Chelsa and Tim had lived with his mother. She knew the old woman had hurt Chelsa at times and she'd confronted her, threatened her. But the tables had been reversed when his mother blackmailed her with evidence of her liaisons, and she'd found herself protecting the woman's actions from Tim. She'd never forgiven Melanie for ruining Tim's life and to punish her she'd taken it out on an innocent child. Even now she hated herself for not confiding in Tim.

But the walls were closing in. She could feel her marriage crumbling away. And now that John was being investigated she'd have to lay low. She couldn't appear to comfort and support him while being the one who had set him up. She wasn't that good an actress. Sooner or later she might crack.

She'd deliberately missed the debacle Dr. Morrissey had arranged between her two daughters and was glad for it. To be in the same room with the girls, Tim and John would have sent her over the edge. Instead, she'd gone to her gynecologist who'd given her the good news that she wasn't pregnant after all. She smiled to herself at that but strangely, she felt her mouth turning down at the corners and found herself fighting back tears. And suddenly she had an overpowering need to see her daughters.

That night she waited until John left for a late meeting. She knew he was lying by the way he wouldn't meet her eyes when he looked at her. No doubt he was visiting his mistress, Emily Watson. Or maybe he'd gone to see his former best friend, Eric Randolph, who had reported him to the SEC. Determined not to let thoughts of John and his mistress deter her, she scanned her closet for something inconspicuous to wear. Finally she discovered a pair of oversized black slacks and dark grey sweatshirt. Without any makeup and her hair tied back, no one would ever recognize her. She left a note on the kitchen counter saying she'd gone out for groceries, although she knew she'd be back before John saw it.

When she arrived at the nursing home, she circled the parking lot several times and was only mildly surprised to see a familiar vehicle. Tim's rusted old Ford Taurus. He'd never upgraded. Why would he? she thought. Even if he could afford to buy a new vehicle, it was in his nature to drive a car until it fell apart. Same way he wore his clothes. Same way he smoked his cigarette butts down to the filters.

She pulled into a parking space several slots away from the Ford and waited patiently. She couldn't go in until he was gone in case he recognized her, and coming back would only mean another wait. She pulled out a flask of Scotch and gulped down a couple of mouthfuls. Immediately she felt the warmth spread through her body. For good measure she had another few swallows, enjoying the feeling of a buzz coming on.

After an agonizing and tedious two hours, Tim emerged, older and thinner than she remembered. For reasons she couldn't fathom she felt an unexplained sense of loss. He was her last connection to her youth, to a daughter long lost to her. She shook away the unbidden memories and concentrated on the task at hand. Once he'd pulled away she was free to leave her car and head into the building. But inside she was at a loss of where to go. First things first, she thought, a restroom. When she was comfortable again, she headed to the information counter. A bored, blue-vested senior citizen with a volunteer badge glanced up from his copy of *RV Life*.

"I'm visiting my daughter, Sienna Cantrell," she said, flashing the guard enough teeth to make his face color up. Makeup or not, she still had it.

The man turned to his computer monitor and perused the room lists. "I don't see her name here as an inpatient."

Melanie hesitated. She hadn't anticipated there not being a record of Sienna. With great reluctance she finally said, "Try Chelsa Moran. I believe they're sharing a room."

A few moments later the man swiveled away from the computer and faced her.

"Found her. Second floor, Room 204. Elevator's at the end of the hall." He nodded over to the left and gave her a gentle, sympathetic smile before he went back to reading his magazine. Hospital for the Hopeless was probably what he was thinking, Melanie figured. She set off down the hall, pressed the elevator button and waited.

Room 204 was only two wards down from the elevator. The door was slightly open. Melanie scanned the length of the corridor but there was no one around. Briefly she wondered if the place even had staff on each floor after hours. It was as shabby and rundown as she had expected. The best that Tim's money could buy.

She pushed open the door and slipped noiselessly into the room, pressing the door closed behind her. It was depressingly dark inside. The street lamps outside the building cast streaks of light across the room so she was able to make out two single beds, separated halfway by a draw curtain. She moved closer to the bed nearest the door and immediately recognized the tiny form lying there asleep. Sienna.

Refraining from touching her, she tiptoed around the bed and behind the curtain. The person in that bed wasn't much larger than Sienna, but she had an IV and monitors attached to her. A steady, rhythmic bleat, bleat came from the monitor, but it wasn't life support. That much she knew. Chelsa, though still comatose and reliant on a feeding tube to sustain life, breathed on her own.

Curious, yet a little uneasy, she took a few steps toward the bed. She hadn't seen Chelsa for years, not since Sienna was in diapers. A range of emotions rushed through her. Love, sadness, regret, all rolled into one. Chelsa hadn't changed other than her body had become more twisted and desiccated with each passing year. It had been an accident. What had happened to Chelsa was irreversible. That she truly believed. But she simply couldn't accept Dr. Morrissey's ridiculous theory of reincarnation, though she could offer no explanation as to what had been happening with Sienna these past few weeks.

Melanie reached down and touched Chelsa's cold, rough

bird claw of a hand and recoiled from the feel of it. She recovered quickly, grasping it gently between her two hands in an attempt to warm it. It was nearly impossible to recognize in this adolescent stranger the child she had known years ago as her daughter. The distorted features, twisted from years of seizures were only a caricature of Chelsa, familiar features inherited from her and Tim. But that's where the resemblance ended.

Still holding Chelsa's hand she sat on the chair next to the bed and placed her face beside Chelsa's. She could feel the wetness of drool on the sheets, but also the warm, fetid breath from the child. Surprisingly there was no revulsion, only an overwhelming sadness at what their lives had become.

Mommy, is that you?

She moved closer to Chelsa until she was almost lying on the bed next to her. Then she felt something in her stomach that made her reel back in alarm. At first she thought it was a flutter from the baby she was carrying, she'd become so accustomed to the thought of being pregnant again. Then she realized it must have been something else. She was not pregnant.

Why did you leave me?

Tears started to fill her eyes. What sort of future would Chelsa have if she awoke? Now she was severely and irreversibly damaged. And if she could find it in her heart to believe Morrissey's theory, in an mental and physical tug-of-war with Sienna. And it was her fault. Tim had been right. She wasn't a fit mother. She shouldn't be bringing children into the world only to hurt them, even if it wasn't deliberate.

She glanced up at the alabaster moon of a clock. It was just minutes after midnight. She sighed, feeling incredibly tired, physically and emotionally. She laid Chelsa's stiff hand upon the bed and leaned back in her chair. The room was so spartan. Tim had his religious artifacts around, yes, but apart from a couple of magazines and CD's, there wasn't much that a teenage girl would like. She gave a rueful laugh. Chelsa had no awareness of her surroundings. She could have been in a bed at the edge of the freeway for all it mattered.

Melanie stood up to stretch her legs, moving to the window side of the bed. An extra pillow was on the other chair.

Careless hospital staff had left a tray of supplies on the night stand. Rubber gloves, syringes, various bottles of medicines she couldn't read in the dim light. Maybe anti-convulsants for Chelsa. Or maybe they were for Sienna. She hadn't been here during the experiment to see.

Don't leave me again.

She glanced at Chelsa once more, so peaceful in her suspended state of half-life, half-death. She began to whisper a prayer from her childhood; the only one she remembered. Tim would be shocked that she even knew a prayer at all. That pleased her.

> *Now I lay me down to sleep,*
> *I pray thee, Lord, my soul to keep,*
> *If I should die before I wake,*
> *I pray thee, Lord, my soul to take.*

She reached over and picked up a syringe from the night table. A choking sob caught in her throat. She swallowed it down. If either of the girls woke up it couldn't work. For a moment she thought she heard footsteps approach the room. She hesitated, not daring to breathe. When she was certain it was just her imagination, she inhaled deeply to steady her nerves and give her courage. Then she made the decision that had been weighing on her mind for weeks.

Chapter Twenty-eight

Rand groaned in his sleep. He could hear his cell phone buzzing in the pocket of his sport coat that hung on the valet stand across the room. He glanced at the clock. It was 5:15 a.m. It had to be a wrong number but when it didn't stop, he pushed Goldie off of the bed, stumbled to his feet and grabbed the phone. It was Kate. She sounded as if she'd been crying.

"You'd better get down to Chelsa's care facility right away. There's been an accident."

"Sienna," he breathed. "Or Chelsa?"

"Neither," Kate replied. "It's Melanie. A nurse found her dead this morning in Chelsa's room. I got a call from John Cantrell. Everyone's at the hospital, police included. It's like a three-ring circus here. The girls, especially Sienna, are going to need you now."

"I'm on my way," he said, getting dressed even as he spoke. Melanie dead? It didn't seem possible. What could have happened to her? Inadvertently his heart began to pound. Figuring it was useless to speculate, he concentrated on getting to the hospital in record time.

When he arrived he found several ambulances blocking the emergency entrance and a couple of squad cars. He recognized Tim's Taurus and Kate's VW. When he tried to enter a uniformed officer held him back.

"I'm sorry, sir. This is a crime scene. You can't go in."

Crime scene? he wondered. What the hell was going on?

He showed the officer his St. Augustus identification. "I'm Sienna Cantrell's psychiatrist. I need to make certain she's all right."

The officer examined the ID closely, then handed it back.

"You can go inside," he said, "but no one's allowed in Room 204 while they're investigating. And don't disturb anything."

"Right." Rand made his way to the second floor and immediately saw Kate. John Cantrell held a crying Sienna. He rushed over to Cantrell.

"How is she?"

"Who do you mean? My daughter or my dead wife?"

Rand felt the blood rush from his face.

"Be careful what you say in front of her," Rand whispered, frowning. "Do you want me to talk to her?"

"Don't you think you've already done enough harm to my family?" Cantrell growled. "I'm taking her home."

Out of the corner of his eye Rand saw Tim Moran emerge from a room down the hall. He was quickly escorted away by a uniformed officer before Rand had a chance to run after him. But he could see that the hand of the officer resting on Tim's shoulder appeared to be comforting rather than accusatory.

"Excuse me," came a voice from behind them. They turned to see a short, swarthy detective wearing an ill-fitting brown tweed jacket and dark wrinkled slacks. He produced a badge. "I'm Detective Alvarez with the Portland Police. No one can leave yet. We have a suspicious death here."

"I need to get my little girl home," said Cantrell angrily. "Her mother's just been killed. She can't stay here."

Detective Alvarez nodded. "Fine. I'll get a statement from you first. Can you leave her with one of the doctors for a little while?"

Cantrell scowled at Rand and passed Sienna to Kate, who hugged her. He pulled out a cell phone, punched in a single number and mumbled a few words before he thrust it back into his pocket.

"It shouldn't take more than a couple of minutes, Mr. Cantrell," Detective Alvarez said patiently. "Come with me."

He was true to his word. Cantrell was back and snatching Sienna out of Kate's arms within fifteen minutes. Just then Rand looked down the hall to see Jennifer, Sienna's babysitter.

An immediate flash of recognition crossed her face, then it was replaced by alarm and undisguised hatred. He sighed helplessly. It was probably better than he deserved.

Detective Alvarez appeared in the hallway again.

"You're next, Doctor Petroski," he told Kate.

She shrugged and followed him into Room 208, which appeared to be serving as a makeshift interrogation room. She shouldn't be in questioning long, thought Rand. She knows less than anyone about Melanie. He wondered where Tim had gone. Perhaps he was with Chelsa. He'd ask Kate after they'd finished interrogating her because it would soon be his turn.

He knew there would have to be an inquest into Melanie's death. Healthy thirty-two year old women didn't just drop dead in a hospital room. At least if they weren't the patient they didn't. And the way the police would see it, if foul play was involved, there were a lot of people who would have been better off with Melanie dead.

Kate emerged from the room appearing pale and tense. When he smiled at her she gave him a brief nod and continued past him. He heard his name being called and glanced back to see Detective Alvarez beckoning to him. He entered the room and took a seat across the desk from the Detective.

The Detective got right to the point. "How do you know Melanie Cantrell?" he asked, pen poised above his notebook.

"I'm her daughter Sienna's therapist." The Detective was scrutinizing him, which made him uncomfortable.

"Where were you around midnight last night?" He scrutinized Rand impassively. Rand was acutely aware that the detective most likely was careful to take in even the most subtle nuance in posture and response, just as a psychiatrist would.

"I was at home watching TV. I went to bed around one a.m."

"That's a little late, isn't it? What were you watching?"

Rand hesitated. "Three Faces of Eve."

The Detective's eyes narrowed. "Hmmmm. Anyone with you last night who could vouch for you?"

Rand stared at him. "No, I live alone."

"That's not what I asked."

"No, there were no witnesses."

The detective peered at him again. "Haven't I seen you around recently?" Rand's heart jumped beats for a second and a sudden rush of bile burned in his esophagus.

"That was a misunderstanding between Mrs. Cantrell and me. It was all cleared up, though." The detective eyed him again.

"Hmmmm. All right. When was the last time you saw Mrs. Cantrell?"

Good question, Rand thought. When *was* the last time? Then he remembered it had been during the consultation with Cantrell and Melanie about Sienna and Chelsa. Wait. No that wasn't it. He'd had Melanie in his office to try and draw her out with the story about MSBP. He took a deep breath and explained his earlier theory about the reincarnation between the two girls and the experiment, which also explained why both girls were in the room together.

"I know it sounds farfetched," he said, noting the detective's skeptical expression, "but at the time we had nothing else to go on. Then yesterday it all became clear and I figured out what we've been missing all along."

"And what's that?"

"I believe Melanie Cantrell suffered from a condition called Munchausen's Syndrome by Proxy. I think she'd been giving Sienna GHB to induce unconsciousness. It's even possible that she may have harmed her other daughter, Chelsa, in the past. Although the medical records don't indicate it, there are a lot of unexplained fractures and injuries passed off to clumsiness. Typical behavior with a Munchausen's patient."

"Why would she do that?"

"To gain attention for herself. When a person feels they are no longer in control of events in their own lives they harm their child so other people will notice them. If they make the child get better before it's proven they're the one inflicting the damage, then they're a hero."

"Hmmm," said the detective again, making notes. "That

would be pretty hard to prove now she's dead, wouldn't it?"

"I have a tape recording of a conversation with her daughter, Sienna, implicating her."

Until that moment he'd forgotten that he'd put the tape and hand-held recorder in his jacket pocket to play for Cantrell and Moran before he put the two girls together. Thankful it was still in his jacket he brought out the tape recorder and re-wound it back to the start. He flipped on the switch and set it on the detective's desk. Then he leaned back and waited for the sound of his own voice speaking to Sienna.

After the tape had played Detective Alvarez folded his notebook shut. "I'm going to tell you the same thing I told the others. This is considered a suspicious death. Until we get the medical examiner's report, no one is exempt as a suspect. So no one gets to leave town. Understand?"

Rand nodded. Then the detective seemed to soften his attitude and said something to Rand that seemed unusual at the time.

"Good luck with those young girls, doctor. They're going to have a tough time for a while without their mother."

Kate was waiting for him outside in the hall. The yellow police tape was still across Room 204 but any investigators were either inside or already done.

"How'd it go?" She eyed him curiously.

"It was weird. But everything's strange right now, so maybe I'm not a very good judge." He took her arm and they started to leave.

"Oh!" Kate's hand flew to her mouth. "I forgot to tell you. Chelsa's regained consciousness."

Rand stopped and stared at her.

"*What?*"

Kate nodded in excitement. "It's true. She was awake and said a few words when the nurse came in and found Melanie."

"Did she see anything? Say anything?"

Kate shook her head. "It didn't seem like it. The police think Melanie died around 12:15 a.m. If there wasn't any noise, the girls would probably have still been asleep."

"Did Alvarez question her?"

"Yes. I don't think he's talked to Tim yet. But now that Chelsa is conscious, they've moved her to active care in the Pediatrics ward at St. Augustus."

Rand grabbed Kate's hand. "Then let's go see her." Suddenly he stopped and smiled in wonderment. "My headache's gone."

When they got to Chelsa's room at St. Augustus, Tim was still with her. Rand thought about asking him to leave so he could speak with Chelsa alone and then decided against it. The man had spent the past six years at his daughter's side waiting for this moment. His prayers had been answered. It was only right that he be allowed to remain in the room.

Rand approached the bed slowly, uncertain as to what state he would find Chelsa. There was no question that any recovery she might make would be slow, painful and often tedious. You couldn't reverse overnight the damage from that many years in a coma. Chelsa was awake. When she saw him she gave him a smile that, due to her long-term condition, looked more like a grimace.

"Do you know who I am?" he asked. He glanced at Tim.

She gave a slight nod, which appeared to be uncomfortable for her because a wrinkle of pain creased her brow.

"How are you feeling?"

This time her smile broadened. "Good," she said.

Her voice was not much more than a croak, but he could make out the words. The condition of her body and posture were unchanged from when he had seen her last, even in a different bed. But at least now there was hope.

He decided not to ask about her mother, or her sister. She might still not be aware of her mother's death or the existence of a sister. She would have already been questioned more than she should have in her delicate state. Instead he chose to ask her just one thing.

"What was the first thing you thought of when you woke up?"

Chelsa's eyes rolled over to look at her father. Her eyes turned back to Rand.

"A bedtime prayer," she said, reciting, "now I lay me down to sleep..."

"I taught her that one when she was a baby," Tim told him with pride in his voice, "and see, she still remembers it."

Rand reached over and stroked her bony stick of an arm. He lifted her hand and bent to kiss it. Then he had a sudden shock. On the inside of her wrist was a birthmark in the shape of a flying bird. It was the same as Sienna's. He laid her hand back down on the sheets and looked over at Tim.

"Take good care of her," he said.

Tim nodded, and though his lips parted, nothing emerged.

Then just as he was about to close the door behind him, he heard Chelsa's voice, her words hoarse and muted. "Dr. Morrissey?"

He turned back and walked to the side of her bed. "What is it?"

"If a person gave you a gift then took it away, would God think it was a sin to take it back from them?"

Chapter Twenty-nine

The next morning before any of his patients arrived, Rand received a visit from John Cantrell. He was wearing the same clothes from the night before, and from the growth of whiskers and his bloodshot eyes, looked as if he hadn't slept. He dropped into the chair facing Rand without asking permission.

"I'm sorry for my behavior yesterday," he said.

Rand waved his hand in dismissal. "We were all in shock. It was a terrible thing. I'm so sorry for your loss." He watched as Cantrell stood and walked over to the window. Distractedly, he straightened the blinds.

Finally Rand said, "Was there something you wanted to talk to me about?"

Cantrell turned to face him. His face was as red as if he were about to have a stroke. Involuntarily Rand's heart went out to him. No matter how their relationship had deteriorated, the man had just lost his wife.

"I needed to tell you what I learned when the detectives questioned me yesterday."

Rand frowned, perplexed. Cantrell heaved a heavy sigh.

"It's hard to know where to begin," he said. "There's been several odd things happening at the office over the past few months."

"Odd in what way?"

"Disappearing funds, forged artwork, my being framed for insider trading."

"Really?" Rand said. He swallowed hard before his next words. "Any suspects?"

Cantrell glanced back at the window.

"Not until yesterday," he said softly. "Until yesterday I'd

been suspecting my assistant, Linda. Even though I had no real evidence to support it, I threatened to fire her."

"What made you change your mind?"

"After I left the hospital last night I searched the spare bedroom Melanie uses sometimes. I found a bank book hidden under the mattress. She has several hundred thousand dollars in a savings account I wasn't aware of."

"Where did she get the money?"

"I found receipts from the sale of my old office furnishings and the new replacements she bought, which were worth far less. I think she skimmed the profits." He hesitated for a few minutes as if trying to figure out a way to share information that wouldn't be construed as incriminating.

"What about the forged art?"

"She'd led me to believe that a painting she'd bought was an original signed Dali. In fact it's just a good quality poster. Either she never bought an original or she substituted a fake later on."

"And the insider trading?"

"When I admitted to Detective Alvarez that I was being investigated he already knew. The Feds were able to track the e-mail that went to a friend from my computer, back to when only Melanie was in the office. She'd set me up, although I don't know why."

"Did she know about your affair?"

"I hadn't thought so, but maybe she did."

It would be hard to hide evidence of another woman from someone like Melanie, Rand thought. Why even try?

"The embezzlement, the set-up: do you think she was getting ready to leave you?" For a man who was cheating on his wife with another woman, Cantrell looked genuinely heartbroken.

"It looks like it, I guess," he said sadly.

"Do you think she'd have taken Sienna?"

"I don't know."

"What do the police think?"

"They think I had motive to kill Melanie."

* * * * *

Tim had scarcely been able to hear the words coming from Detective Alvarez's mouth, so overwhelmed was he with conflicting emotions. Melanie was dead. Chelsa was alive and conscious. His dreams had come true. No wait, he hadn't wanted Melanie dead. Had he? He'd hated her at one time but that was long ago. He'd learned to forget her. Forgive her.

Suddenly he was aware that the detective had been repeating his name for several minutes. He glanced up, still in shock over last night's events.

"Mr. Moran," Detective Alvarez said, "please answer my question."

"I'm sorry," said Tim. "I didn't hear you."

"I asked what time you left the hospital last night."

Tim thought back, his mind still swirling. He looked at the wall. Had it been nine, ten?

"I think it was about 10:30 p.m.," he said, blinking rapidly. "Yes, that's about right because I got to the church around eleven to pray."

"Did anyone see you?"

Tim reflected. There had been a couple of people in the church, but no one he knew. Reverend Maloney was rarely there that late and besides, since his disastrous visit to the hospital years ago to baptize Chelsa, Tim preferred to avoid meeting him face to face.

"No one," he said.

"That's too bad," said the detective. "Melanie Cantrell is your ex-wife, correct? And the mother of your child, Chelsa Moran, who was in Room 204 the night of her death?"

Tim nodded. "That's right."

"Did you and your ex-wife get along?"

"I hadn't seen her in almost six years."

"Didn't she visit Chelsa?"

"No, she stopped soon after she became pregnant with Sienna."

The detective studied him carefully then made some notes on his pad. "How did you feel about the fact that she was having another man's baby while still married to you?"

"I was glad to see the last of her." Immediately he regretted his words for the detective quickly jotted more notes.

"What do you think she was doing in that room last night?"

"Maybe her conscience got the better of her and she finally decided to visit."

"You don't really believe that, do you, Mr. Moran? From what I understand, she wasn't aware Chelsa was still alive."

Tim's stomach growled from nervousness. He slammed his fist into the center of it, hoping it wouldn't erupt into a worse situation. He was pretty sure the detective was trying to goad him into saying something incriminating.

"No."

"Or maybe she was trying to kill Chelsa?"

Tim shook his head vehemently. "She'd never do that."

"Not even if it meant saving the life of her other child?"

"What do you mean?"

"I've been fed a fantastic, and yet almost plausible, story about how there appeared to be only one soul shared between two girls. If one of them died the other could go on living a normal life." Tim didn't answer.

"Did you come back to find her trying to harm Chelsa?"

"Of course not!"

"Have you ever thought about what would happen if Sienna were to die? That Chelsa would regain her soul and live a normal life?"

"That's ridiculous."

As Detective Alvarez leaned back and watched him, Tim's stomach erupted again. Had he ever consciously considered it? He had to admit it had crossed his mind the day they'd experimented with Chelsa and Sienna in the same room. But he'd never kill a child so Chelsa could live. Even though he believed Sienna had robbed Chelsa of life, of a normal existence. And then it hit him. In reality it had been Melanie who, in becoming pregnant, had robbed Chelsa of her soul. She had given Chelsa life, only to take it away.

Detective Alvarez was trying to get his attention again.

"Mr. Moran, please do not leave town. We may need to question you some more. You may wish to talk to an attorney."

Tim nodded, feeling numb with fear. If they were to arrest him for Melanie's murder, who would look after Chelsa?

Chapter Thirty

Melanie's death, at first considered suspicious, was eventually ruled a suicide. Her blood alcohol level was over one point and traces of GHB had been found in her system. A single needle mark was found on her left arm where it appeared she may have injected an air bubble to bring about a fairly rapid, though not pain free, death. Any one, or a combination of these, could have killed her. Rand was having difficulty imagining or accepting that a woman with as much determination to survive as Melanie would actually take her own life.

He placed a call to Dr. Elias, who had performed the autopsy on Melanie, to get whatever further insights he might have. But Dr. Elias seemed as surprised as anyone.

"She was a healthy woman. Vibrant, beautiful..."

"Yes," Rand said impatiently. "But can you say definitively that it was suicide?" There was silence for a few minutes.

Finally Dr. Elias spoke.

"I thought that at first. But the more I examined the location and angle of the puncture wound from the needle, the less I think she did it herself."

"Then there was someone else? It was murder?"

"I didn't say that."

Rand frowned. "What about the alcohol. The GHB?"

"Accidental, inadvertent." He heard a sigh. "Can't honestly say. Maybe if we'd known her state of mind at the time of ingestion."

"Well, let me ask you this," Rand said, trying to mask his frustration. "Was there any question of murder? Do you have reason to suspect either her current or former husband?"

"No, I don't." Dr. Elias sighed.

"Then what do you think?" he asked, exasperated.

"I really don't have any answers. The cause of death is inconclusive. Maybe it was just her time to die."

Rand finally had to accept Melanie's death for what it was, suicide, an accident, or perhaps inconclusive as the medical examiner's report stated, Dr. Elias's esoteric explanation notwithstanding. Delving deeper would not help anyone, certainly not her daughters.

Though the mystery surrounding Sienna's blackouts had been resolved to the satisfaction of the doctors, and Chelsa's awakening was nothing short of miraculous, Rand was aware of loose ends that needed tying. It took him a few days, but when he finally sorted out what they were he knew he needed a friend by his side. He called Kate.

"Would you come for a drive with me today?" he said, wondering if he sounded too vague for her to accompany him without further explanation.

"Anywhere special?"

"To see an old friend." There was a long period of silence between them. He knew he almost didn't need to ask. Kate would be there for him. Wherever or whenever he needed her.

After meeting in the parking lot outside an ultra-modern, glass and cedar-beamed Seniors' Residence, they walked inside together and headed to the elevator. Aware of the destination, Kate pushed the button for the third floor. They stepped out and with her leading, stopped outside the door of a room near the end of the hall.

Kate said, "You go in. I'm here once a week. He's probably sick of seeing me." Rand gave her a hug that ended up lingering a few minutes more than he'd intended.

"I won't stay long."

Outside Dr. Silverstein's door, he hesitated. There was so much he needed to say to the doctor, so much he wanted to tell him. But this visit wasn't really about that. Today it was about Sienna. He pushed the door open and stepped inside.

There were two men in the room playing cards on a folding card table between them. One was an elderly Asian man, the other was a tiny, pale skeleton in a green pastel, patterned hospital gown, with a mane of shocking white hair. And that was the only way that Rand was able to tell it was Dr. Silverstein. The other man stared at this new visitor until finally Dr. Silverstein turned around.

"Well, look what the cat dragged in," he said. "Come in, my boy, and watch how this fellow cheats." He winked at his friend and set down his cards. "How have you been?"

Rand realized he was staring and glanced out the window when tears started to well up in his eyes. "I'm fine, thanks. It's good to see you. I came to give you an update on Sienna Cantrell's condition." He blinked rapidly. "She's made a tremendous comeback, although she lost her mother in the process."

Dr. Silverstein gave him a rueful smile. "Sometimes these things happen." He brightened. "I was right, wasn't I? Getting you involved."

Rand laughed. "Yes, you were right. How did you know?"

"I didn't. So often it's just guesswork. Trial and error."

He looked closely at Rand. "You haven't changed much, boy. Where's your sidekick?"

Rand grinned, a little embarrassed. "You mean Kate?"

Silverstein tilted his head slyly. "Yeah, you know, that Kate Petroski. You should take her out some time. She's a nice girl. Not Jewish, but nice just the same."

Rand laughed out loud. "Dr. Silverstein, I'm not Jewish."

The elderly doctor winked. "I can't fix everything."

Back out in the hall Kate was reading a magazine while she waited for him. She was wearing a soft shell-pink sweater that brought out the darkness of her eyes. Once again he was struck by how beautiful she was. Aware of how strong his feelings for her had grown.

He went over and gave her a kiss on the cheek so she couldn't see the tears in his eyes. When he was finally able to compose himself he pulled away. She smiled at him, surprised but not displeased. Then her expression sobered when she saw his face.

"He gave you the talk too, huh?"

Rand nodded, hardly able to get the words out. "How long?"

"Not long."

"What is it?"

"Melanoma. It's metastasized. Remember how he used to go to Mexico every winter? Come back as brown as a cocoanut. Well, it finally caught up with him."

They walked out of the retirement home together, not speaking. There wasn't really anything to say. Dr. Silverstein had changed their lives in more ways than they could count. It was their duty to pass on the gifts he'd given them.

The last thing on Rand's 'to-do' list was to make a trip to eastern Oregon where as a child he'd vacationed with his family. After a three-hour drive through the mountains he finally reached the rolling, windswept farm land that had once belonged to his parents.

The lake hadn't changed in fifteen years. There had been no building, nor development; no encroachment of society. The only difference was the last time he'd been here it had been encrusted with ice and snow. And of course, the body of his dying sister. But now it was surrounded by bulrushes and reeds.

As he stood staring at the lake, the mosquitoes began to pester him, just as they had when he was a child. He and Carrie. He remembered how she'd cried as he'd tortured one that had feasted on her arm, maliciously pulling off its wings and legs, it's body full, red and taut with her blood.

"That'll fix him," he'd said. "He'll never eat another living soul." Carrie had laughed out loud, the high pitch of her eight-year-old voice ringing out sharply across the water. But that had been in the late summer. There were still six more months before she died.

He'd finally come to terms with his role in Carrie's death. Was it her fate to have been born, only to die so young? She'd been like one of those beautiful bulbs on a string of Christmas lights that burn brighter than the others. They fascinate you and draw you in. But they're always the first to burn out.

Relinquishing the guilt was the hardest thing he'd ever done. Having Sienna recover and Chelsa return from the dead had heartened him, finally giving him hope that he had a purpose in life. Who knows where our destiny lies? he thought. Who knows how much time we're meant to have on earth? He smiled to himself at his theory of Chelsa's reincarnation. Of course, it had been only that. A theory. A fantasy. A dream that had no basis in fact.

But maybe, just maybe, it could be real. Who was he to say? And if it was real and he could believe, then maybe Carrie was out there waiting to come back to him. He'd probably never know for certain. Until one day when his eyes would catch those of a stranger's and for an instant there would be a flash of recognition, the kind you get when you feel you've met that person before. It was all he had to hold on to.

He took one last look at the pond that had taken Carrie away from him, then turned and headed in the direction of his car. Then he heard a sound that made him stop. It was a child's laugh, so faint that at first he thought it was only the chirping of the chickadees, hopping from branch to branch in the thick-leafed vine maples. He heard it again, and at the same time felt a tug on his sleeve. Then just as suddenly it was gone and he knew it was Carrie saying goodbye.

There was just one thing left for him to do. He got into the car, turned the key in the ignition and began driving back to Portland. With one hand he reached into his pocket, pulled out his cell phone and pushed the automatic dial in his address book. His mother picked it up on the third ring. He hesitated for a few seconds before he was to make the admission that should have been done twenty years ago.

"There's something I have to tell you," he said.

ABOUT THE AUTHOR

Leigh Goodison grew up in British Columbia, Canada and moved to the United States in 1992. She is also the author of the medical thriller, *The Jigsaw Man*, the first in the St. Augustus Chronicles, *Wild* Ones, a young adult/coming of age novel, the nonfiction handbook *The Horse Trailer Owner's Manual*, and *Goodies from the Great White North*, a recipe book/cooking memoir.

Leigh's short stories, articles, essays and poetry have appeared in dozens of publications across North America. For many years she worked in the medical and legal fields, subject matter that often influences her books. Leigh has owned horses since she was eight-years-old and still has three Arabian mares. Currently she lives in Washington state.

www.leighgoodison.com